Jesus My Son: Mary's Journal of Jesus' Minist t
takes the reader into some of the private mo l
in His mother Mary's daily journal. We are t y
come from a mother's heart, as she shares with us the love for her Son and family.
You will experience both heartbreak and joy as Jesus' mother tells of some of the
daily experiences in the life of Jesus. The stories and accounts found in *Jesus My
Son: Mary's Journal of Jesus' Ministry* are scholarly and are an extrapolation of the
stories of Jesus we find in Scripture. Mary Bailey's writing stays true to Scripture
and offers wonderful insight into the days and nights of Jesus.

The reader will experience moments of joy, pain, heartbreak and love as these
stories of Jesus unfold. This book would be a useful addition to the library of every
Christian who loves studying the Bible, and especially the life of Christ.

Ted Foley, PhD,
Clinical Psychologist and Theologian

In a touching and well-told story of Mary's life as the mother of Jesus, the author
portrays this remarkable woman in a voice which evokes all the emotion the
plot conveys. *Jesus my Son: Mary's Journal of Jesus' Ministry* is an inspiration to
everyone who reads it.

Sunny Serafino, author of *Forgiven* and
Finding Amy, 2011 Royal Palms Book of the Year (unpublished)

Mary Bailey paints a whimsical portrait of Mary, the mother of Jesus, from his
conception to the beginning of his ministry. With imagination and tenderness
she attempts to make Mary come alive, with all the struggles, and the wonders,
and the fears, and the delights that must have marked her path. She draws
from a variety of early Jewish traditions to describe the world Mary may have
experienced. Driven by a bold, pious imagination, her pictures of Mary and Jesus
are tender and loving. The reader will find much on which to ponder from this
creative work.

Stephen Pattison, Ph.D., Senior Minister,
Capital City Christian Church, Kentucky

Mary's vivid imagination and her detailed research carry us back to the first
century and give us insight into the heart and soul of the mother of our Lord.

Todd Schwingel, Minister,
Sebring Christian Church, Florida

Also by Mary Bailey

Jesus My Son
Mary's Journal of Jesus' Early Life

Jesus My Son

MARY'S JOURNAL OF JESUS' MINISTRY

MARY BAILEY

WESTBOW
PRESS
A DIVISION OF THOMAS NELSON

Copyright © 2012 Mary Bailey

All rights reserved. No part of this book may be used or reproduced by any means, graphic, electronic, or mechanical, including photocopying, recording, taping or by any information storage retrieval system without the written permission of the publisher except in the case of brief quotations embodied in critical articles and reviews.

Illustrations by Jimmy Johnson.
Cover painting by Liz Lemon Swindle @ www.reparteegallery.com

Scripture taken from the Holy Bible, New International Version®. Copyright © 1973, 1978, 1984 Biblica. Used by permission of Zondervan. All rights reserved.

WestBow Press books may be ordered through booksellers or by contacting:

WestBow Press
A Division of Thomas Nelson
1663 Liberty Drive
Bloomington, IN 47403
www.westbowpress.com
1-(866) 928-1240

Because of the dynamic nature of the Internet, any web addresses or links contained in this book may have changed since publication and may no longer be valid. The views expressed in this work are solely those of the author and do not necessarily reflect the views of the publisher, and the publisher hereby disclaims any responsibility for them.

Any people depicted in stock imagery provided by Thinkstock are models, and such images are being used for illustrative purposes only.

Certain stock imagery © Thinkstock.

ISBN: 978-1-4497-3374-2 (sc)
ISBN: 978-1-4497-3375-9 (hc)
ISBN: 978-1-4497-3376-6 (e)

Library of Congress Control Number: 2011961930

Printed in the United States of America

WestBow Press rev. date: 1/4/2012

Mary's Journal is dedicated to:

Mothers
who continually pray for patience,
perseverance, and an unwavering faith
as they encounter the trials of motherhood.

Readers
of *Jesus My Son: Mary's Journal of Jesus' Early Life*
whose kind words encouraged me to continue Mary's journal.
Without you, this book would still be patiently waiting.
Nothing is as patient as a novel waiting to be written.

Sisters
especially, my sister, Betty, who has shared
the highlights and the trials of this journey.
Even Mary realized the importance of a sister.

Grandchildren
Who brighten the lives of grandparents.
Of course, I have to mention my grandchildren
who inspired some of the entries of this journal:

Chase, the eager fisherman
Autum, the enthusiastic writer
Sydney, the compassionate sister
Zach, the avid sportsman
Sheridan, the zealous talker
Suzette, the inquisitive listener
and Saylor, the loving child

My journal is as full of love and appreciation as Mary's.

Foreword by Joe E. Brown
Minister and Evangelist

For the period of five years I had the privilege of serving as minister of the Oakland Christian Church in Franklin County. During my ministry I became a friend of my sister in Christ, Mary Bailey. My wife and I spent many hours in her home. Mary and I would travel in the hills of Franklin and Scott Counties calling on people inviting them to come to church. I preached a series of messages on the birth and life of Jesus Christ. One Sunday morning my message told how our Lord was not born of a rich family but of a poor one. In the sermon I used the Old Testament Law concerning the purification of a woman after the birth of a male child (Leviticus 12:2) and the offerings they brought for the purification.

> *"When the days of her purification are fulfilled, whether for a son or a daughter, she shall bring to the priest a lamb of the first year as a burnt offering, and a young pigeon or a turtledove as a sin offering, to the door of the tabernacle of meeting. Then he shall offer it before the Lord, and make atonement for her. And she shall be clean from the flow of her blood. This is the law for her who has borne a male or a female."*
> (Leviticus 12:6-7).

God knew that not every family in Israel could afford to bring a lamb for sacrifice at the birth of a child. Therefore, He also allowed the lesser sacrifices of two turtledoves or two young pigeons. Jesus' family offered the lesser sacrifice (Luke 2:22-24) at birth. This shows that Jesus did not come from a wealthy family. With this inspiration, Mary Bailey has captured the ministry of Jesus through the eyes of His mother, Mary.

What if we could listen to Mary's heart as she pours out her emotions in a journal? What insight might we gain from her unique view of Jesus' ministry?

The words of Mary's journal are as accurate as possible. I have added background elements to the scripture to provide a glimpse into the environment at the time Jesus walked on this earth. Looking into the depth of Mary's heart, I tried to make these entries more than the usual rendition of the stories of Jesus' ministry.

Whenever possible, I connected His ministry with the prophecies that were foretold hundreds of years before the incidents actually happened.

Mary amplifies every emotion a mother feels today. Her unwavering faith is a model for all mothers. My prayer is for readers to know and love the same son Mary loved.

Acknowledgements

This book could not be written without the help of many preachers who prepared informative sermons full of fuel for the fire that burns inside me to present Mary's view of her son's earthly life. I listened intently to glean every idea I could use for my stories. When I reached an impasse in my writing, a preacher or someone would offer a spark to keep the stories flowing. I have given credit to the people who inspired an entry.

I also want to thank:

Faithful friends who have read and commented on my work
A special thanks to Ted, Betty and Anna

the Avon Park Wordsmiths for their valuable critiques

Jimmy Johnson for his unique and distinctive illustrations

Ted Foley for his positive suggestions which provided a richer story

Joe Brown for explaining
the initial inspiration behind Mary's journal

Sunny Serafino for her editing expertise and tedious scrutiny
which greatly enhanced the story

Last, but not least, I must thank God for allowing me
to believe that Mary really might have kept a journal
so we could learn of the human side of His son.

Table of Contents

The Word became flesh and made his dwelling among us.
John 1:14

Mary Senses a Change

My motherly instincts have filled my mind with the need to continue my journal this evening. The anticipation of a dramatic change has wrapped around my body as tightly as the swaddling clothes are wrapped around our newborn babies. As with any mother, my heart grows heavy thinking my oldest son, Jesus, will soon move out of my house to begin the mission of his heavenly Father.

This is my first entry since Cousin John came to visit a few months ago. I still remember the conversation Jesus had with John that day in our back yard. John paced back and forth in his bare feet and camel skin loincloth as his unruly hair bounced every time he threw his arms in the air. From his actions, I sensed he had been visited by a messenger of God who placed in motion the beginning of their destiny. I feared Jesus would immediately follow John, but that must not have been God's plan.

When I visited Elizabeth over thirty years ago and John leaped in her womb and God gave me the beautiful song, I knew this day would come. Our sons have been chosen to fulfill the prophecies of our ancestors. Ever since the angel Gabriel visited me, I have anticipated and tried to rush God's plan for this fulfillment. His amazing proclamation that I had been chosen to carry God's seed for His son, our Messiah, has guided my entire life.

I often read the journal entries from those unsettling days and understand even more why Joseph did not believe me. I am glad the angel did finally visit him, or he would never have taken me for his wife. Instead, he probably would have had me stoned for adultery. Who in their right mind would expect God to choose a peasant girl like me and a carpenter like Joseph to be the earthly parents of our Messiah? Certainly, no one expected him to come from Nazareth.

Whenever I spoke my doubt, I can still hear my mother's consoling words "God looked at your hearts and saw that both of you were worthy to fulfill this awesome request. You know nothing is impossible if God is with you."

For twenty-six years, Joseph and I anxiously anticipated the fulfillment of this promise. Since Joseph retired to his heavenly home nearly four years ago, I have been waiting alone. I pray this kingdom will arrive before my Lord also calls me home.

Why does He delay in establishing His kingdom? We are in desperate need of a Savior to deliver us from this harsh Roman rule. At thirty, my son is more than capable to rule a kingdom. The knowledge and wisdom he possesses never ceases to amaze me. He can quote nearly the whole scroll of Isaiah and probably Jeremiah too. Sometimes I wonder if he helped write them.

Since John's visit, the churning in my stomach has not ceased. If I was not busy making preparations for my youngest daughter, Sarah's wedding; I fear I would lose my mind. Someday I may possess the patience of Job, but my Lord has not found fit to bless me with such today.

Jesus did some miraculous things in our home, but they were only for our family. I remember a few years ago when Leah's father, Silas, the village sandal maker, had an accident with the cutting tools which left him completely blind. Jesus appeared troubled over the incident for some time. He knew he had the power to heal Silas' eyes, but he also knew his Father had not yet given him permission.

I am thankful for the special powers God allowed him to perform for our family when he healed James' broken hand and revived my darling Sarah. Joseph only saw the miracle when Jesus prevented a cart of lumber from falling on his brothers. Even being an eyewitness to that event, Joseph still did not understand the awesomeness of his foster son's powers.

Jesus would not permit me to tell about the miracle he performed when he revived Sarah. He told me his time had not yet come. I saw these little things quite often and knew of his miraculous powers, but Joseph constantly worked in his shop and did not even know they were happening. I kept these things hidden in my heart because I knew Joseph would only worry. My dear Joseph, it has been over four years since you left to be with your heavenly Father, but I still miss you as if you left only yesterday. I pray you knew the depth of my love.

Joseph died wondering about the meaning of Gabriel's promise of a mighty kingdom. I regret he did not see the fulfillment of that promise. When I first told him God had chosen me to be the mother of our Messiah, he initially thought that I had committed adultery. His reaction forced me to flee to my cousin Elizabeth's to escape the possibility of being stoned as punishment for my unfaithfulness.

Even though the angel did eventually appear to Joseph and he took me as his wife, he never really forgot he doubted my words. He would often wake in the middle of the night and whisper in my ear, "I am so sorry for ever doubting you." Oh, Joseph how I wish you could do that now.

I must continue my writing and remove myself from the grief of those days. The joy of each bright new day offers so much more. The wait of these last thirty years with Jesus by my side in our earthly home has not been easy, but the experience has been remarkably rewarding. Tonight, I do sense my waiting is about to end. Although the anticipation of this change terrifies me, my skin tingles with the excitement.

Knowing the importance of this journal, Joseph encouraged me to write as much as possible. I remember how he marveled at my writing ability, which he first discovered on our wedding night. I sat on the floor at the table recording the events of the day while Joseph slept alone in our wedding bed over the oven. He had vowed we would not consummate our marriage until after the birth of my son. Joseph knew of the prophecy that the Messiah would be born of a virgin and did not want to disavow that knowledge.

Awakening in the middle of the night, he came and sat beside me and watched in amazement. Girls my age were not allowed to learn these skills. I am thankful my parents believed in the importance of girls needing an education also. I told Joseph that God looked at my heart and saw not only my willingness to accept the challenge of raising His son but also my desire to record the events of Jesus' life. We both acknowledged our role to help people believe in Jesus when the time comes for him to inherit his kingdom.

Although people are expecting a savior, they would never expect him to be from Nazareth—or the son of a carpenter. Our leaders have always taught that our savior will come from royalty, proclaiming in a thunderous voice, waving a mighty sword to deliver the children of Abraham. Apparently, God wanted His son to live a very normal childhood. His arrival only stirred the hearts of the animals and the lowly shepherds when they obeyed the instructions of the angels and followed the bright star that led them to the stable in the cave where we were forced to stay that crowded night in Bethlehem. I shudder when I think of those days spent in that cave.

Today my family is very normal. We have never lived a luxurious lifestyle. Joseph insured we were always fed and clothed, but we could never afford the rich clothes or the fancy belts and jewelry of the wealthy. I still recall the one time I wore the vibrantly colored clothes of royalty.

A few days after I gave birth to Jesus that night in the stable, my dear friend Luke, the village doctor, came by with some food and clothes for us. He had a plush, beautiful, soft, white blanket for Jesus and a beautiful blue wrap with a pure white head covering for me, which I wore nearly all my stay in

Bethlehem. Standing in that rustic cave holding my newborn son, I knew the pride of a queen who wears those luxurious clothes as she holds her newborn baby in a pure white blanket. Kissing his tiny little hands and feeling his soft breath on my cheeks, I fell in love. That moment, we created a bond that will never be broken. No matter what happens or what Jesus is required to do from his Father, he cannot take away that bond of a mother's heart.[1]

This entry fills the last of this scroll. The papyrus and ink is sometimes so hard to find, especially for a woman. I must stop for now and pray that my Lord is pleased with my writing and will provide another scroll soon. I know there is going to be so much to write about in the near future.

Dear Father, thank You for the writing supplies You have always provided. I pray I have followed Your wishes with the words I have written and You will continue to encourage my work. I thank You also for the honor of giving birth to Your precious son. When I think of the awesomeness of that gift, I am humbled. Most people still think the deliverance of Your son will take place in some glorious mansion, but instead You chose a lowly stable. What will people think when they realize the Messiah lived right in their midst all this time? Please help me pave the way for their understanding.

---

1   This is in reference to the painting *Mary's Heart* by Liz Lemon Swindle, used for the cover of *Jesus My Son: Mary's Journal of Jesus' Early Life*.

Then He went down to Nazareth with them and was obedient to them.
But His mother treasured all these things in her heart.
Luke 2:51
When (Naomi) saw (Ruth) was determined to go with her, she said no more to her.
Ruth 1:18

Mary Enjoys Writing and Reminiscing

When I used the last of my scroll a few weeks ago, I wondered if God would think my need for writing important enough to provide another one. After today, I am convinced that, if I am doing what God wants me to do, He will find a way to make it possible.

My heart dances with joy as I unroll the large beautiful scroll a traveler left at the carpentry shop today in exchange for some expertly crafted mezuzah to hang by his door. As commanded in the laws of Moses, I am sure he will have a scribe write the proper scripture text on the strips of linen to place in the little boxes to welcome his guests.

Joseph made the one we have over our door and as visitors visit our home, they kiss their fingers and touch the mezuzah to receive the blessing of the house. I am pleased the gift of craftsmanship has been passed on to the younger Joseph. He spends many hours perfecting his work. The man must have greatly appreciated the handiwork of the little boxes because he took several to put over each door in a new house his son had built.

Although I am sure he could pay for the items, he did not have room to carry them and this scroll. He asked Simon and Joseph if they could accept this beautiful scroll as payment. Knowing how I love to write and noticing the full scroll stored in my treasure box, they were eager to accept the barter. As usual, my Lord found a way to encourage me to keep writing. I feel He realizes how important my stories will be some day. After waiting thirty years, I sometimes wonder if that day will ever come. God reminds me daily that He is in control and things will happen in His timeframe, but sometimes I forget.

Oh, how I love the rich feel and beauty of the papyrus as it fills with the words my Lord has placed in my heart. Having to contain them for so long, at times I felt my brain might explode. Like a little child with a new toy, I could not wait to open the scroll to begin my writing again.

With a full bottle of ink, a new quill, and a fresh supply of papyrus, I am ready to catch up on the happenings of my family since my last entry. While I have the time, it is important to write because I sense the duties of my life are getting ready to change. I may find myself in a situation where I will not be able to write or find writing material.

Writing on this scroll gives me such pleasure, I may write all night. Wonder what my children would say if I was still writing when they woke up tomorrow morning? They would not say a word, knowing the enjoyment this gives me. I shall begin my writings tonight with an update of each of them.

I now have two adorable grandsons and two more grandchildren on the way. I expect one of them to be my first granddaughter. Joseph, my first grandchild, just turned five and his brother, Jesus, will soon be three. My oldest daughter, Elizabeth told me last week she is expecting again. Simon and Leah, who are now living in the room Joseph and I shared, expect to give birth in a few months. My family is growing as fast as the rock rabbits in the dessert.

My main concern now is the wedding in a few months of my youngest daughter, Sarah. We are fortunate the groom and his family have graciously asked to host the event at their home in Cana. Our house is so small, I am afraid we are not able to accommodate such an event as Joel and his family has planned. We only have to make the dress and the veil and anything extra Sarah might desire. Her happiness over this wedding has filled the entire house. Even her brothers smile as soon as they walk in the door to see her dancing around humming a joyful tune.

Since a two-day walk separates the two families, Sarah has chosen to forego having the groom come to our house to carry his betrothed and her party to his house to claim her as his wife. She agreed we would send Judas ahead of our party to notify Joel when we have arrived near Cana. Joel will then meet our caravan and from there he will take the bridal party to his house for the beginning of the celebration. I love the traditional weddings, but I am pleased Sarah allowed this change in the procedures for the convenience of everyone involved. Her love for Joel is so strong, she would agree to anything to speed up this process.

Once Sarah leaves this house, I fear it may resemble a tomb. Even with all the boys here, her absence will echo through the rooms. I will miss the mother and daughter talks we have enjoyed this last year after I moved in with her to give the room Joseph and I shared to Simon and his wife, Leah, so they could enjoy a bit of privacy.

The bond between mother and daughter cannot be filled with sons or daughters-in-law. Leah is a wonderful daughter-in-law, but she will never allow me into her life as a mother. After she entered our home as Simon's wife, I more fully understood the uniqueness of the bond between our ancestor, Naomi, and her devoted daughter-in-law, Ruth.

The carpentry shop still provides the needs of our family. When Joseph became sick, Jesus took over the management of the business. He kept all the boys busy working and patiently taught them the tools of the trade. Since Joseph's death, they have all worked together to keep the business going as they knew their father would have wanted. The work prospered under Jesus' keen eye, but in the last years most of the duties have been passed to his brothers.

Jesus is a great businessman mainly because of his patience when dealing with the customers. He always gives fair and accurate estimates. If there is a misunderstanding, Jesus always gives the customer the benefit of the doubt. James grew angry over the money loss one time, so Jesus graciously handed the task of estimating to him. James does not complain any more, but we do not always have happy customers.

A few years ago Jesus began losing interest in the shop. As the firstborn son, he felt an obligation to help Joseph as long as he lived. Jesus is required by law to care for his parents until their death. He knows I will always have a place with my daughters. The end of that obligation offered Jesus a freedom to live his own life. Only his Father knows what that may be.

Joseph had taught Jesus every aspect of the trade, but had taught Jesus' brothers only specific tasks. Jesus wanted each of them to learn everything so they could work together after Joseph died. Their eagerness to learn hastened the process. With the skill level they now possess, Jesus does not feel accountable and appears restless when he works in the shop.

Jesus has discreetly given his brother, Joseph, a bigger role in the leadership of the business. Joseph seems more interested than the rest of the boys because God has chosen to pass their father's gift and love of the craft to the younger Joseph. Jesus takes Joseph to every job now and sometimes allows him to go alone. Since John's visit a few months ago, Jesus chooses to spend more time under the tree in our back yard where he talks to his Father, and less time in the shop.

I can sense something is about to happen which sends chills of delight mixed with fear throughout my body. Thirty years after Gabriel's visit is longer than I expected Jesus to be with us. When Gabriel visited me and said I had been chosen to have God's son who would inherit the kingdom of David,

I expected something miraculous to happen much sooner. Joseph and I both waited for that promise to be fulfilled.

My heart still aches when I think of the guilt Joseph carried for not believing my story. I tried many times to convince him it had to happen that way or I would never have gone to visit Elizabeth where I learned so much about the birth process and the foretelling of all the prophecies of John and Jesus. I shudder to think how awful that night in the cave might have been if not for the experience of helping Elizabeth through John's birth. My Lord knew where I would be when our son arrived. He wanted to prepare me for that situation as much as possible. All that night, I could hear the midwife's instructions and Elizabeth's calm voice encouraging me, telling me what I needed to do. Their presence filled that humble stable.

Joseph lived most of his life caring for someone else's son, but he never once complained. I often wondered if he expected more. If he did, he kept his secret well. Since Jesus acted like any normal little boy, we had a difficult time thinking of him in any special way.

By his actions, I can sense Jesus will leave soon to complete the mission his Father has prepared. Who knows what my role will be in that part of his life? I only know I am a bondservant of my Lord to do as He instructs and I will always love Jesus with a special part of my heart.

Dear Father, I want to thank You for allowing Your son to live with us for so many years. Whatever this kingdom might be, it cannot be any more glorious than the life with which You have chosen to bless us. I may soon have to give him to You, but You will never take away the memories. Give me the understanding to know when this time comes and the wisdom to accept Your plan. As the end of this day draws near, I thank You for the blessing of this beautiful scroll. You have richly blessed my writing since the day of Gabriel's visit. I pray You will continue to use me as a vessel to write the words to the story You would have the world know.

Is not this the carpenter's son? Is not His mother called Mary, and His brothers,
James and Joseph and Simon and Judas? And His sisters, are they not all with us?
Matthew 13: 55-56

Mary Describes her Family

I rolled up the scroll and prepared to retire for the night. Passing by the rich material, I could not resist the temptation. Writing on this scroll gives me such pleasure, I decided to write a little longer. The soft illumination of the full moon still provides ample light for my writing.

Although the purpose of my writing is to enlighten the world of the life of God's son, our Messiah, I am compelled to also write about all my other children. The thought of Jesus' brothers and sisters discovering this journal someday and thinking I did not love them as much as their brother breaks my heart.

When they realize the true identity of Jesus, I hope they will understand why his stories fill most of these pages. I have assured each of them of their special place in my heart. Sometimes I feel my heart is so full of love it might explode. With the addition of two more grandchildren, my heart will just have to grow a little bigger. Of course, Joseph's death created a huge void to fill.

The psalmist says we are not to puff up with pride, but when I think of my children, my heart swells with much delight. In a world where children constantly rebel against their parents, God has blessed me with loving, caring, and mostly respectful children who are normal in every way. As with most families, there were times when some of the children forgot who they were. Thankfully, the foundation Joseph and I provided encouraged them to return home after "sowing their wild oats." They always came back better, stronger young men than when they left. God allows young people the freedom to test their faith. The testing of our faith is the building up of perseverance, and each child tests in a unique way. James is the one who likes to try his faith. He seems to rejoice in the trials presented before him. Judas is the one who usually succumbs to the temptations he encounters.

Jesus has always been my peacemaker and protector. After Joseph's death, Jesus became the father figure for the rest of the children. He fixed all their aliments and pains. If one of the boys had a broken heart because he had been scorned by one of the local girls or bullied by one of the other boys, Jesus comforted their hurting. He has some miraculous God-given gifts for healing the obvious as well as the not so obvious wounds. His words of wisdom have helped all his brothers and sisters at one time in their lives.

I remember not too long ago Elizabeth came for a visit with anger steaming from her body. Jesus saw her approaching the house and ran to meet her. He sent her sons to me as he took Elizabeth over by his tree to talk. I watched from a window as her shoulders shook while Jesus gently held her and listened. A while later they came in the house with Elizabeth a little red-eyed, but smiling.

When I searched for an explanation, Jesus smiled and whispered, "I had to remind her that Amos had to increase his work hours to reconcile the debt caused by moving to that new house. For that reason, he could not help put the house in order before this next baby is born. After all, she is the one who insisted they move before the baby arrived. Sometimes we have a hard time realizing the consequences of the decisions we make based on our desires instead of our needs. I helped Elizabeth evaluate the situation and better understand Amos' detachment. Perhaps he is worried about the debt of the new house along with the addition of another mouth to feed. Amos' aloofness does not mean he loves her any less. They will be fine and Amos will come home to a more caring and thankful wife tonight."

I recalled the time we moved into this house. My desire to have everything settled in its place consumed me. I think that is the only time I lost my temper with Joseph. My mouth did not open for days. Joseph would go to his shop and stay until I had retired for the night. The boys would even take his food to him. My mouth opened in awe the night he delivered a beautiful treasure box he had made for me to store my writings. He smoothed the top as flat as still water so I could write on it. There is even a little hole to hold a bottle of ink. He set the box by our bed and said, "You needed something beautiful for your new house." Believe me, since that day Joseph had a more caring and thankful wife. I cannot remember ever being mad at him again. I must return to my story before I ruin this scroll with teardrops from my memories.

The girls in the village admire Jesus' handsome appearance, but he has never shown a great interest in anyone except his Father. Often when the younger children played, Jesus would sit under the tree in the back yard with a little bird on his shoulder. The other children learned to respect his need for solitude. In this house full of siblings, there is not a lot of opportunity for quiet time.

My wish is that of any mother—for all my children to be happy. Jesus appears to be happy, but lately, there seems to be something missing. Instead of the joy I once felt when anticipating Jesus' kingdom, I now experience fear.

When I am near him, I sense a change. His attitude, his presence, his body are going through a transformation that I cannot describe. I can only fear it and pray that I can accept it. Every time I saw Jesus perform some miraculous deed for his family or read in the synagogue, I remembered the prophecy of Simeon when we had taken Jesus for the redemption ceremony in the temple. The prophet looked at me and, shaking his head, said that a sword would also pierce my heart. Lately, I have felt his prophecy has barely touched the surface of my pain. I eagerly, but cautiously, await my Lord's guidance for His son.

James is still my provider. He spends a lot of time hunting and fishing to ensure we have meat on our table. I have encouraged him to take Judas with him as much as possible. Judas needs to spend more time with his brothers and less with the crowd that is always tempting him to do rebellious things. As many times as James has tested his faith, he has managed to overcome the temptations and has matured into a very dependable young man. He is a good influence for Judas because he knows the temptations Judas is experiencing. I wish James could just tell Judas what to do, but second hand experience cannot satisfy the desires of the flesh.

I still worry when James begins to express his adamant views on some things that are not the popular belief. Like most young men his age, he is not fond of our Roman rule. Of course, no one in our village has good feelings about our current government. When the Roman soldiers come storming in our village, I have stressed to the children to seek cover. If the soldiers suspect a man has not paid the proper taxes, it is nothing for them to capture a son or a daughter for payment. When that happens, that child is gone forever. We live in constant fear of the Roman soldiers and I fear James is becoming too outspoken about his feelings.

Elizabeth is still my beauty queen, but she has acquired a more mature attitude. Her heart has always been in her dancing and her singing, but now she performs for the adoration of her children. Once she became a mother, her life completely changed. Just like me, whatever her wishes for her future might have been, they vanished the moment she felt the warm soft breath of her newborn child on her lips.

She still loves to make the beautiful clothes we could never afford to buy. Now she sews them for her family. The well-being and cleanliness of her children are top priority for her. She will soon give birth to her third child, who, I am hoping, will be my first granddaughter.

Although she and Amos have had some disagreements, he has always been very good to her. Most husbands today will not allow their wives to express any emotion, but Amos welcomes comments from his wife. I have silently watched as a smile appeared on his lips from some brave announcement Elizabeth would proclaim. Their relationship is much healthier than most of the married couples in the village.

All my other children adore their brother-in-law and nephews. Thankfully, Elizabeth and Amos live close enough to visit often which is good for all of us. It is heart warming to have young children in the house.

Next there is Joseph, the image of his father. I am glad we waited to name this one after his father because he not only looks like him, his actions mirror those of Joseph. I watched Joseph the other day and stopped to take in the scene. My heart swelled with love as I recalled the same scene with my darling husband. I wanted so badly to run and hug him. I do not watch him anymore—the pain is too strong.

He is also the quietest of the lot. He never speaks unless someone speaks to him. His silence is good for getting his work done, but not for helping the customers. Thankfully, Simon does love to talk and enjoys managing the business of the shop.

Joseph is also especially gifted with the numbers. Even before his father's death, he took care of the calculations for most of the jobs. Although the priests often ask Joseph to help teach mathematics in the synagogue, he has never wanted to do anything but work in the shop. He has a fear of speaking in front of people, even the small children.

Like his father, he has a gift for crafting masterpieces. With experience, his skills will rival his father's. Upon his father's death, Joseph begged to be more involved. He spends most of his time in the shop working on a new design for a customer. Using his mathematical abilities, he has come up with some clever creations.

He is also beginning to show a little interest in Ettezus, one of Sarah's friends. Every time she comes to visit, Joseph will come out of his shop to see her. I think they may have even shared a word or two. I know that took a lot from Joseph, but he is always smiling when she is around. He watches her the way my Joseph used to watch me. Oh, what wonderful memories come to mind?

Next there is Simon, my first son to marry. He and Leah will soon give me another grandchild. It has been a joy having Leah with us. When I moved into Sarah's room, the other children questioned my decision—especially Sarah. But it did not take long for Leah's soft manner and willingness to help persuade the other children to accept her as one of our own. Simon watched her work so hard in her parent's sandal shop. Now he strives to make it easier for her and eagerly helps with whatever she is doing. It warms my heart to watch them together. I know they are as much in love as Joseph and I were. All the boys are willing to comply with her wishes. Their acceptance provides much comfort, because if I must leave for some reason to be with Jesus, she will be the woman in the house assuming the role as their mother.

Joseph and Simon have a good relationship concerning the business. Simon deals with the customers and Joseph does the work. As unfair as it may seem, it works for them. Simon still spends much time at his father-in-law's sandal shop helping the poor man continue his business after the accident left him blind in both eyes.[2]

Simon will make a wonderful father. I cannot wait to have another grandchild. No matter how many you have, the birth of each one is just as exciting as the birth of the first. But that first one will always be my joy. I do not love my first grandbaby, Joseph, anymore than I love his brother, Jesus, but watching my daughter give birth to a first child, my first grandchild, created an impression that can never be duplicated.

My next child is Judas. Judas, Judas, Judas! What else can I say? At eighteen, he is finally beginning to learn the meaning of respect. A few months ago, right before he turned eighteen, he left with a group of young men to "explore the world". They were gone for over a month and he returned a different person. He just told me one day he was leaving. I tried to reason with him, even seeking guidance from Jesus who just shook his head as if to tell me, "Let it be."

I knew the rebellious group he accompanied meant trouble, but I also knew he needed to experience life himself. Of the six who left, Judas is the only one who has returned home. The other parents have no idea where their children are. They often come by to ask Judas about their son or daughter. Judas either does not know or is unwilling to talk. When he came home after spending a few weeks in Jerusalem, the others were still there with plans to continue on their journey to explore the stories from the other cities. We have heard about the idol worship of some of those religious sects. I am just thankful Judas chose to return home.

He would not speak about what happened that month, but I think he learned a valuable lesson in relation to family and growing up. I still see him staring into space with that 'what if' expression. I think he sometimes feels responsible for leading the group on the trip.

After Joseph's death, Judas never seemed to grasp Jesus as the new father figure. I sometimes had the feeling Judas resented the discipline Jesus tried

---

2   Mary Bailey, *Jesus My Son: Mary's Journal of Jesus' Early Life* (2010), 151

to impose upon him. We all allowed Judas a little more freedom than we should have. I know Joseph would never have tolerated some of the actions we did. I am afraid we have paid for all that freedom mixed with a lack of discipline.

Judas recently became interested in a wonderful young girl in the village. She is from a respectable family and will be a good influence on him. I am afraid his first girlfriend helped lead him astray. No one has ever said, but I think she may still be with the other young men who have not returned. I pray for her parents. I cannot imagine knowing your daughter is living with a group of men in some of those towns which are known for their sinful way of life. I am thankful Sarah has never shown any interest in leaving home. She really did not have a chance, since, at the age of twelve, she became enamored with the young man, Joel. She is afraid to leave, hoping he may surprise her with a visit.

Sarah is my baby doll and my miracle child. The miracle Jesus performed at her birth gives her a special place in my heart. As my last child she will always be my precious little baby. Her servant's heart is apparent in everything she does, especially, when she is singing beautiful lullabies to her nephews when they are here. My Lord graciously did not bestow upon her my limited singing ability.

The stars are still directing her path. She often tells me how the stars have influenced her day. Usually, I hear this after she has been a little testy and I have had to remind her of her place in the family. She loves to boss her brothers who would do anything in the world she asks, but sometimes she forgets they are not her slaves.

The day she met Joel at the well, the stars told her to go there. I knew the relationship had increased when Joel and his father, Zachary, made a special trip to see me and Sarah's brothers, of course. When he brought his father to speak to us, my heart sank. His father politely asked if Joel could take Sarah as his wife. They knew we did not have much to offer, but Joel's admiration for Sarah's beauty and tender heart did not require much. He offered a price that I jokingly tell Sarah we could not refuse. My father never did tell me the value Joseph offered for my hand. I think there were times when Joseph wished he could have made an even exchange.

Joel possesses many good qualities we could not have found in anyone from Nazareth. Believe me; I have searched, because I could not bear to think of my baby girl moving so far away. Sarah did not give us a chance to look very hard. Once she met Joel, she knew immediately he would become her husband. I will never forget the day she came running to the house to tell me of her awesome find.[3]

Joel's parents came to visit one time to see who had smitten their son so. Sarah with her servant's heart quickly persuaded them with her outer, but more importantly, her inner beauty. They left pleased with their son's choice. When only the father came back the last time, I knew the reason for his visit. I am happy for them because I feel certain Joel will take great care of my little girl. Her absence will leave a deep void in this house, but maybe Simon and Leah will have a little girl to ease the loneliness. It always amazes me how our Father can take a seemingly sad situation and provide a most joyful replacement.

I cannot forget to mention my darling little girls who are in the arms of my Lord at this time. The sword of pain still pierces my heart when I think of Deborah and Ruth, but the pain is a little duller each day. When I think of them with my eyes closed, the scene I now see is Joseph, healthy and strong, holding them and telling them a bedtime story as he did for all his other children. What a relief that image creates.

I am saddened that my darling Joseph will not be here to give his precious little girl to her new husband or to experience the other events of our lives, but in my heart, I feel he is watching from a higher view—one that will give him the ability to care for all of us a little better. From his view I hope he can feel the strong love his children, including Jesus, possess for their father.

I praise my Lord for my wonderful family. Each of my children is unique in their own way. Some may try my patience a little more than the others, but each one holds a special place in my heart. Who would have thought when Gabriel visited me those many years ago this would have happened? My journey is not quite finished, but I feel my role as Jesus' mother must lessen. It saddens me to think my family no longer requires the care I once had to provide, but it also allows some freedom to discover new things.

If only I can receive the patience to accept these changes. My desire is to follow Jesus on his journey and continue to record my version of his life. From a mother's view, I know my stories will be different from others. I can only pray that people will have an open mind to accept the words my Lord has placed in my heart. The fulfillment of the promise is near and I must prepare my family for what is to be.

---

3   *Jesus My Son: Mary's Journal of Jesus' Early Life*, 178

Oh, my, I think the morning sun may be trying to peak over the horizon, but sleep cannot compare to the joy of writing about my family on this beautiful scroll of papyrus.

My dear Lord, thank You, thank You, thank You. I love You and goodnight (maybe I should say good morning). As always, I look forward to the joys this day may bring.

John wore clothing made of camel's hair, with a leather belt around his waist,
and he ate locusts and wild honey.
Matthew 3:1-12; Mark 1:1-8; Luke 3:1-9; John 1:6-28,
"Behold, I am going to send My messenger, and he will clear the way before Me.
And the Lord, whom you seek, will suddenly come to
His temple; and the messenger of covenant,
in whom you delight, behold He is coming, says the Lord of hosts.
Malachi 3:1

News of John's Message

My hands are trembling as I write the disturbing news we heard today about Cousin John. Some travelers came by the shop while I watched Jesus and his brothers. Since men do not usually like to speak in front of women, I stepped outside to let them conduct their business, but stayed close enough to hear their words. The travelers told about a rebellious man who came from the wilderness and ate nothing but berries, locusts and wild honey. They said he girded his loins with clothing made of camel skin with a leather belt around his waist. He preached some kind of nonsense about repentance and love—a much different message from the teachings of the scribes and Pharisees.

A sharp pain pierced my heart as my boys and the travelers discussed the many rebels who are trying to unite the people against the Roman rule under which we now live. The man they talked about proclaimed to be the forerunner of someone even greater whose sandals he would not be worthy to loosen or untie. Wanting to hear more, I prepared a vessel of water to offer some refreshment.

Roars of laughter could be heard as I neared the door. Even my sons enjoyed the ridicule of this young man until one of the travelers began telling the background of the rebel. Supposedly, the Lord had visited the father in the temple and gave him this child as a gift even though his wife had passed the child bearing age. They continued to say the man's father, a priest, had been deemed speechless before the birth of his son. The priest claimed to have been visited by an angel who told him he must call his son John. The vessel of water fell to the ground and shattered as Jesus bumped into me in his haste to leave the shop.

James tried to change the subject, but the men were not finished with their story. The travelers went on to say many people were following this crazy man to the Jordan to be immersed in the water to wash away their sins. "Can you believe that?" one of them said. "Water is going to wash away our sins! What about the blood of the sacrifices required in the Law of Moses?"

Another one exclaimed, "Who does this man think he is? Our Messiah? A crazy man living in the wilderness is going to be our Savior? How preposterous can any one man be?"

The men continued saying people from all around, even some from Jerusalem, Judea, and everywhere around the Jordan, were coming to hear this crazed man to confess their sins. This rebel baptized each one of them in the murky water of the Jordan. They said he told the people he baptized with water but the one who would come after him would baptize with something called the Holy Spirit.

How can this be? I know this is John they are talking about. Is Jesus this man coming after him? Is this Holy Spirit with which he is going to baptize a part of the promised kingdom? Is my long wait finally over? Jesus has appeared distraught since John's visit, but I do not believe he was prepared for the news we heard today. He spent the rest of the day under the tree talking to his Father.

The travelers even said John called the Pharisees and Sadducees a brood of vipers. I just knew that rebel spirit of his would cause him trouble. This reminds me how the Pharisees and Sadducees questioned Jesus when he stayed behind in the temple at the age of twelve. They dismissed his questions and comments because of his youth, but with John being a grown man, his actions will not be overlooked so easily.

The men said even the leaders were asking this rebel if he might be Elijah or one of the prophets, but he said "No." When they asked who he was then, he started quoting from the scroll of the prophet Isaiah. I know they were referring to the scripture which foretells of "a voice of one crying in the wilderness, make straight the way of the Lord." Every day I sense more of the impending fulfillment of Isaiah's prophecy of my beloved son.

I heard all this from the open doorway. When the travelers left, I stood there with the shattered pitcher still lying on the floor. James came over to help pick up the pieces and to ask if I heard the disturbing news.

"Could they possibly be talking about our cousin John?" he asked with deep concern in his voice. "The news greatly distressed Jesus."

"I know," I said pointing to the tree where Jesus sat with the bird on his shoulder.

The rest of his brothers came to stand with us. We watched silently as Jesus lowered his head and fell to the ground on his knees. His body shock as he rocked back and forth. We all suffered from the pain the news had provoked in our beloved son and brother.

As the sun began to set, Jesus came up behind me, put his arm around my neck and held me for some time. Then he gently turned me around so he could look intently into my eyes and said, "Mother, you know I must be about my Father's business."

Those words I had previously heard caused my heart to stop. The parched feeling in my throat prevented any words from forming.

Jesus stared into my eyes as he continued, "The day we have been anticipating has arrived. As you know, John is preparing the way for me. I heard you and Cousin Elizabeth discuss this day many times before her death. It should not be a surprise to you. We may not see each other again until my kingdom is delivered. Mother, just as you have always loved me, I will always love you with a special part of my heart. Goodbye, dear mother and thank you."

His gentle kiss, before he turned and walked out the door, still burns on my forehead.

When his lonely figure disappeared from sight, I rushed to the shop to tell James. As the words poured from my mouth and the tears poured down my cheeks, James could only smile.

"Mother, you know Jesus has been talking about needing to visit John to discuss some very important news. The travelers this morning only confirmed this need," James said closing the shop for the day.

"Somebody needs to talk some sense into John's dense head. With that thick unruly hair, it may take a hammer to pound it in!" James said, trying to lighten the situation. He took my arm and escorted me back to the house. Seeing my distress had not left, he added, "Do not worry, Mother. Jesus is a grown man. You have taught him well how to care for himself."

James thinks Jesus has simply gone to visit his friend. I cannot help but think it is much more. What is John preaching that is so moving to Jesus? I told James I must go see what is happening to John. I owe that much to my dear friends, Elizabeth and Zachariah.

Seeing the determination in my eyes, James said the travelers mentioned John preached near the Jordan. If I insisted on finding him, he suggested maybe we could start that way tomorrow to check on the reason for all the commotion. Since Jesus left so late in the day, James thought maybe he would stop at Elizabeth's for the night to tell his little nephews one last story. They will deeply miss the grand stories from their loving uncle.

Tomorrow James and I plan to get up early and go straight for the Jordan. Maybe we can talk to John and hear his explanation. John has always possessed a little different attitude. I remember repeatedly asking Elizabeth if John could spend more time with us thinking Jesus' gentle spirit might influence John a little. She would look deep into my eyes and smile. "Dear, Mary," she would say putting her arm over my shoulder. "Do you think I do not see how my child acts? His ways are somewhat different than most young boys, but my Lord has chosen to give me a young boy so full of life and spirit. I do not think He would want me to stifle what He has so carefully designed."

We dropped the matter completely, but I did try to convince John to stay with us after the death of Elizabeth and Zachariah. He would hear nothing of it, but insisted on staying with the group in the dessert. Elizabeth told me he often stayed with them since the time they protected him from Herod's decree regarding the death of all two year old males after Jesus' birth. I am afraid that group may have influenced him more than we realized.

Those religious and devout men constantly study the prophecies. It has been said they see themselves as guardians of mysterious truths that would govern the life of Israel when the Messiah appeared. Some people even believe they are the ones the prophet Daniel said would guide the Jews in the time of turmoil.

I cannot believe they have taught John to act like the wild man the travelers described. Although they are considered by some to be rebels, they are held with great esteem in many religious groups.

If I could talk to John, I know I could find the truth. Elizabeth and I had known since the day I first visited her that a link existed between John and Jesus. We both knew our sons were given to us by God. If only I could speak with her again. I do miss my dear friend. She could tell me more of what the future holds for them. I have an odd feeling this is the beginning of something as extraordinary as his birth.

John's message must be about Jesus. It appears my thirty year wait may be coming to an end. I look forward to this marvelous kingdom, although I have no idea what this kingdom may hold in store for me or Jesus. It must be different than any kingdom to which we have been accustomed. Jesus is too meek and mild mannered to show any sign of desiring any recognition or glory as a king.

Dear God, I beg You to help us understand John's actions. What strange circumstances would compel a child to so drastically turn from the teachings of his parents? Please be with Jesus as he searches for him. Give them both understanding and wisdom. You must understand my need to search for John to learn the truth. I know You have tried to prepare me for all these events, but deep in my heart I hoped they would not happen. The prophecies of Isaiah foretold of this day, but forgive me if I am not willing to let my son go even if it is to fulfill Your divine prophecy. A mixture of emotions is running wild in my mind. You have blessed me with a wonderful son for thirty years. Now I look at the future not only with great anticipation but with great fear also. Dear Lord, I beg You to enlighten my mind and my heart to these happenings. Fill my mind with understanding and wisdom and my heart with enough strength to see me through.

Then John gave this testimony: "I saw the Spirit come down
from heaven as a dove and remain on him.
I would not have known him, except that the one who
sent me to baptize with water told me,
'The man on whom you see this Spirit come down and remain
is he who will baptize with the Holy Spirit.'
I have seen and I testify that this is the Son of God."
Matthew 3:11-17, Mark 1:9-12, Luke 3:3-22, John 1:29-34

John Baptizes Jesus

After the long trip to the Jordan and the emotional drain of today's events, I convinced the boys we needed to stop and find rest for the night. We were able to find an inn in a small town on the outskirts of Bethany beyond the Jordan. The path must be a byway for the caravans traveling from Nazareth to Jerusalem. I have a small room with a cot, but the boys chose to sleep outside. This privacy gives me a chance to write while the day's events are still fresh in my mind.

The innkeeper looked very suspicious when I asked for a small amount of papyrus and some ink. I explained my sons needed to write a message to send to their brother. Someday I will be able to write in public and shout to the world that a woman has a brain just like a man. Well, maybe I will not, but my prayer is that my daughters will. If Sarah ever gets a chance, her voice will be heard. Her determination is quite stronger than mine. Living in a house full of boys has forced her to express herself loudly, but I must stop my rambling and return to my story for I have much to write.

Early yesterday morning, James and I quietly prepared to slip away while the others slept, but the other brothers would have no part of it. Simon agreed to stay with Leah and Sarah and tend the shop. Since Leah is expecting their baby any time now, he is not going to leave her side. I love the way he is such a devoted and caring husband. His actions remind me so much of Joseph. Sarah also wanted to come, but graciously agreed to stay behind and help Leah. I also think it is time for Joel to make another visit. That period of separation required before a wedding is becoming shorter and shorter.

The early rays from the sun barely peeked over the horizon as the boys and I left for the Jordan. After overhearing them discussing various ways to carry me, I insisted we take the donkey for me to ride when I grew tired. Without him, I would not have been able to keep up with the pace of the young men in the scorching heat. A few times I forced the boys to rest, when I noticed they were struggling. They were determined to spend only one short night on the road before reaching our destination.

As we approached the Jordan, we could hear the rumblings of people talking long before we reached the river. The crowd listening to John's preaching and waiting to be immersed by him stretched as far as the eye could see. It took forever to reach a place where we could see the river. The message John preached about the baptism of repentance for the forgiveness of sins had to seem foreign to the people there, but they were eager to learn more and accept this new way of thinking. His message completely ignores the sacrifices required in the Laws of Moses.

It is with much regret that I admit I understand why the religious leaders are questioning what John is saying. I know who John is, but I also sensed his words might be blasphemy. Soldiers in the crowd constantly whispered to each other. If the crowd had not been so big and so intent on being baptized by John to receive whatever he offered, I fear the soldiers would have arrested him. I believe they feared for their lives had they tried to take John by force.

I do not know where Jesus had been unless he spent some time with Elizabeth and his little nephews. We got to the edge of the water just as Jesus walked out from the crowd. As soon as John saw Jesus, he started telling the crowd, "This is the one I have been talking about—the one whom I am not even worthy to wash the feet of."

John came out of the water to meet Jesus. As they talked, I could tell the conversation agitated John. Finally, John shook his head and raised his hands as if to say, "I give up. Have it your way."

John took Jesus by the shoulders, hugged him and led him into the water. Then he said something I could not fully understand. Silence absorbed the crowd as John immersed Jesus into the water just as he had been doing everyone else.

When Jesus emerged from the water, the strangest thing happened. A form like a dove descended from heaven and landed on his shoulder. A ray of bright light appeared that reached all the way from the heavens to Jesus standing in the water. A deep, loud voice roared from the clouds. People in the back of the crowd heard it just as clearly as the people standing next to the water. I clearly heard the voice of my heavenly Father say, "This is my beloved son in whom I am well pleased."

My heart stopped as James grabbed my shoulders to keep me from collapsing. I knew my son had gone and God's son had come to take his place. The crowd gasped in amazement as the earth shook from the power that emanated from the scene. God's thirty year plan had been put into motion with the immersion of His son by the one He had sent to prepare the way.

When I think of what may happen to this beloved son I have nurtured from a newborn child to a grown man, my body trembles. I have known from the beginning that he belongs to my Lord, but he is still my flesh and blood, my son. I want to protect him. Why must I give up this one that drank life from my bosom and felt these warm arms around him for so many years? Why me? Why him? Why did he have to be so loving and good? The piercing of Simeon's sharp sword in my heart tells me he is gone.

After the baptism, Jesus disappeared. I ran through the crowd looking for him. Someone said he headed toward the wilderness. I tried to catch John's attention, but the crowd in the water waiting for their turn prevented any conversation with him. When we started to return home, Jesus could not be found. I know he is thirty years of age and capable of taking care of himself, but it is so unlike him to be so disrespectful. He has always been considerate of my wishes. He did not even acknowledge our presence by the river today, but there were so many people gathered around, he may have not seen us. Right now I wish I could touch him and take him home and find out more about this baptism John is performing.

His brothers and I did not get immersed today. We do not fully understand what this new message is all about. I must first talk to Jesus to find out more. When we left, hundreds of people were still in the water waiting. I even saw some of the soldiers and leaders waiting on the shore. I do not think they were interested in his preaching, but more interested in the reaction of the crowd.

Why is it so hard for people to believe what they see with their own eyes? Shortly after the incident, many were saying they heard the roar of thunder when the ray of light appeared. How can people be so deaf? I did not hear thunder, but the voice of my Lord acknowledging His son, our Messiah—the one we have been anticipating for years. Are their hearts so hardened they are blinded by the truth, even though they know this prophecy has been proclaimed by nearly all of the prophets?

As difficult as this is to admit, I must say that when I stop to reflect on today's incident, I cannot fault their disbelief. I witnessed all these things with my own eyes; the miraculous birth, the miracles Jesus performed, the hours he spent meditating with his father, and I still find myself questioning what I just witnessed.

Oh, my dear Lord, what is going to happen? How can I help Jesus if I doubt? Strengthen my faith and show me the truth. Please be with Your son through this journey I now dread. Jesus is gone and I cannot do a thing for him. You must keep him safe. Thank You for allowing me to experience the awesome baptism today. I always knew Jesus communicated with You as he sat under the tree with the bird on his shoulder, but I have never heard You speak as I heard today. You are an awesome God.

And Joseph her husband, being a righteous man and not wanting to disgrace her,
planned to send her away secretly.
Matthew 1:19
When His own people heard of this,…they were saying, "He has lost His senses."
Mark 3:21

Mary and Her sons Discuss Jesus' Baptism

We finally made it home after a long, hot trip. The boys are resting while I sit in the moonlight writing in my journal to preserve the happenings of the day. This morning I heard the boys scurrying outside just before the sun rays flooded my room at the inn. They were eager to get home. With my writings from the night before tucked away in my tunic, I met them at the door.

The dirt roads shed a layer of dust over our sandaled feet as we quietly plodded down the beaten path to Nazareth. Sparks of excitement charged from the group, but no one had anything to say. After some time, Judas interrupted the tense silence. From his tone, I could tell the boys had discussed the events from yesterday. "Mother, what do the actions of Jesus mean? And John, why is he acting this way? Does he not realize he is going to get in trouble with our leaders?"

Joseph and James nodded their heads in agreement. I prayed a silent prayer for God's help to say the words I needed to explain the true Jesus. They needed to know the whole truth.

"Boys, let us rest a few minutes. I have something very important to tell you," I said as I looked for a place to sit. "As you know, Jesus and John have been friends for some time. What you do not know is the complete story of that miraculous friendship. Please listen closely as my Lord gives me the words to explain."

I told them of the visit from Gabriel with the proclamation that I would conceive a seed from the Holy Spirit who would be the Messiah of the world. I told them about my visit to Elizabeth shortly after this salutation. I could not tell them of the reason for my hurried visit. I cannot destroy the respect they have for their father by telling them he did not believe my story. They were told I went to help and learn from her. I will never tell anyone of the humiliation Joseph felt when the angel finally appeared to him after he doubted my faithfulness and I hurried to Elizabeth to escape possible stoning for adultery.[4] Hopefully, that secret will die with me.

4   *Jesus My Son: Mary's Journal of Jesus' Early Life,* 7

I explained some of the things Jesus had performed while at home. How he had saved their lives when the cart almost rolled over on them. How he had breathed life into Sarah after her lifeless birth. James remembered falling out of the tree and the pain from his arm, but he did not remember Jesus doing anything but touching the hurting spot. He cried too hard to see the broken bones protruding from the skin. They listened intently and gasped a few times. I could tell they did not fully believe my story.

Judas jumped from his seat and exclaimed, "Mother, to what lengths would you go to protect Jesus? I know you would not lie, but I also know how love can sometimes misinterpret even the slightest gestures."

He marched down the path waving angry fists as Joseph silently joined him.

"Mother, why did you wait so long to tell us this? Maybe we could have helped you or helped Jesus. Where is he now? Do you think we need to go find him and bring him back before he and John both get into even more trouble?" James shouted pacing up and down. I could not tell if he believed me or just wanted to find out the truth. He left to join Judas and Joseph.

Only the donkey stayed to hear my muffled cry. We continued the trip under a blanket of silence. When we arrived home, all the boys fled to the shop ignoring the delight of their sister to see them. Sarah looked at me with questioning disbelief as she helped me dismount the donkey. Without comment, she took the donkey to feed and water him. Simon ran to the shop to hear the story from his brothers as Leah tenderly put her arms around my shoulders to help me to my cot. Bless her heart. She has less reason than anyone to understand, yet she seemed to sense the turmoil emerging around us.

We have not yet seen Jesus. Maybe he knows we all need some time to gather our thoughts. Perhaps he needed to talk to John for awhile. I wish he had told me his plans. It is a mother's right to worry—no matter how old our children are. I am exhausted and going to bed to end this punishing day. My prayer is for Jesus to be here in the morning and for his brothers to understand.

Dear Lord, give us an understanding heart. My heart aches for the confusion I have planted in the boy's hearts. They do not understand and will not until You find fit to soften their hearts to the truth. Will You do the same for the rest of the people? If his family cannot believe, how can anyone else accept the story I have to tell? I pray for guidance of the truths I must tell and those I must also keep secret. I beg for the wisdom to separate the two.

At once the Spirit sent him out into the desert,
Mark 1:12-13

Jesus is Missing for Ten Days

Tonight I am writing to relieve the tension in my body that is waiting to erupt at the slightest movement. I have walked a beaten path from the shop to the house, hoping Jesus might appear. He has been gone ten days without one word and I am sick with worry.

His brothers are relieved he has not returned home. They say he is following John, and he will be home soon. I am not so sure. We have not continued our discussion, but time has eased the tension created from our previous conversation. Perhaps Jesus is giving a lesson from King David who often wrote of the healing power of time.

Jesus has always been considerate of my feelings. Worry is not a word I would ever use to define my relationship with him except for the time when he was twelve and Joseph and I lost him in the temple in Jerusalem. After searching for three days, we finally found him. He told me then I should not worry because he must be about his father's business. Maybe he is doing that now, but he could have told me. I find it hard to believe he has been here for thirty years and in an instant he can disappear without a word. How can his mission on earth be complete with the miraculous occurrence of his baptism?

Does my Lord think I have forgotten about my son just because he has finally become His son? Why does He not send Jesus home? God knows all things. He knows I am worried sick. I guess He also knows I have no reason to worry, because Jesus is safe under His wings. Why do I keep forgetting? When I take the time to stop and think who Jesus is, I know my worry is unfounded. I wish I could stop being a mother as easily as Jesus has stopped being my son. But God did not make mothers like that. We are destined to worry and fret over our children from the day they are conceived until the day our mind does not allow us to worry anymore, as my mother did, or we encounter death—whichever comes first.

James tries to console me by saying Jesus has gone to live his own life and will not come back home to stay. He says I may have to be content with the rest of the brothers and let Jesus go. Although James loves Jesus, I sometimes feel he may be a little resentful of Jesus' attitude. James has never liked for Jesus to sit by the tree for hours ignoring the work that must be done in the shop. James is a believer in work. He must do so much work before he can enjoy any free time. If he is not working in the shop, he is out hunting to provide food for our family or helping some of the neighbors. He would not be content if he could not enjoy his work.

When Jesus began to lessen his responsibility around the shop after Joseph died, James became annoyed. As the first born son, Jesus felt responsible for our care until our death. With Joseph dying at such a young age, Jesus' responsibility disappeared. He knows if I need someone to care for me, Elizabeth or Sarah will become my caregiver. I could even stay here with Simon and Leah. My well-being does not give Jesus a minute of concern.

If I could only find John. I am sure he knows of Jesus' whereabouts. Perhaps they are together reminiscing over the good times they shared or catching up on the last few years when they did not see each other. It had been almost five years since John visited before the last time when he came to spend a few hours with Jesus. When he left that day, I thought he acted strange and that maybe an angel had visited him. All I can do now is pray for their safe return.

Dear God, only You know where he is. Set me free from this worry so I can carry on with my daily life. It is sad to waste all this time on worry when I know in my heart that You are going to take care of Your son just as You do all Your other children. You have some business for him to complete and are not going to let anything happen to him until Your plan is finished. I just pray You allow him to come home safely to share that destiny with all of us. May his brothers find in their hearts a reason to rejoice over their brother's safe return?

The word of God came unto John, the son of Zechariah, in the wilderness.
Luke 3:2

Jesus is Missing for Twenty Days

If worrying is what I did the last time I wrote, I do not know what I would call what I am doing today! The anxiety in my mind has become like a volcano waiting to erupt. John came around yesterday—alone. He has not seen Jesus since the day of his baptism. John said he and Jesus had a disagreement over the need to be baptized. John told Jesus he did not feel qualified to baptize him and asked Jesus to baptize him instead. Jesus insisted he must be baptized by John just as all the others have been.

I remember seeing that conversation when John threw his arms up in surrender. John did not think Jesus needed to be baptized since he is God's son, but Jesus insisted he must be baptized in order to fulfill all righteousness. Only after Jesus' insistence did John agree to immerse him in the same manner as everyone else.

I asked John about a statement he had made to the crowd. When Jesus approached him, I heard John tell the people, "A man comes after me who has surpassed me because he was before me. I myself did not know him, but the reason I came baptizing with water was that he might be revealed to Israel." I asked John to explain how he did not know Jesus since they are cousins and have been friends since they were born.

John said he and Jesus knew each other as earthly cousins, but that Jesus had been around before the beginning of time in heaven with his Father. John did not know Jesus as that person, but God had revealed to John that "The man on whom you see the Spirit come down and remain is He who will baptize with the Holy Spirit."

John further explained that Elizabeth and Zachariah had revealed to him that Jesus possessed a special relationship with our heavenly Father. John did not know God would reveal his son's identity as the Messiah until the dove representing the Holy Spirit rested on his shoulder and the voice spoke from heaven. I clearly heard that voice speak from the heavens and knew Jesus' Father had acknowledged him. People around me said the wind only howled. Why are people so afraid to hear the truth at times? A voice loud enough for the entire crowd to hear spoke and said, "This is my son." How can people dismiss it as a natural happening?

Reluctantly, I must admit Jesus' brothers did not believe they heard a voice either. Walking back home, they discussed the baptism and wondered about its meaning. Even though I explained the nature of Jesus' birth, they have difficulty believing their mother gave birth to a baby who had been conceived by the seed of God. It is unbelievable that the brother they played with, worked with and lived with is the Messiah. I do understand their disbelief. For thirty years they saw nothing to indicate Jesus could be anything but a normal brother. They never realized all the miraculous things he performed for our family when he lived with us. Hopefully, this absence from their brother will allow them the needed time for reflection.

Jesus has not been seen since the day he was baptized. John thought he returned home and did not even know we were there to watch. John spent the next few weeks baptizing the crowds as they came seeking his righteousness of repentance and salvation. John said he had to slip away from the crowds to come today. I heard the boys ask John about his message and how he conceived the idea. John explained that the word of God came to him while he lived in the wilderness. He knew the time had come to prepare the way for Jesus. I know his brothers listened and heard what John said, but I can tell they are not entirely convinced. It did appear their hearts were softening a little.

John said when he started talking to people, they were so eager to listen to his message. Some actually thought he might be the Messiah, but he quickly told them he only came to prepare the way. He could not contain his delight that God revealed Jesus' true identity through the Holy Spirit in the form of the dove to the crowd that day. John said he had always suspected Jesus was the Messiah, but the revelation from God confirmed his suspicion without a doubt. I know from experience how reassuring God's revelations can be.

What could have happened to Jesus? Why would he just go away without telling anyone? If he were younger, I would scold him when I find him. And I will find him! In my heart I know his Father is protecting him, but I just wish I could talk to him. Will I ever understand what is going to happen? I know Jesus is God's son, but he is also mine. And I love him deeply. I knew this day would come, but I expected it to be much sooner. I never thought I would have him for thirty years so he would become such a big part of my life. How can I just forget my son? Has he gone home to live with his Father without the earthly kingdom? Without even telling us goodbye?

Dear Father, You chose me because You knew I had enough faith to get me through, but, Father, does it have to be so hard? Does my heart have to be torn apart with not knowing? I am again beginning to wonder why You would chose me since I am having such a difficult time dealing with his disappearance. Why You would chose me, a common person, I cannot even begin to comprehend. If I did not have my faith and my prayers, I fear my mind would be gone.

So, dear God, I continue my prayer. Please take care of my beloved son. Bring him home safely. Give me the understanding I need to comprehend what is happening and the peace that comes from knowing You have control and he is still Your son. I cannot imagine You bringing him to earth to encounter some hideous death. Forgive me when I forget and worry like any mother.

For He will give His angels charge concerning you, to guard you in all your ways.
Psalm 91:11

Jesus is Missing for Thirty Days

Thirty days! I can hardly write tonight with the volcano inside my body that is becoming impossible to control. My patience to accept God's plan is so thin, I believe I could see right through it. Where is he? How is he eating? Where is he sleeping? Has some wild animal devoured him by now? Why is he doing this to me? If it were not for his brothers and Sarah, I would be out there looking for him. They will not let me go.

Like her brothers, Sarah cannot accept what I have told her about Jesus' birth. She sees him only as a loving caring brother. She cannot think beyond what she has seen. She knows I would not lie about something this spectacular, but she chooses to close her eyes and her heart to the truth. I sometimes think she feels I am getting old and my memory is failing me. Her condescending attitude when I tell her all the things that have happened is beginning to annoy me. I have not let any of them read my journal for fear of what they will say. I certainly cannot let them read the part about Joseph's disbelief. I may have to mark those words out of my journal completely to protect Joseph's memory.

They all say Jesus is old enough to take care of himself and he will come back when he is ready. The more I try to explain the circumstances of his birth, the more they close up their comprehension. God has not chosen to open their minds to the truth yet. My Lord must have some need for their disbelief now so he can reveal the truth at a later date. I know Jesus is a miracle baby and I am so proud of who he has become—until now! But still, in the midst of my worry, I know he is doing what he thinks he must.

If Sarah's wedding plans did not have us all running around like wild rock rabbits, I would be full of sickness over the grief I feel. The wedding is in a few weeks and everyone is busy preparing things for her move to Cana. With the death of Joseph, Jesus is supposed to present her to Joel. She will be so heartbroken if he is not there. She has planned everything to the minutest detail and needs Jesus to be there. James is more than willing to perform the duty, but Sarah is afraid James may arrive in his hunting clothes, not bathed and smelling of the wild animals he hunts. James is not one to care much what people think of his appearance. I am certain Jesus will not disappoint the little sister whom he breathed life into the day she was born.[5]

Ever since John's last visit, I had watched Jesus stand and stare into space. He would sometimes play his harp for hours at a time. His prayers during those last weeks were heart wrenching. When the travelers came and said John was baptizing in the Jordan, Jesus dropped everything to go see him. He had been waiting to hear that news for some time. A powerful force compelled him to search for John. He did not even wait for us to accompany him. If we had not rushed, we would not have seen the miracle of his baptism. Jesus' knew he needed to be baptized by John. I do not even think the dove descending on his shoulder surprised him. He and John stared at each other and smiled that same understanding smile they have been sharing since they were young boys.

James is very adamant that all is well and Jesus is only doing what he has wanted to do for some time. I wonder how much Jesus has talked to James since he has so willingly accepted the fact that Jesus has been missing for such a long time. Does he know more than he is saying? Has Jesus revealed his whereabouts to James and he has chosen not to tell me? I will be so angry if I find out James has known all along. I do not think he comprehends what is going on, but I think John's testimony helped soften his heart enough to at least listen to my story.

Dear God, it has been thirty days since anyone has had any contact with Your son. Does that not concern You? Do You think it is not important for us to know where he is? You could not have sent him to earth just to experience John's baptism. There must be more. What about the throne of David he is to inherit? Please help me understand. I know I should not worry, but dear God, I cannot help it. I am sorry, but do not forget I am merely an earthly mother. I do not have that omniscient power You possess as his heavenly Father. The future is so very uncertain for me. I have diligently searched the scriptures and can find nothing about our Redeemer disappearing for thirty days. Forgive me Father, but You must remember, You are the one who made mothers this way.

Surely, You have not sent Your son to earth just to torment me.

---

5   *Jesus My son: Mary's Journal of Jesus' Early Life,* 153

Wherefore art thou, my Son?

My faith is strong
but my heart is grieving.
I am only human.
Why has my God not heard my plea?
Where is my son—Your son?
They are one and the same.

Forgive me if I forget,
but I do not have Your heavenly knowledge
to know that all is well with him.
I cannot see him.

I only know he has been missing too long.
Has he befallen bad times?
A hungry animal
a crazed man
a natural disaster
could all take his life from me.

Almost forty days have passed.
Why has he not contacted me?
I am his mother.
I should know.
Do You, my Lord, have him?
Did You call him home?

Why am I so in the dark?
I have done nothing but love and cherish
the son You gave me.
How could You do this?

My soul cries out to You
just like King David's.
Deliver me from this terrible
pit of grief from not knowing.

Can You see my pain?
I beseech You my Lord
as King David beseeched You.
"Answer me when I call to You,
O my righteous Lord.
Give me relief from my distress;
Be merciful to me and hear my prayer."
Deliver me from this void of knowing.

Jesus, full of the Holy Spirit, returned from the Jordan
and was led by the Spirit in the desert,
where for forty days he was tempted by the devil.
He ate nothing during those days, and at the end of them he was hungry.
Matthew 4:1-11; Mark 1:12-13; Luke 4:1-13

Jesus Returns Home after Forty Days

I had to stop everything to share my happiness with my journal. Praise God! I think. I did not know whether to welcome him home with open arms or send him to the roof for punishment. Jesus came home today acting as if he had been on a short walk to visit a few friends. He did pick up a few cousins and new friends along the way.

I have tried to keep myself busy with Sarah's wedding preparations so I would not lose my mind with worry. Today I was pouring my energy into sewing Sarah's veil, when I looked up to see Jesus standing in the doorway. My heart leaped for joy as I rushed to greet him. Soon Sarah and all his brothers were gathered around him. Judas showed some reluctance, but eventually welcomed his brother home. It seems this lengthy absence has done wonders to free the doubt of Jesus' siblings.

He should look frail and sickly from being gone for so long, but his physical appearance is amazingly normal. I do not know how he managed to live and evidently, he does not care to tell anyone. That mystery may never be solved. The only explanation I can think of is that he must have fallen and hit his head and suffered from memory loss. I really do not care what happened. I feel blessed he has returned home healthy and safe.

When I told him of my worry, he just stared at me as if to ask "Why?" He mumbled something about being with his Father as Simeon's sword again pierced my heart. If only I understood more of this mission and could see through that deep layer of privacy that surrounds him. I must get used to the fact that he does have some important business to perform.

I do not know where he picked up his cousins, James and John, or the brothers, Andrew and Peter, or their friends, Philip and Nathanial, but they are outside sitting around Joseph's shop talking as if nothing ever happened. Even Judas has chosen to listen to their stories. In their rejoicing of his return home, they have forgiven him for the worry he has caused us. My wayward son has returned home, I must stop and prepare a celebration feast in his honor. They must all be starved.

Dear Lord, thank You for answering my prayer and bringing my son and his new friends home safely. Please forgive me for being an earthly mother and doubting Your intentions. Had I only believed what I knew in my heart? A wonderful feeling of peace surrounds me just by being around Jesus and his new followers. My earthly cares disappear when I am resting in the quiet comfort of his presence.

Nathanael said to him, "Can any good thing come out of Nazareth?"
Philip said to him , "Come and see." .
Matthew 4:18-22; Mark 1:16-20; Luke 5:1-11; John 1:35-51

Mary Meets Jesus' New Friends

What a glorious day! We enjoyed a wonderful celebration with Jesus and the friends he brought with him. After being sufficiently fed they are now on the roof resting. I am thankful for this additional time to spend with my journal. Today I took a step closer to understanding Jesus' mission. The delightful conversation with the men during our meal helped ease the anger of Jesus' brothers. They may not believe him yet, but they were awed by the stories of his friends.

Nathaniel, one of the men, is from Cana. He said his first thoughts about Jesus when he heard he lived in Nazareth were, "What good can come from Nazareth?" I told him I wondered how people would react to his home town. Nazareth is not looked upon as one of the holiest villages. Everyone has always assumed the Messiah would come from the holy city, Jerusalem.

Nathaniel told me Jesus knew everything about him—things no one could possibly know. Jesus convinced Nathaniel to leave everything and follow him when Jesus told how he had seen Nathaniel resting by a fig tree before their meeting. We discussed how difficult it will be for him to convince people that he really is this Messiah foretold by the prophets.

After seeing all that has happened in the last few months, I am certain this is the beginning of his kingdom. When I saw Jesus being baptized and the acknowledgement of his Father, I knew the transformation from my earthly son to my Lord's heavenly son had taken place. I now realize his Father needed those forty days to prepare Jesus for his mission.

After waiting so long, I almost had given up hope of that promised kingdom and the mansion in which we would live. Today I realized why it has taken so long. God had to wait until I could follow Jesus to record as much of his ministry as possible. He knows how important my journal is in telling this version of his son's life. Only God knows what place I will occupy in this upcoming part of my son's life.

My family is such that my responsibilities are all being handed down to some very capable hands. Leah has willingly taken over most of the household chores. Even with the impending birth of her first child, she still provides all the needs of her brothers-in-law. After the Sabbath, Sarah will leave for Cana for her wedding. James will go with me to be with Jesus. Simon, Joseph and Judas will be tending the carpentry shop. None of them could bear to lose the shop. As long as they have that shop, they have a part of their father. It will be a family business for a long time.

Of course, Simon will soon be tending to his own family, including the baby who is due any time. While we are gone, they will manage things. The other boys will soon find their mates and will either move into our house or build one of their own. At this point, I do not believe any of them will ever move far from home. I had wondered about Judas moving away, but after his venture, he seems content to stay close to home.

Sometimes we must let our children go in order for them to appreciate their family. Once they reach a certain age, we cannot live their life for them. I have watched as children who were forbidden to explore any outside interests, run away at the first opportune moment to escape the restrictions placed upon them by their parents. Discipline is important in raising a child, but children must also be given freedom to explore.

I have nothing that will keep me from following my son wherever he goes except for a few grandsons which I will have to come back to visit occasionally. I already miss them just thinking about not being able to see them.

My job in this mission is to record the events as I see them. I know God will direct me in what to say so I am not worried about my work. I feel if God thinks it is important, I will be writing about it. It is going to be a remarkable but uncertain time. Not knowing what the future may bring, I only know I must write as I see it. The sign of the dove on Jesus' shoulder at the baptism let me know that all is well and my job is complete except for the recording. God gave me a gift for writing and I plan to use it as much as possible. As long as He provides the materials I need, I know I am fulfilling His plan.

Dear God, You are so mighty. I stand in awe of Your greatness. Why did You choose me—such a lowly person to be the mother of such a wonderful king? May his kingdom come peacefully and spread throughout the world. May his words be spoken with wisdom as I know they will be since You are guiding him. Please keep him from the hand of evil and love him as I have loved him. As children grow up, mothers must let them go. The void left by Jesus leaving will soon be filled with new grandchildren, but it will never be the same. My heart aches but also rejoices, when I think of the changes I must witness.

The tempter came to him and said, "If you are the Son of God…"
Matthew 4:1-11; Mark 1:12-13; Luke 4:1-16
Man does not live by bread alone, but man lives by everything
that proceeds out of the mouth of the Lord.
Deuteronomy 8:3
You shall not put the Lord your God to the test.
Deuteronomy 6:16
You shall fear only the Lord your God; and you shall
worship Him and swear by His name.
Deuteronomy 6:13

Jesus Heals Leah's Father and Tells Mary of His Temptation

Dear Journal, it is with a grateful heart that I write my entry tonight. Today Jesus explained his mysterious disappearance and confirmed without a doubt his almighty powers.

This morning Sarah, Leah and I were inside going through things, getting ready for Sarah's move to Cana, when Jesus walked in and stood by us for a long time just watching. I could tell he had something on his mind, so I took a break.

Jesus asked if we could take a walk. Always eager to spend more time with him, I handed Leah my items and followed Jesus down the road toward the village. Breaking the silence, he finally said, "Mother, there is something I have wanted to do for some time, but have not been able. Do you remember the day of the accident when the sharp cutting tool blinded Leah's father, Silas, the sandal maker? I feel my Father caused that incident to test me. I wanted to heal Silas' blindness, but my Father would not allow me. I too had to learn that He has a reason for everything. Now it is time to perform that healing."

Jesus continued, "My Father had a plan as we now know. Simon and Leah would never have married had that accident not occurred. When you and father offered Simon's services, you had no idea things would end like this. You have to admit, Leah is a welcome addition to our house full of boys. She cares for them like they were all her brothers. So something good did come out of that bad incident."

Not fully understanding his words, I chose to remain silent. We walked along the path making small talk until we arrived at the sandal shop. Miriam and Silas sat at a work bench while Miriam directed Silas' hands as they worked on a pair of new sandals. Jesus and I greeted Silas and Miriam with a proper hug. Then Miriam and I walked outside as Jesus sat down beside Silas.

We were having a delightful talk about our pending grandchild, when a smiling Jesus appeared at the doorway indicating he had finished his task. Silas stood in the doorway with Jesus. As Jesus and I started back home, Miriam went to help Silas back into the house.

We had gone only a short distance when I heard Miriam's scream. I turned in time to hear Silas exclaim, "Look, Miriam, it is a miracle! I can see. Jesus made me see. He healed my eyes! Look, Miriam, touch them. See, they are healed. What a joyful day for us. I promised Jesus I would not go outside and show everyone my delight until after the Sabbath. Then we can proclaim it to the heavens."

"Thank you, Jesus," Miriam called after us as she hugged her jubilant husband.

Jesus looked at me and said, "I will have a peaceful sleep tonight."

"Why can he not tell?" I asked.

"It is not my time, Mother. This gift from my Father cannot yet be known publicly. I trust they will not tell anyone until it is permitted. My day in the synagogue will be ruined if my abilities become known before I leave here."

We walked the rest of the way in silence until we neared the big tree. He sat down and motioned for me to sit beside him. "Have you been wondering about my disappearance these last forty days?" he began. "I have always tried to respect your feelings and regretted that I could not supply an explanation before my Father called me to the wilderness."

"Finally," I whispered as relief flooded my soul. I waited attentively for his explanation. I could not help but feel his pain as he described the time he had spent alone in the wilderness. He said immediately after he left the baptism at the Jordan, the Holy Spirit directed him to the wilderness where he fasted and prayed for forty days. No wonder he looked so thin!

He continued his story of how the angel Michael (I call him Satan) had visited him and tried numerous times to tempt him to deny his Father. I could tell the visits disturbed him. He said at first, Satan had appealed to his bodily needs by requesting him to turn some stones into bread. Satan knew he had not eaten and tried to convince Jesus that his Father would have wanted him to stay healthy and provide his needs. Satan told Jesus that any son of God should be able to perform such a simple deed. Jesus said he quoted the words of our great leader Moses and told Satan, "Man does not live on bread alone, but on every word that comes from the mouth of God."

Next, Jesus said the angel took him to the holy city and stood beside him on the highest point of the temple. Jesus said Satan looked at him with a sly grin and said that any son of God should be able to jump down and let the angels come and lift him back up. Jesus said he simply smiled at him and said, "It is also written: 'Do not put the Lord your God to the test'."

Jesus said Satan again tried to tempt him by taking him to a very high mountain. They were observing all the splendor of the world when Satan said he would give the kingdoms of the world to Jesus if he would only bow down and worship him. With that Jesus said he told him "Get away from me. For it is also written: 'Worship the Lord your God and serve him only'."

Jesus smiled and said Satan finally left him alone. Immediately, the angels came and attended to his needs and restored his health. We both sat in silence for some time. I could only think of the pain he had to endure and wondered how this prepared him for his kingdom.

Through our discussion, I realized his Father had presented him with the same worldly temptations every person on earth encounters with their lust of the body, their pride of their possessions, and their constant quest for power. He had not spared any earthly temptations from His son.

As I finally have time to write this, I am so thankful God allowed Jesus to tell me the story so I could preserve it for all to know. It is important for people to know he has endured everything any human will ever face. Every temptation he encountered, he answered with a quote from scripture. The Holy Spirit who ministered to Jesus and protected him is the very same one that ministers to and protects us. What an awesome thought. If Jesus had not told me these things, how would the world know? People tend to think because Jesus is the son of God he will easily live the perfect life. But with these forty days of temptation, God has shown the world that just like Jesus, we too can conquer any temptation with scripture He has provided. We must know without a doubt that our faith will see us through.

We continued our walk to the house with everything looking a little brighter. The shadow of doubt that had once covered my world had been removed. All at once, sunshine streamed from the heavens as birds again were singing their happy tune.

My heart wants to rejoice for the revelation of our Messiah. Instead, my mind is filled with apprehension of what Jesus may have to endure because he is God's son. I do know that whatever befalls him, he will be directed by his Father who will share the same feelings I do as we observe the escalation of our shared son to his kingdom.

Dear Lord, I believe this may be the last private conversation I will have with Jesus. You have proven You are preparing him for whatever plans are in place. I still know he will receive a kingdom, but I am beginning to think it is not the one I have been expecting all these years. I am thankful You have given me the ability to record these events so the world can be enlightened by his life and Your willingness to treat him equally with all of Your other children. It is comforting to know You love each of us so much You are willing to let Your only son suffer the same temptations as all believers. I am so blessed among women and You are still the awesome God I have loved for so many years.

The two disciples heard him speak, and they followed him.
John 1:35-51

Jesus' First Followers Discuss Their Feelings

Thank goodness we only have one more day after tonight before the Sabbath. Sarah has completely exhausted everyone with her orders and demands. After we had eaten our meal tonight, Sarah and I began making preparations for our Sabbath meals. Jesus again walked to the door and stood there for some time to watch us. Just like the shepherds on the night of his birth, he appeared to be etching the scene in his mind to carry with him as he continues his journey. I sensed him silently telling us goodbye.

When we finished the necessary preparations, I went outside to listen to the men while Sarah went to her room to finish packing for her move to Cana. I cannot bear to watch her pick up things and hug them only to place them back knowing there is not enough room to take all her precious treasures. One time she picked up the scroll from which Joseph had read her the last story before his death. She quickly put it down and said with a quivering voice, "Simon will need to read this to his child." It is too heartbreaking to watch. I have to leave the room. I cannot believe this long-planned wedding is only a few days away.

Usually, the bride would wait with her attendants for her groom to come and carry her off to the wedding ceremony, but since the wedding is going to be at Joel's, she agreed to compromise with that tradition. Most wedding ceremonies last around seven days. Sarah's will be shortened because she insisted Elizabeth must come and serve as her attendant. Elizabeth agreed to bring her sons and stay two nights but no longer. I think Sarah appreciated an excuse not to celebrate the full time. She just wants to marry Joel and then begin her new role as his wife. She will be a caring and loving companion for her husband.

Later Jesus and his brothers were sitting around listening to the men tell how they had so willingly left everything to obey Jesus' command to follow him. Andrew said he and Peter were fishing one day, contemplating the message of John, when Jesus came by and called out to them to "Follow me, and I will make you fishers of men."

Andrew said, "We never looked back. We left our nets immediately and followed him."

"We did the same thing," James said. "We even left our father, Zebedee, in the boat mending the nets with the servants. He is probably still yelling like the roar of thunder!"

Jesus' brothers enjoyed a good laugh since they have heard that roar and knew exactly what James meant. Oh, my, I can just see my sister, Salome, when Zebedee returned home to tell her of the day's events. It is good she has other children and a few grandchildren to occupy her time. I believe she will understand when Zebedee tells her it is Jesus they are following.

I am glad Jesus is surrounding himself with good, caring people. We used to see James and John occasionally when the boys were growing up, but they were fishermen and we were carpenters so our paths seldom crossed except for the festivals. Our religious celebrations have always been a gathering time for family.

I often wondered how James and John could be such mild mannered men when I looked at their father. Everyone in our family wondered how the boisterous Zebedee could ever choose Salome as his wife. They appear to be as different as night and day, but in our house Salome had never been shy to speak her mind. Zebedee had a reputation as the best fisherman around and made a good living with his fishing abilities. Most people thought of him as a loud and boisterous man. My father did not accept his unusually high barter until Salome convinced him she desired to be Zebedee's wife. My sister has always desired the finer things in life.

Her decision allowed Joseph to ask for my hand. My father would never have allowed me to be betrothed before Salome. I remember saying a silent thank you when they finalized their agreement.

Another fellow named Phillip also accompanied Jesus. He is a tall, lanky man from Bethsaida, like Andrew and Peter. His friend, Nathaniel, who earlier had expressed his reservation about our Messiah coming from Nazareth, is the last one Jesus chose. The men are all pleasing to the eye, but do not possess unnatural beauty. To say they are anything but average in looks or intelligence is an understatement. Peter is the only one I know who leaves a family behind. An unlikely group of men to help Jesus establish his kingdom, but I am sure they each possess hidden gifts.

My role in this new period in Jesus' life will diminish for many reasons. For one, Jesus implied it could be very dangerous for any of his loved ones to follow him. The message he has to tell is much different than the belief of people today and will probably not be accepted by any of the spiritual leaders and certainly, not the Roman rulers. Also, he says he must concentrate on the fulfillment of this message and cannot be concerned for our safety. If we follow him, he says he will not be able to recognize us as his family. How can I ignore a son of whom I am so proud?

I have waited for this to happen for so long, I had almost given up hope of that promised kingdom and the mansion in which we would all live. Now that the time is near, I realize how wrong I may have been. Is there even going to be an earthly kingdom? Will we live in a mansion? I wonder if God knew I would misinterpret Gabriel's message so badly. Did He plant the thought of David's throne in my mind to keep me alert for signs? If He did, it worked. The thought of that mansion has been in the back of my mind since that proclamation. When our house became so crowded, I would think of the spacious rooms in the mansion where we would someday live. The hope of something better has made this life bearable.

These things had to happen in this time frame to allow me to follow Jesus so I could record as many of his activities as God will allow. I have nothing to keep me from following him wherever he goes except for my dear little grandchildren. Although I will miss them, I rejoice for the caring and devoted parents who have made their family a top priority. They need my prayers more than they need my presence. I can offer those wherever I lay my head.

My job in this mission is to record the events as I see them. I know God will direct me in my writings, so I am not worried. If He thinks an event is important, I will be writing about it. It is going to be a remarkable time. I am still uncertain about the particulars of His kingdom, but I am certain I must write the things I see.

The sign of the dove on his shoulder at the baptism let me know that all is well and my role as Jesus' mother is complete. My new role is scribe. God gave me a gift of writing and I plan to do as much as possible. If I am doing what He wants, I trust He will provide whatever I need.

After everyone had gone to bed, Jesus and I silently sat under the stars. He took my hand and gently kissed it. "Thank you, Mother, for being such a gentle-spirited person," he said. "You can rest now for your work is complete."

Little does he know that a mother's work never ends? Whatever he endures, I will endure. Whenever he rejoices, I will rejoice. Simeon's sword has pierced my heart many times and it will not rest in its sheath until I am no more.

"I know your Father is in control as He always has been," I told him through misty eyes. "I am thankful He allowed Joseph and me the freedom to raise you as we wanted. We have given you the love and guidance of a normal family. Do not judge your brothers too harshly for not fully believing in you. They know you lived a normal life with us. They do not understand how you can be this almighty redeemer who is going to free us from our slavery to the Romans. You must be patient, for Your father will soften their hearts and they will believe in due time."

"Dear mother," he said still holding my hands, "the slavery you speak of is none of my concern. I came not to free you from trials, but to make your trials bearable with the hope of a glorious kingdom. I know this thought may be foreign to you, but you will understand in due time, as will the rest of my family. But you will go through some trying times before they believe and accept what I have to say. I wish I could hide these next few years from you, but, I am afraid you must endure as any mother would."

His words pierced my heart so deeply, I could not respond. My mind hovered just beyond comprehending his words. I think he is trying to prepare me for some very hard times. He knows what he must do and he is depending on the Holy Spirit to lead him through this journey.

Dear God, I want to ask You to reach from the heavens and take him to be with You to spare him this uncertain journey which will end in Your heavenly kingdom. I sense that is not Your plan. Forgive me if I go against his wishes and choose to follow from a distance. I promise to stay out of his way as he completes his mission and Your plan.

Your beauty should not come from outward adornment, such as braided hair
and the wearing of gold jewelry and fine clothes.
Instead, it should be that of your inner self,
the unfading beauty of a gentle and quiet spirit, which is of great worth in God's sight.
I Peter 3:3-4

Sarah Prepares for Her Wedding

This hectic period of preparing for Sarah's wedding is finally over. She completed her ceremonial cleansing and has been in a state of purification for some time. These last few days the cart has been loaded with her treasures to take to her new home. The strong backs of Jesus' friends were an unexpected blessing. Sarah did not have much until she realized she now has six strong men to help carry her prized possessions.

She is not about to leave behind any of the masterpieces Joseph made for her. Being the baby for nine years before his death, she became the sparkle in his eye—especially the last year of his life. When Joseph grew sick and could no longer get out of bed, Sarah stayed by his side as much as possible. All the children took turns sitting with him, but Sarah would often slip in an extra turn. Girls just have a gift for soothing the anxieties of a sick person. The boys could barely stand to watch him suffer. Joseph tried his best to hide the pain when they were by his side, but we all knew how unbearable those last days were. I thank God that my children understand He gives special gifts to certain people. They were willing to let Sarah do what they could not.

The last thing Joseph made in his shop was a crib for Sarah just like the one he made for Jesus. I remember the crib my parents sent to Cousin Elizabeth while I spent those three months with her before John's birth. As soon as I recognized the beautiful craftsmanship of Joseph's hands, I knew I could safely return home. I can still recall the relief I felt that day. He only made one other crib for Elizabeth when she expected our first grandchild. He knew he would not be here for Sarah's first child, but wanted to give her a special gift from his hands. That crib will go to Cana if Sarah has to carry it on her back.

Joseph remembered the manger Jesus used for a crib and vowed his children and grandchildren would have a better place to lay their heads. He kept his vow. I think he felt he had let me down by not finding a room or bed for Jesus that memorable night. Although we both knew God planned everything that happened, we still felt we had disappointed God.

The memories of thinking my baby would bounce out from the unbearable ride on the donkey, frantically searching for a room, the first glimpse of the crowded stable, and the unnerving visit of the shepherds are not the best memories, but when I go back and read about those happenings in my journal, I also recall some of my fondest memories.

Poor Joseph. He spent his entire life caring for someone else's son, but he never once complained or treated Jesus any differently from the rest of the children. My heart grows heavy when I think Joseph will not be here to present Sarah to her new husband, but I am glad Jesus came home in time to fulfill that duty.

Apparently, Joel's father has a nice big house where at least Elizabeth, her sons and I can stay, but I am sure the boys will be sleeping outside under the stars. Since we must travel such a long distance, Joel's family agreed to take care of the wedding preparations. The only thing necessary for a successful wedding is plenty of wine and good food. If the wine is good and plentiful, guests do not notice much else.

Joel comes from a family of carpenters who also have a trading business. If his father had not given Joel the trip with the caravan for his eighteenth birthday, Sarah would never have met him. I do not know if that is a good or bad thing, but I do know God planned the meeting. They are very much in love and will have a happy life together. It will be quite different for Sarah not being around all her adoring brothers. They all know she had a special birth, but no one knows what really happened except Jesus and me and the people who will eventually read my journal.

Since tomorrow is the Sabbath, the cart had to be loaded to be ready to be on our way early the next morning. If all goes well, we will arrive in Cana in time to help with some of the wedding preparations. Joel's family is making most of the arrangements since we agreed to have the wedding in Cana. Sarah plans to move there anyway, so the decision was easy. Plus, I wanted to see where she is going to call her new home.

Some young girls are more concerned with an outward appearance with their braided hair, gold jewelry and fine clothes. Although Sarah does possess an outward beauty, her inner beauty of a gentle and quiet spirit is of much greater worth in God's sight. Joel and his family know they are receiving a special jewel for a wife and daughter-in-law.

I am pleased to know she will be living with a good reputable family. I am saddened we could not help more, but Joel's family insisted they would supply everything. Hopefully, they have planned for the crowd we will now be taking.

I have sewed a beautiful veil to go with her new wedding tunic which I will personally carry. I do not trust any of those young men with those precious pieces of cargo.

When this wedding is over, I plan to spend some time with Jesus. I want to see what he and John are preaching. Plus, I cannot stay in this house without Sarah. I want to be here to help Leah with her new baby, but with Silas' eyesight restored, Miriam will be able to come by often to visit and rock her first grandchild. I know of that special bond with the first grandchild, especially if it is your daughter's.

Dear God, I pray You will be with us on our journey. May we have a safe and uneventful trip? Also bless the union of these two children with as much happiness and as prosperous a life as Joseph and I had. May their marriage be blessed with as many children as there are stars in the sky. I pray Sarah will never suffer through the pain of losing a child as I almost did with her.

And he came to Nazareth where he had been brought up; and as was His custom,
He entered the synagogue on the Sabbath, and stood up to read.
Luke 4:16-30; Isaiah 61:1-2

Jesus Attends His Hometown Synagogue

Oh, my! What a day this turned out to be. This morning I awakened early with the excitement of spending the day with all my family, including Jesus and his followers. There is no way I could have anticipated today's outcome.

As the sun slipped over the horizon, we climbed the knoll to the synagogue for our weekly worship. On the way, Jesus' followers were talking about him preaching in some synagogues during their trip from the Jordan. They remarked how everyone praised his speaking abilities. They said people were astonished that he spoke with such authority about the writings of the prophets. I have often heard him speak in our synagogue with that same conviction and authority. The presiding priest always eagerly handed Jesus the scroll of Isaiah to read. Things happened a little differently today.

When we arrived at the synagogue, the priest greeted our family and new friends. Sarah, Leah and I took our seat in the back with the women while the men proceeded to the benches reserved for men. The priest eagerly welcomed Jesus to the platform to read the scripture for the day. As usual, the priest selected the scroll of Isaiah from the large collection. When Jesus first began reading at age thirteen, the priest would open the scroll to a particular scripture, but since Jesus usually ignored them and picked his own reading, they eventually stopped opening it.

Today Jesus unrolled the large scroll and started reading:

> *"The Spirit of the Lord is upon me,*
> *because He anointed me to preach the gospel to the poor,*
> *He has sent me to proclaim release to the captives,*
> *and recovery of sight to the blind,"*

When Jesus read this line, he looked at me and smiled. I noticed Miriam and Silas were not at the synagogue this morning. I assumed they were waiting at home bursting with eagerness to tell their daughter the good news.

Jesus continued reading the chosen scripture.

*"to set free those who are oppressed,
to proclaim the favorable year of the Lord."*

When Jesus handed the scroll to the priest, all eyes in the room were on him. Jesus looked at the crowd and said, "Today this scripture has been fulfilled in your hearing."

It must have taken some time for the words to sink in to those thick skulls, because everyone spoke well of Jesus' reading and talked about how gracious the words fell from his lips until someone looked around and said, "Is this the son of the deceased carpenter, Joseph? How can he fulfill this scripture?"

Jesus then began quoting one of the proverbs, but the crowd became so disorderly I could not hear the words. His friends later told me he spoke about things he had been doing in other synagogues.

The men, our neighbors and friends, became furious when Jesus said, "A prophet is never welcome in his hometown." Above the murmuring of the men, Jesus quoted a scripture about Elijah and Elisha only being sent to minister to a very few. I feared the men were going to stone him right there for blasphemy, but he slipped out of the crowd and everyone finally settled down and went their own way.

We all, including Jesus' new friends, walked down the knoll with our heads hung low. Sarah could not believe our friends could say such things about Jesus. The reaction of the people we have known since we moved here years ago astounded us. What did Jesus say that infuriated them so? I always thought they would have a hard time believing the Messiah has been growing up in their midst for all these years, but I never expected such a harsh reaction. I probably would have reacted the same way if one of our neighbor's sons said those same words. Since they do not know of any of his miraculous powers, they have no reason to believe him. I wonder what they will think when they see Silas walking openly down the streets, greeting them by name.

Jesus must have gone on to Cana because he did not come home. I believe he thought it might put us in danger. I hope he is safe. It worries me that people here are not able to accept who he is and what he is preaching. Even James and the rest of his brothers are still reluctant to believe him. I saw the shocked look on James' face as he listened to Jesus this morning. If I had not witnessed the miracle of Silas and had that talk with Jesus the other night, I also would have doubted. I know Jesus is receiving direction from his Father, but his message is so new and different from the teachings we have been hearing for years. In the people's eyes, Jesus is considered a blasphemer because his revelation as the Messiah contradicts the teachings of our current leaders. They do not understand the source of his message.

Dear God, please help the people understand his mission. I know You have a plan for Jesus, our Messiah, but I have a difficult time seeing it become a reality. Unless You soften the hearts and change the attitude of the people, they will never believe. Give us the wisdom and understanding we need to accept his revelation.

On the third day a wedding took place at Cana in Galilee.
Jesus' mother was there, and Jesus and his disciples
had also been invited to the wedding.
John 2:1-2

Mary's Family Travel to Cana

Tension filled the air this morning as we started toward Cana. Sarah's usually bubbly attitude changed to disappointment when she realized Jesus did not come home last night. I assured her he would not break his promise and would arrive at her wedding. She accepted my explanation and continued making the final preparations.

I hated to leave Leah with her baby due any day, but she promised she would wait until we returned to deliver my grandchild. I secretly hope for a girl, but Simon, like most men, wants a son. I smiled as Simon hugged and reassured me they were in good hands. If necessary, I am certain Simon could deliver the baby with the same efficiency Joseph delivered Jesus.

As we walked toward Cana, I saw Silas and Miriam running toward our house. What a glorious meeting for Leah to know her Father can now see as a result of Jesus' wonderful powers. Maybe this will persuade Simon and the men of the town to believe in Jesus' miraculous ability. After the incident in the synagogue yesterday, I understand why Jesus had sworn them to secrecy until after the Sabbath. Jesus knew of the reaction of the people to his proclamation. How differently would the people have reacted if Silas had been there with his sight restored by Jesus? Only God knows that answer.

We stopped to pick up Elizabeth and her two little boys. At first, Elizabeth thought she would stay home and not take her two sons to the wedding, but Sarah shamed her sister for lack of interest. Toting two toddlers with another one on the way did not seem like a feasible trip for Elizabeth. I am thankful Jesus' friends were here to help.

To Peter's delight, little Joseph followed him around like a shadow. I understand he has some children of his own at home. It is hard for me to believe a man could leave his family and follow Jesus with the future so uncertain. Peter has no idea when he will return home to see his family. Andrew said Peter's recently widowed mother-in-law moved in with them a few weeks before he left. Maybe he needed to get away for awhile. There are very few men who can live in the same house with a mother-in-law for any length of time. No matter how much they care for each other, the situation creates tension. I have seen similar circumstances in families in Nazareth when the men would come to Joseph's shop and stay for hours just to escape their home life. But in this case it did allow Peter the freedom to follow Jesus, knowing his wife had help at home.

We arrived in Cana later than we expected. Traveling is harder with a large group, especially if one of them is a young girl with premarital jitters, one is a mother expecting a child, and two of them are high-spirited little boys. I stopped counting how many times Sarah told the boys to be careful or the men to slow down so her treasures would not be broken.

As promised, Joseph and Judas went ahead to notify Joel we were arriving. Joel and his army of brothers came to where we had rested and took Sarah, Elizabeth, and Ettezus, Sarah's friend who joined us at the last minute, to his house. I have never seen Joseph smile as he did when Ettezus fell into step with our party shortly after we left.

She smiled at Sarah and said, "Do you really think I am letting you go to that foreign country without my approval? If I do not like what I see, you will be coming back to Nazareth with me. Understand?" She quickly glanced at Joseph whose smile spread from ear to ear.

"Of course," Sarah said. "I would not have it any other way." She hugged her friend as they joined arms and proceeded along the road.

The girl's presence lifted my spirits, because I did not want to be one of Sarah's attendants of the bridal party. With only Elizabeth, I would have been forced to participate. Three is an acceptable number for Joel and the groomsmen to carry back to their house.

Joel and his brothers "stole" his bride and her attendants while the rest of us supposedly slept. We waited awhile then followed at a distance. Sarah did not mind that the groom did not claim her at her home. Some traditions are not nearly as important as young girls think them to be. Her dear friend and loving sister by her side were all she needed.

We arrived at Joel's house drained from the long trip. While we discussed waiting to unpack in the daylight, Joel's brothers came out with torches and quickly took care of everything. Joel had taken Sarah to the bridal chamber to consummate their wedding while the rest of the attendants joined us. What a blessed night this will be for the new couple.

Sarah's spirits received a boost when Jesus joined us along the way. I expect he had gone to have a private talk with his Father after the synagogue disturbance yesterday.

Joel's family welcomed us with open arms. His mother, Rolyas, had beds prepared for everyone, even Jesus' followers. His father, Zachary, ushered all the guests to their designated spot. Of course, it did not take long before all the boys were on the roof talking and laughing with Joel's brothers, whose beds they were given.

Jesus and I sat and talked to the parents for a short time before turning in ourselves. We wanted to ensure the acceptance of this family for Sarah. Before the parents retired to their room, they pointed to a table in the corner and invited me to use anything there. They could not hide their smile at my shocked reaction. Evidently, Sarah and Joel had discussed my ability to write. Most young girls would not be eager to expose such a trait, but Sarah must be proud of our abilities. Thanks to our hosts, this entry is written while it is fresh in my mind.

Tomorrow will be a busy day preparing for the celebration of the great union of our two children. Traditionally, the bride and groom would stay in their chamber for a week until the final feast. I cannot see Sarah staying away from the celebration longer than one night. I expect to see both of them early tomorrow morning. I must stop writing and get some rest. But first I must thank my heavenly Father for the many blessings He has given me.

Dear Lord, thank You for a safe and uneventful journey. But, I am even more thankful for the wonderful people who have come into our lives through Sarah and, especially, for the beautiful papyrus they have provided. I know You have blessed Sarah with a bright future. May Your blessings fill the union of these two young children and this family as they begin their life together. I pray for Your approval on the festivities of the coming days. Bless this house and all who dwell therein.

For this reason a man will leave his father and mother and be united to his wife,
and they will become one flesh.
Genesis 2:24

Mary Helps Prepare for the Celebration

Today has been a busy but blessed, fun-filled day. When I awakened this morning, the aroma of fresh baked bread filled the air. The bowls of fruit and eggs on the table greeted our arrival in the kitchen. We ate and became more familiar with each other. After the meal, Peter and Andrew took the two small boys for a trip through the town. Nathaniel left to visit his family while we were in Cana. He did not say if he would rejoin our group or stay with his family. I hope he comes back. I like the young man. Sarah and Joel have not yet emerged from their chamber, but I expect to see them any moment.

Rolyas insisted on giving us a tour of their home as her servants began cleaning up from our meal. As we entered each room, I immediately noticed the familiar well-crafted Mezuzah on the doorposts. They reminded me of the ones Joseph used to make. Rolyas said Zachary had purchased those on a trip from Jerusalem and had one of the scribes in the synagogue write the required scripture on the fine linen sheets as blessings for their guests.

We soon discovered they had been made by Joseph. The father said he got them from a carpenter in Nazareth many years ago as he traveled back from Jerusalem. He had admired the fine workmanship and had bought several for his parents and sons. He tried to return to the small one-room shop filled with beautiful crafts, but on his next trip the shop had been closed. Joel's father did not realize the house where Joel took him to meet Sarah's parents belonged to the same family. He had only met Joseph on the first trip. It is amazing how our Lord brings people together.

I noticed the beautiful decorations throughout the entire house. In one corner of the house the Shabbat or Passover items used on ritual occasions were displayed. I made a mental note to watch the young boys carefully around that corner. A simple Tallit, the prayer shawl, also hung in a corner. The wooden columns supporting the roof were made of marble with exquisite designs on the top and bottom. Rich purple cloth hung from the windows and doorways. Compared to our house, this one looked like a mansion. God has blessed this family Sarah has chosen. The father and brothers all appear to be righteous men. When we arrived all the married brothers came to help us, but soon left to go to their own homes. Joel is the last one to marry. With his good looks, I am surprised he is still single.

Flowers hung throughout the house in preparation for the wedding. Tables were set with the most exquisite cloths and napkins. The dishes were of fine china instead of clay like ours. I feared the two boys would knock them off the table in their hurry to explore the new surroundings. I silently rejoiced that Peter had taken them for the day.

After sighting a hand-crafted senet game on a shelf, I thought how wonderful it would be to have a tournament before we return home. The boys lost interest in the game after Joseph died. I would like to see them start playing again.

Every time I see one of the games, I recall the wonderful doctor who cared for me in Bethlehem. He would bring his game to the stable and we would play and talk for hours.[6] I wonder what ever happened to his two sons. My heart broke when I heard the news of Doctor Luke's death while trying to protect his baby as the Roman soldiers came through carrying out Herod's decree to slay all male children two years old and under. We were told his wife took his two sons and moved north to escape Herod's harsh rule. I pray God has kept them under His care.

After our tour we returned to the kitchen. Rolyas gave me a tour through her cabinets laden with jars full of spices such as salt, onions, garlic, cumin, coriander, mint, dill and mustard. Crocks full of wild honey and syrup sat prominently on the shelves. Someone constantly replenished the bowls of dates and grapes placed on the tables.

Rolyas surprised me by allowing me to assist with the food preparation. From the amount of food prepared, I assumed she and her daughters-in-law had been cooking for days. At first I thought she would have her servants fix the food, but Rolyas insisted no one could prepare this special meal as well as she could. Before they were able to afford the servant's help, she had prepared the food for her older son's weddings. Now the young ones expected their mother's fine cooking. Like me, she could not bear to disappoint them, but she did seem grateful that this one completed that task. She did not think she would be able to prepare many more feasts, and she did not trust anyone else to make the preparations.

While cooking, we laughed about our big families and how easily we could stretch a meal to feed as many mouths as were present. Her boys were

---

6   *Jesus My Son: Mary's Journal of Jesus' Early Life*, 58.

about like mine. An open invitation existed for anyone present at meal time. I never knew if the preparations were for our nine family members or a dozen. Our families are different, but they are also very similar.

Just as I predicted, Joel and Sarah emerged to join in the festivities. A smiling Sarah told us how Rolyas and her daughters-in-law had prepared the wedding bed with candles and lace and had filled the house with fragrant flowers.

Joel and his brothers had built a small house at the edge of their property. Customarily, rooms for the newlyweds would be added to their parent's house. Rolyas told me Joel insisted on building a separate house for them. He did not want Sarah to have to endure the constant flow of people coming through his parent's big house. After experiencing the busy house today, I appreciate Joel's wisdom.

The small two room house reminds me of the one Joseph had bought for us when I returned from my visit with Elizabeth. It will be big enough for them until they have a house full of children. I am glad Sarah and Joel were able to experience that wonderful union of two people when they become one in the eyes of God. After our wedding celebration, I still see Droopy standing beside me as I wrote in my journal while Joseph slept on our bed above the earthen oven.[7]

Because of the prophecies that our Messiah would be born of a virgin, Joseph and I chose to wait to consummate our marriage until after my purification period. I can tell from Sarah's smile that her union with Joel was as fulfilling as our first time together. I still shudder when I think of that blessed experience God made for a man and woman when they unite as one.

As we laughed and enjoyed our work, I noticed one of the daughters-in-law appeared somewhat subdued. She helped with the preparations only when given a direct order by her mother-in-law. Earlier I noticed this same daughter-in-law left the kitchen as soon as Sarah and Joel arrived for their meal. I hope there is no conflict with the young girl. I have heard other mothers at the well tell of the jealousy of their daughter-in-law whenever another one joined their family. Apparently, it is difficult for some girls to share the affection of family members. Sometimes the young girls become very selfish and jealous of the attention placed on a new member who joins the family.

We finished the day with another glorious meal for everyone present. Jesus and his brothers and Joel and his brothers ended the evening with a friendly

---

7   *Jesus My Son: Mary's Journal of Jesus' Early Life*, 35.

tournament of senet. A joyous roar filled the room when Joel beat Jesus in the final game for the championship. Jesus smiled at me and graciously congratulated Joel on his remarkable ability to play the game. I wanted to play, but enjoyed talking to the women too much. Plus, since none of the other women desired to play, I questioned how my request might be received.

I again noticed the distant daughter-in-law who did not participate in the activities, but chose to stay at a distance from the group. I watched as Jesus followed her outside. He returned a few minutes later smiling.

"Is everything all right?" I asked.

"Yes, Gabriela had some self-pity issues," Jesus replied. "She has been in this family almost three years and has yet to produce a grandchild. With Sarah's presence, she fears her status will diminish in the eyes of her in-laws. As I am sure you have noticed they do adore their grandchildren."

"I am aware of their devotion for their granddaughters, but I did not realize Gabriela had been barren for so long. Does she have some woman problems?"

"Not anymore," Jesus said with that same knowing smile.

"Thank you," I said breathing a sigh of relief. "I feared she might be jealous of Sarah and cause problems with her and her new family."

The small cloud of anxiety hanging over my head disappeared as Jesus took my arm and shepherded me to the rest of the family.

Thank You, my dear Lord for the powers You are now allowing Jesus to display. I predict Sarah and Gabriela will provide new grandchildren within a few days from each other. Oh, what a wonderful God You are. I cannot write enough words to declare Your glory.

When the wine ran out, the mother of Jesus said to Him, "They have no wine."
John 2:1-11

Jesus Performs His First Public Miracle

What a relief to just relax and share the day with my dear journal. The last two days have been exhausting, but our reward came when Jesus presented Sarah, adorned in her beautiful wedding garments, to Joel at the ceremony. Our efforts were paid back sevenfold for every minute spent sewing and decorating her dress and veil.

Joel's eyes glistened as Sarah, Jesus and I marched around the canopy seven times before Jesus presented the radiant bride to her waiting groom. I cannot find the proper words to describe Sarah's beauty. Her sparkling, white dress made from some shiny material given to us by one of our travelers glided along the floor. The beads (another gift) we sewed around all the edges glistened in the sunlight. Sarah had spied the material some time ago, and had hid it under her cot anticipating this day. Using every inch of the material and all the beads we also created an extra long piece that flowed as she walked to meet Joel.

The veil, made of matching material, only much thinner, hung to her waist in the back. It also had a row of beads sewn around the edges. We never could have afforded to buy the material for her clothes but thanks to the travelers, there could not have been a more beautiful bride found throughout the country. Sarah looked like a queen who had just stepped out of her mansion.

Young Joseph stole the show as he stood still and proud holding the ring for Joel. One of Joel's little nieces spread the flowers for Sarah. Our family has grandsons and Joel's family has granddaughters. Perhaps Sarah or Gabriela will give them a grandson this year.

I knew when Sarah came home from the well that day after seeing Joel, it would not be long until this day. Selfishly, I prayed it would not happen because I know my house will be unbearable without Sarah. But the law of nature and boys and girls is more powerful than even a mother's desire. I am thankful it has taken two years.

For the celebration the aroma of the fresh baked bread again filled the air. The display of cheese, vegetables, fruits and eggs on the banquet table could not have been prettier in any mansion. The center of the table held platters filled with delicious roasted lamb for this special occasion.

I sat back and watched the festivities as Jesus and his followers mingled with the ever growing crowd. The people were eager to see the family the new bride had brought with her. Apparently, the news of Jesus' preaching had spread to parts of Cana.

Everyone danced and partied most of the evening. At one time Sarah approached me and said the supply of wine had run extremely low. Either more people attended than they expected, or they did not realize people would enjoy the wine so much. People were crowded into the house and garden area. Our family accounted for a good number, especially, with Jesus' six followers. To run out of wine at a wedding is a disgrace to the family. I saw the servants anxiously talking to each other. I looked at Jesus and whispered "They have no more wine."

When he smiled and looked at me with that same smile I have grown to love, I knew without a doubt he would "fix" the wine shortage, but he said, "Woman (I have heard him use that term of endearment only once before when I insisted he talk to a friend who had come to visit Elizabeth), what does that have to do with me? My hour has not yet come."

Ignoring his question and comment, I walked over to the servants and told them to do whatever he says. Jesus calmly told them to fill the six 20-30 gallon stone pots setting by the door, with water. These were the pots that usually held the water used for ceremonial washing of hands—not the drinking water or wine. Surprised at his instructions, I moved out of the way to allow him his freedom. When the water pots were full, he told them to give a cup to the headwaiter who took a drink and immediately called for the bridegroom.

My heart sank waiting for his complaint to Joel. Jesus must have seen the disappointment on my face because he simply smiled. I could not understand how he could disappoint Sarah by creating such inferior wine. I knew without a doubt Jesus had the power to fix a simple wine shortage when he had the power to breathe life into this little sister.

The headwaiter looked at Joel and asked, "Why have you saved the best wine to be served last. Usually, people serve the bad wine after people have had enough to not notice the difference."

I held my breath as Joel sipped the liquid from the stone pots.

"Where did this superior vintage come from?" he asked searching the servants for an answer.

I breathed a sigh of relief as one of the guests came and ushered him back to the party. He never knew the source of the new wine, but the servants did. Each of those servants became believers of Jesus' power today.

Jesus' followers also were impressed with the miracle he performed. God allowed this simple miracle to reinforce their belief after the scene in the synagogue. I heard them discussing on the way here about the disturbance and their uncertainty of the man they had given up everything to follow. God knew their doubts and used this sign to verify the faith they had shown in Jesus.

I see the lives Jesus has changed and wonder what else will change because of the things he does. What changes must I go through before his work for his Father is finished?

Dear God, I hope the pride You had for Your son today matched my feelings. As I think about it, my heart grows heavy knowing this is just the beginning of the end. I knew Jesus could not disappoint his baby sister today—or me. He has always tried to satisfy my wishes. At times he told me You would not allow him to grant my request. I later understood why. You have a plan for everything and although we try to interrupt that plan, You always manage to bring us back where we need to be. I wonder what other great miracles You have in store for us? Help me, Father, to know what I can and cannot ask of him. Thank You for allowing him to make this day for Sarah even more special. You have abundantly poured out Your blessings for our family and Joel's.

And amazement came upon them all, and they began…saying "What is this message?
For with authority and power He commands the unclean spirits and they come out."
Matthew 4:13-16; Mark 1:16-28; Luke 4: 31-41
Surely our griefs He himself bore, And our sorrows He carried;
Yet we ourselves esteemed Him stricken, Smitten of God, and afflicted.
Isaiah 53:4

Jesus Performs Healings in Capernaum

I begin my writing tonight with a heavy heart. After the celebration, Sarah and Joel left for their new house. A lone tear slid from my eyes as I watched my baby girl wave goodbye knowing it would be some time before I would see her again. The tear quickly evaporated as I thought of the joy she would soon experience. I am happy for her, not sad. Tonight she will again experience the unique pleasure God has created when a husband and wife unite as one.

The conclusion of the celebration and the soothing powers of the wine settled upon everyone so we decided to spend one last night with our gracious hosts. Early the next morning, I hugged my little grandsons and bid Ettezus, Joseph, Judas, and Elizabeth farewell as they headed back toward Nazareth. After conveying our sincere gratitude to Joel's family for the wonderful celebration, James and I followed Jesus and his new friends to Capernaum.

We were not sure if Nathaniel would chose to stay home with his family or rejoin our group. After we had walked a very short distance, we heard him whistling a joyful tune as he fell in line with the other men. Good, I think Nathaniel is a righteous young man.

Jesus knew Peter would welcome this opportunity to see his family since they were nearby. Peter grew homesick for his own children while playing with Elizabeth's boys. Like obedient sheep, the rest of us are just following. The men said they have never been hungry and most of the time they sleep outside. Tonight we are at Peter's house, where thankfully, I have a cot and a place to write.

Since today is the Sabbath, we worshipped in the synagogue where Jesus again amazed the people with his teaching and message of authority. While he preached, a man possessed by the spirit of unclean demons cried out with a loud voice, "Let us alone! What business do we have with each other, Jesus of Nazareth? Have you come to destroy us? I know you are the Holy One of God!"

My body trembled when Jesus looked at the demon and commanded, "Be quiet and come out of him!"

The demon threw the man down among the people and came out without causing the man any harm. The man jumped up and began talking and walking as a normal person. He left, praising the teacher who had healed him. The people were filled with amazement and wonder and even a little fear. They were looking around asking how Jesus could possess the authority to command unclean spirits. Everyone left going their own way eager to spread the story throughout the area.

We left the synagogue and arrived at Peter's house only to find his mother-in-law lying on a cot burning up with a high fever. After witnessing Jesus' mighty power, Peter implored him to heal his mother-in-law. Jesus rebuked the fever and the woman immediately got up and started waiting on us. The quick healing amazed everyone. She eagerly began making preparations for a feast to feed the group. I helped her prepare a huge meal, although Jesus did not get to eat much. The news of his healing power spread quickly and people came from everywhere to see him.

The rest of that day, people swarmed into the small house. He only had to lay his hands on them, and they were healed. The great prophet Isaiah spoke of this when he said our Messiah bore our grief and carried our sorrows.

Many other people came to be healed. Some of the demons shouted, "You are the Son of God." Jesus tried to quiet them because he did not want them to spread the word. The wild-eyed, rowdy men left as quiet, humble servants.

I am following him with constant amazement. How can he do this? This is far beyond anything we had hoped for in a Messiah. How can the son I gave birth to have such authority over the demons? I know God is with him always, and He is really the healing power, but how? I have tried not to doubt his capability, but I am amazed that the son who came from my womb can possess such miraculous powers.

Dear God, please suppress my questions and doubts. I know who Jesus is and yet I still am amazed at his powers. Open our hearts, Father, and place upon us the gift of comprehension to understand the amazing things we witness. Even with our eyes wide open, we are blinder than all those he has healed today.

Mary Bailey

Good-Bye Sarah

My baby girl is gone.
Her room is empty
except for me.
But what am I without her.

I cannot grieve for my loss,
but must rejoice for her gain
of a righteous man
who also loves my God.

May they share many years
of wedded bliss
as husband and wife
in the eyes of God.

A new home
A new love
A new life
A new set of parents.

I do not lose a daughter.
I gain a son to love as my own.
I will love them both equally and
pray they love equally in return.

Although she is mine,
I know I must share her joy
with another family
who now claims her as daughter.

Two families with a common bond.
Sarah has a new mother,
but she cannot hold Sarah's heart
as I have done for many years.

I pray she will love my daughter
as I will love her son
as my own
for he is.

May the new couple be bound together
in love and respect
for each other and their families
with a ribbon of mutual love.

He said to them, "Let us go somewhere else to the towns nearby,
so that I may preach there also; for that is what I came for.'
Matthew 4:23-25; Mark 1:21-2:12; Luke 4:31-5:26

Mary Returns to Nazareth While Jesus Proceeds to Jerusalem

What a delight to place the scroll on top of my treasure box and record the events of the last few days. My scroll is the only thing I have to give this desolate room some life. Without Sarah this room would be unbearable, if not for the simple gift of my journal. I wish one of the boys would marry soon so I could give them this room. They all share a room, but they would never take this one from me unless they marry and require the privacy. The entire house echoes with the absence of Sarah's contagious laughter.

Jesus stayed in Capernaum for a few more days while James and I returned to Nazareth. He and his followers planned to continue to the towns throughout all Galilee preaching in their synagogues and casting out the demons as they make their way to Jerusalem.

I did not expect the reception we received upon our arrival home. People were waiting along the path to our house to talk to Jesus. One of the servants at the wedding in Cana had been through the town looking for the man who had changed the water to wine. Some of these people were the same "friends" who had nearly stoned Jesus in the synagogue the Sabbath before we left for Cana. We told the people that Jesus and his followers had gone to the temple in Jerusalem and would not be coming back this way. I did not stay long to talk. Home and maybe a new grandchild waited.

People looking for him were disappointed, but I am afraid some were more curious than anything else. I heard them talking about magic and spirited powers like those the sorcerers possess. People in Nazareth know I gave birth to this man. They cannot believe his powers are from a heavenly Father. How can someone that miraculous ever come from Nazareth? Why is it so much more difficult than it should be? They are not magical powers. They are gifts from a heavenly Father to his earthly son. Oh, my! It *is* an unbelievable story.

I fear Jesus will have a very difficult time wherever he goes convincing people he is the Son of God. When we left Capernaum to go our separate ways, he hugged me tightly and gently kissed my forehead. His eyes misted as mine did. Again, I felt this would probably be our last embrace for some time. His Father's mission is his life now and I am not a part of his work. Doing the will of his heavenly Father is totally his focus.

I wish Joseph could be here to see what is happening. Would he believe easier than I have? If not, it would not be because of his lack of strength or commitment to God, but because of his unconditional love for Jesus. He could not have endured some of the remarks the people were saying today. God knows what we can endure and gives us no more.

I did not understand his baptism at first. The trip to Capernaum gave him a chance to explain. The kingdom Joseph and I waited for is not on this earth. His Father will call him home when the time is right to prepare a kingdom we can all inherit. He told me this kingdom is beautiful beyond belief. No eye has ever seen nor can any mind comprehend what God has prepared for his children.

Everyone will have the chance to inherit it because of the sacrifice Jesus must make. I do not know exactly what the sacrifice might be and I fear the answer too much to ask the question. The only requirement to inherit this kingdom is to obey his message and love each other. All the sacrificial requirements commanded by the Law of Moses will be washed away by Jesus who will be the final sacrifice.

I heard him say those words, but what do they mean? Is God actually going to shed the blood of his own son for a sinful people like us? Surely, my Lord could not sacrifice His own son as the priests sacrifice the lambs upon the altar. This concept is so radical from all our teachings. With the message he is preaching, how will he ever convince people. And how long are the scribes and Pharisees going to let him contradict the Laws of Moses? His message is destroying their livelihood. Can they afford to let him continue much longer?

I asked if I could go with him, but he sadly shook his head. Finally, he explained that it would be too difficult for me. He said he would never again recognize us as his mother or brothers. For our safety, he will never return to our home in Nazareth. His family is now his heavenly Father and his followers. He walked away toward Jerusalem and James and I headed back to Nazareth dragging very heavy hearts.

Dear God, Your son has returned. What can I do to prepare myself for the rest of this journey Jesus must walk? As he turned away this morning, I felt Simeon's sword shred a slice from my heart. The wound is so deep; I fear the bleeding will never stop. The pain has taken up permanent residence in my soul. Can You replace this pain with the peace of knowing all is well with him? My mother's instinct tells me that peace will not come to pass for some time.

He testifies to what he has seen and heard, but no one accepts his testimony.
The man who has accepted it has certified that God is truthful.
John3:32-33

Simon and Leah Have a Daughter...and a Son

At least for awhile, God has taken my weary, saddened heart and lifted it to the highest heavens just by the sound of a baby's cry. I am relieved the wait is over and I arrived home in time to witness Leah's delivery. I remember my relief when my sister and cousins came to help me through my deliveries.

Early this morning, James and I walked down to visit Silas and Miriam while Leah slept. She stays exhausted from carrying such a large bundle. When we first arrived home, I made the comment that her huge belly looked as if it would crack open any minute.

Miriam and Silas wanted to know about the wedding and all the news of Jesus. Silas said the people in Nazareth were amazed when he and Miriam walked down the streets smiling and laughing. The reaction of his friends astounded him.

"No one wanted to believe Jesus had done this," he said with disappointment drenching his words. "I told them he only touched my eyes and I could see. They tried to suppress my happiness with their criticism. They even laughed when I told them. How can we convince them, Mary? They must believe what he is doing is from a divine source. They could only call him the carpenter's son. They cannot see the truth right before their faces!"

James and I stayed much longer than we intended. Miriam sent some handmade baby clothes for Leah. Sewing all those sandals made her an excellent seamstress. The tiny little shawl and tallit will be so beautiful on a newborn baby. They are quite different from the swaddling cloths I had to wrap around my first baby, but not as eloquent as the shawl and blanket Dr. Luke brought us. I praise God for giving our children a nice warm home instead of a stable to give birth to their child.

As we approached our house, I heard screams coming from inside. James and I rushed through the doorway just in time to hear baby Sydney Katherine scream with an angry cry from the swat Simon placed on her little bottom.

"She did not breathe," Simon said as wild-eyed as any of the demon-possessed men Jesus had healed. James and I burst into laughter as I wrapped the beautiful little cloths around my newborn granddaughter. Holding her close to feel her soft gentle breath on my lips lifted a ton of weight from my heavy heart. Leah's shrill scream interrupted my moment of happiness. James ran from the room and I held Sydney Katherine tightly as her father delivered her little brother.

"Twins!" I exclaimed. "Simon, you have twins! James, come in here and hold this baby so I can help," I shouted toward the door.

James reluctantly entered the room and tentatively reached for baby Sydney Katherine. I pushed her into his chest and grabbed some more cloths to wrap around another screaming baby.

"Miriam told me Leah might have twins. Leah's grandmother had a twin brother, but he had not lived for a full day," Simon said trembling as he handed his new son to me.

I laid Zachary Joseph and Sydney Katherine in Leah's arms as her face beamed with pride. She held them until fatigue overtook her and she drifted to sleep. James and I took the babies into the other room to allow Leah some rest until her newborn children would require the attention only a new mother can give.

Emotions overcame me as I laid the twins in the crib Joseph had made for Jesus. Because of our hasty retreat to Egypt, Jesus did not sleep in it until he was nearly two years old. As each of my other children were born, Joseph would lay them in the crib and smile the biggest smile. He took so much pride in his cribs.

My dear Lord, thank You so much for the blessing of a granddaughter and a grandson. Home will not be nearly as lonely now that You have given us replacements to fill the void Jesus and Sarah have created. This house is going to be very busy again. Please keep all of us safe in Your arms.

He said, "Take these things away; stop making My Father's house a place of business."
John 2:13-22
Zeal for Your house has consumed me, and the reproaches
of those who reproach You have fallen on me.
Psalm 69:9

Jesus Cleanses the Temple

My blessings are overflowing for these lovely little twins God has chosen to send me to occupy my wandering mind. I think I would go crazy if it were not for the joy of cuddling these precious little bundles. There is no time to think with the constant feeding, changing and rocking of baby Zachary Joseph or Sydney Katherine. I try to help Leah as much as I can, but only she can feed them and that is almost a constant task. As soon as one finishes, the other one is waiting to take over. Poor Leah. I do not think she has had a full hours sleep for over a week now. Simon and I take turns handing them to her.

I feel fortunate to find this brief time to update my journal. There are many things I need to write. I fear I will forget if I do not write the incidents soon after I hear them.

Nearly every day travelers come by telling us more stories of the man the people are calling the teacher. Some have even implied he must be possessed by demons. How can they think all those good deeds are coming from a demon? I am amazed at the logic of some people's thinking. Many of the guests know we are the teacher's family, and update us with the latest news as they have done for years. Others are only passing by for a few hours rest and some refreshment. They report the latest news, but are not as kind as those who know us.

Years ago, I got upset at Joseph for constantly inviting travelers to stop and rest in his shop. I never knew how many were going to be at our table. Joseph would go to a job and come back with someone he met along the way who needed some refreshment or just a few minutes rest. He reminded me of the help we received on our trip to Bethlehem. Had it not been for the hospitality of a few people, I am not sure I could have survived that trip. Just as I felt I could go no further on poor Droopy, a stranger would wander by and offer us some rest in his home. Without those refreshing breaks the trip would have been unbearable.

It did not take long for word to spread that Joseph welcomed weary travelers. Once they stopped, they always came back on their return trip.

There were many times when I thought we would not have enough to feed everyone and our big family, but we never ran out of food. It always amazed me how the food would stretch to feed as many as were eating. Many of the travelers would bring gifts for the children and sometimes something for me. Often when I had used the last of my scroll, a traveler would just happen to have one to exchange for some food and water. They were always thankful for our hospitality, and I greatly appreciated their gift. I could not complain, because their tales of far-away places always delighted our children.

Now I am seeing the children of these travelers stopping to visit. I am thankful for the stories they bring of the teacher. If someone knows Jesus is my son, they are always respectful to us. If they are new, they are usually laughing and making fun of his actions. Many people think he is some kind of sorcerer or someone with magical powers. They do not see him as our true Messiah, the son of God. A young man forgot where he was the other day and exclaimed, "Can you imagine someone from Nazareth thinking he is the new Messiah? How absurd."

My dear son, will people ever believe you? Will you be destined to carry this disbelief forever even after you return to your heavenly father? Oh, I can only imagine what a glorious reunion that will be.

Today a traveler had been to Jerusalem for the celebration of the Passover feast. He told how this wild man claiming to be a Messiah, the son of God, made a scourge and drove the money changers from the temple, pouring out their money and overturning their tables. Even the people selling doves for the sacrifices were forced to leave. People have been trading their wares in the temple for years. Jesus has changed from the mild mannered son I raised into a zealous son of his heavenly Father.

I remember in our studies once, I read from the book of the Psalms of King David about how zeal for his father's house will consume the Messiah. Jesus was a young man at the time, but he looked at me and said, "Mother, you will remember that scripture someday." He was right. Today that scene is ever so fresh in my mind.

The travelers laughed telling how Jesus told the people that if they destroyed the temple, he could raise it up in three days. Has he gone mad? It took more than forty-six years to build that temple. How can he possibly think he could rebuild it in three days? The travelers were amazed so many people believe his message and are following him.

If he is not careful, he is going to get in trouble. I am surprised he has not already been arrested. Removing sellers from the temple takes a lot of money from businesses and taxes from our Roman government. The leaders had to be upset with him. I know he is not possessed, but I know he has changed.

Dear God, his zeal for You has completely consumed him. It appears he wishes to make the Pharisees and scribes angry. He needs Your protective arms around him to keep him safe from those who will not believe his teachings. I must go and care for baby Zachary Joseph who is demanding an audience. What a blessing these twins have been for our family.

Now there was a man of the Pharisees, named Nicodemus, a ruler of the Jews;
John 3:1
Then the Lord said to Moses, "Make a fiery serpent, and set it on a standard;
…everyone who is bitten, when he looks at it, he will live."
Numbers 21: 8-9

Nicodemus Visits Mary

It seems every time I have reached the limit of my worrying, my dear God sends someone to ease my mind. Today the peace came in the form of a man of the Pharisees named Nicodemus. He came to my house and requested to speak to the mother of the man they call Jesus. My sons drilled the man with questions until they were sure he meant no harm. Unsure of why I would be singled out by a Jewish ruler, I approached the man with apprehension. Fearing the worst news of Jesus, my heart hung close to the ground. Why else would someone of such importance visit me in Nazareth?

The man told me my son had asked him to visit and tell me the latest news. Jesus and his followers are traveling throughout the area of Judea baptizing people and telling them of his kingdom. My ears immediately perked up to hear more. Why would God send this complete stranger with this news of the acceptance of Jesus' abilities?

Nicodemus said he went to Jesus in the dark of the night for fear some Pharisees may not agree with his desire to hear what Jesus had to say.

"I know your son is come from God for no one can do the things he does unless God is with him," Nicodemus told me.

"Please tell me more," I begged, eager to hear from someone who had actually talked to Jesus. "What else did he have to say?"

"I wish I could tell you everything, but I cannot remember it all," he said. "Let me tell you what I can recall. Jesus told me I must be born again in order to see the kingdom of God."

"Born again? What does that mean," I asked sitting on the corner of my stool.

"You are asking just as I did," he said smiling. "I asked how an old man like me could re-enter his mother's womb and be born again. Jesus talked to me for some time. We talked about being born of water and the spirit instead of re-entering our mother's womb. He spoke with such confidence.

"He asked how I could believe heavenly things when I do not believe the earthly things he tells us and cannot accept the testimony of those who have seen.

"Your son said to me, 'As Moses lifted up the serpent in the wilderness so must the son of man be lifted up; so that whosoever believes in Him shall not perish, but have eternal life'."

"Is this the fiery serpent Moses set on the standard to judge the people?" I asked.

"Apparently, your son is giving life just like the serpent. I had to come and see the man's mother," he continued. "To tell you the beautiful words he spoke. I hope you can explain them to me. I searched and searched to find Jesus' home until God led me to this carpentry shop. After passing the interrogation of your sons, I finally got to speak to you."

"You must forgive them," I said with a smile of appreciation. "So much has happened this last year, they are wary of all strangers."

"I do understand. I thought it quite touching," he said, continuing with his story. "Jesus told me, 'For God so loved the world that He gave His only begotten son, that whosoever believes in Him shall not perish, but have eternal life. For God did not send His son into the world to judge the world, but that the world might be saved through Him'."

Nicodemus paused in deep thought and then asked, "Can you tell me what he is saying?"

"I wish I could tell you the full meaning of his words," I said, feeling God directing me to tell him more. "I only know that after the angel Gabriel visited me, the Holy Spirit overshadowed me and I conceived the seed of God to give birth to His son. This seed is now the man to whom you have been talking. The angel also promised this baby would be the Messiah who would inherit the throne of David, and his kingdom shall have no end.

"I have not received understanding beyond that. I am sorry I cannot help you, but I cannot tell you how much you have helped me by your visit today," I replied, taking his hands and just holding them. What a relief to hear some news of Jesus from someone who has spoken to him.

"Do you understand what he meant when he called himself the light that came in the darkness? He said people loved the darkness better than they loved the light. Can you explain that?" Nicodemus questioned.

"My son is truly the light. My God sent his son to shine among the evil darkness of the world. How I wish the world would accept this light. Even you said you went to him in the dark of night. Are you afraid to recognize the light he offers?" I asked.

Nicodemus sadly shook his head in answer to my question. "I fear my colleagues are not as trusting of your son as I am. Perhaps their approval is more important to me than your son's at this time," he said hanging his head in despair.

Not wanting our conversation to end, I asked if Jesus had said anything else.

"He only asked if I would visit you to tell of the latest news," he said. "We talked for some time until I had to return home before the light of day. I know I will see your son again. I feel God has sent me to help him in some way."

My heart is filled with happiness knowing Jesus has such a friend among the nobles. To know that a Pharisee is willing to help Jesus gives me some hope that others may also.

The visitor left and I hurried to write his story. The words of hope float from my heart as my hands write them on this beautiful scroll.

Alas, I must close my scroll and attend to Sydney Katherine. Her lungs are every bit as powerful as her brothers. I am so thankful for a patient Leah who adores her two children and cares for them with such ease. With her abundance of milk, they are growing quite plump...and, I must add, adorable.

My dear Lord, I thank You so much for sending Nicodemus to ease the concerns I have of Jesus' work. You have not given me the enlightenment to fully understand his words, but I am indeed thankful for the hope You have sent through this stranger. I pray, Father, for the wisdom and understanding to accept the things Your son is doing for, truly, he is mine no more.

John also was baptizing in Aenon near Salim, because there was much water there;
and people were coming and were being baptized.
Matthew 4:12; Mark 1:14; Luke 4:14; John 3:22-4:3

More Stories of Jesus' Work

We had not heard many more stories since the leader, Nicodemus, came to visit us. I hoped things had settled down a bit, but apparently we had only experienced the calm before the storm.

Oh, my! The stories we are hearing now. I have nearly wrung the skin off my hands. They say Jesus and John are both baptizing. Could there possibly be some conflict between their teachings? One of the travelers said John's disciples discuss the baptisms of Jesus who now baptizes more than John. I do not believe their mission is meant to be a competition.

God has given both of them special abilities to be used together—not to cause conflict. Maybe Jesus is doing this to take some pressure off John. I heard John had greatly irritated Herod and some of the Pharisees with the truth of his teaching. The latest story is how John confronted Herod for having his brother killed so he could take his sister-in-law for his own wife. How cruel can one man be? How can God make Herod just like he made John and all my sons? What can happen to a man to make him become so merciless of human life? What evils has he encountered? How could Herod think God made his life so much more important than anyone else's?

We also got the news that Jesus is drawing such huge crowds wherever he goes that his life is sometimes in danger. Because of his healing powers, everyone with a disease is desperately trying to touch him. The crowds have turned into mobs. Someone came by and said he drove out evil spirits who were crying out that he is the Son of God. I witnessed a similar incident in Capernaum. I can sense a difference in the attitude of the people who are telling us these stories. A few months ago the people who were filled with doubts of his power are now filled with amazement and wonder at his abilities.

One of the travelers, a friend who often stops by, told us Jesus had chosen some other good people to be with him and to also preach. I know the first six he brought home with him were good companions. I am relieved to know he is surrounding himself with more good men. There is safety in numbers.

They said he also gave those he chose the same powers he has to drive out demons and heal the sick. How is Jesus able to pass that same authority to other people? Jesus received his abilities from his heavenly Father. These followers are mere humans who are receiving this divine ability.

My dear God, again I come to You with a mind overflowing with questions. Can you bestow upon me the ability to understand the stories we are hearing? How can You expect me to hear and not wonder what is happening? You know mothers are never free from worrying about their children. He may be Yours, but he will never be removed from that special place in my heart.

Jesus said to her (Samaritan woman at the well), "I who speak to you am He."
John 4: 4:42
They buried the bones of Joseph, which the sons of Israel
brought up from Egypt, at Shechem.
Joshua 24:32

Jesus Meets the Samaritan Woman at the Well

I am so glad I have my dear journal to record my stories. Just being able to write the accounts I hear, brings some relief from the fear caused by the reports.

Some travelers came by today saying Jesus had spent a few days in Sychar talking to the Samaritans. They were not happy with this association, but I am pleased. I hope he visited my friend Christina. I remember the blessing of her hospitality when I had escaped to visit Elizabeth after Joseph did not believe my account of the source of the child I had conceived. Meeting Christina at the well provided a safe haven for my rest. In those few days, God gave me a new friend I will always remember. I hope Jesus will remember Christina from my writings and will pay her a visit. I would enjoy hearing an update on her life with her demanding aunt.

After my visit with Christina, I had a different view of the Samaritans than what we were taught by our religious leaders. Just because they worship on the mountain at Shechem, where the bones of Joseph were buried, instead of the temple at Jerusalem, should not make a person's soul unclean. They received that mountain as an inheritance from Joseph. Christina loved her place of worship as much as I do the temple. We worship the same God. How can the place where one worships make a difference? I am beginning to think Jesus is trying to convince us of that truth.

I fear people are not going to look too kindly on him spending time with the Samaritans. All our lives we have been warned that the Samaritans are unclean people with whom we should not associate. Had it not been for that unclean Samaritan, Christina, I do not know what would have happened to me that day. She saved me from going with that evil caravan master.[8]

When Jesus talks to her, I hope he tells her he is my son. Although we only spent a few days together, she will remember me. The travelers said Jesus talked to a woman at a well and told her everything she had done including all her sins. Could that woman be Christina, the kind, considerate, righteous young girl who spent most of her life taking care of an ailing, demanding aunt? The traveler said that because of this girl's testimony to Jesus, many of the town's people had also believed. Maybe God had these plans for her ever since the day He directed me to her path. She would easily believe Jesus because of the truths I told her that day.

Apparently, Jesus associates with the sinners as well as the righteous. He has broken all the manmade public barriers that have been in place since the Law of Moses. The sinners are as much a part of his teachings as righteous, devout men. My dear son, your compassion for the lost has caused Simeon's sword to pierce the very depth of my soul. What shall become of you?

I cannot help but wonder what this is doing to his already shaky relationship with our leaders. He has caused a lot of commotion and upset a lot of the scribes and Pharisees. How is all this leading up to his great kingdom?

I think it is time for me to distill all these rumors myself. He said he would never recognize me as his mother again, but I can still follow from a distance. I need to hear what he is teaching. They said it is even dangerous for him to enter a house because the people swarm wherever he is. Maybe I could persuade him to come home for a few days to see his new little niece and nephew. I will greatly miss rocking little Sydney Katherine and Zachary Joseph asleep at night, but I know one of their uncles will gladly take my place. God has blessed me with a daughter-in-law who is totally devoted to her children and husband. I have to say Leah is the answer to the prayer I have been praying since the day each of my sons were born. I have prayed for wives who would love God above all and my son and her children next. What a wonderful marriage that attitude creates.

Another traveler came by one day and said the scribes and Pharisees are now saying Jesus is possessed by Beelzebub. How can they think the devil drives out his own demons? Why would they even think Jesus is an evil spirit?

I pray he will come home and rest for awhile until things calm down and the danger subsides, but I seriously doubt that will ever happen again. Tomorrow morning I will tell my sons I am leaving to find him. Wonder if I can sneak away from them? They do not need to see him acting this way. They are having enough trouble dealing with all this news.

Dear God, please lead me to Jesus and help me persuade him to come home for some well-deserved rest. I know he must do Your work, but I fear for his safety. I beg You to spread your protective wings over him and my friend, Christina.

He came again to Cana of Galilee where He had made the water wine.
Mark 1:15; Luke 4:15; John 4:43-54

Mary Prepares to Visit Sarah in Cana

My sons would not allow me to go to Sychar in search of Jesus. They feared it would be too dangerous. Instead, Joseph suggested I go to Cana to visit Sarah. It has been some time since her wedding and we recently received news she is expecting a baby. I think she must have had a wonderful, fulfilling wedding night. I reluctantly, but willingly, agreed to visit Sarah and let Jesus be for the time being.

My sons think it would be dangerous for me to search for Jesus. In the back of my mind, I feel they are trying to protect me from the disappointment of what he has become. They do not agree with most of the stories we hear about his teachings and associating with sinners and demon-possessed men. Lately, they have only heard bad things about him. People seem to have forgotten about all the miracles he performs. Why does God allow people to believe the worst and ignore the good in men?

When Judas left home for a period of time, everyone in the village rushed to tell me the news of all the bad things the group did and never once told me about how they had helped a widow woman in Nain who had a young son. They helped her gather the crops her husband had planted before he died. To show her appreciation, she had them kill a fatted calf and fixed them a feast of a meal before they left. Judas has often mentioned this story to us, but none of the town's people know of this one. They only remember the stories of the wild parties where some travelers had seen him.

James is going with me tomorrow to visit Sarah. He has become so restless since Jesus left. He does not want to work in the shop anymore. He still hunts some, but not like he used to. Our meals consist of bread, fruit and the vegetables we can find in the city. Every once in a while a neighbor will need some work done and will offer to pay us with a lamb or a calf. What a treat we have on those days. The fragrant aroma of roasted lamb coming from our huge earthen oven brings all the boys to the table on time. We try to get word to Elizabeth and Amos to bring their children over and eat with us on those occasions. My heart is the fullest when all my family is together enjoying a wonderful meal and each other's company as they share memories.

God is so wonderful to give us grandchildren as we age. They are special little creatures that so easily steal our hearts with their smile and a simple little hug. I remember the day my parents came to visit when Joseph and I first came back from Egypt. They were so eager to see their almost two year old grandson. Although Jesus had not seen them before, he sensed they were special people and eagerly sat in their laps and allowed them to dote on him. I now understand how they felt. There is no warmer feeling than the breath of a my grandchildren as they plant a kiss on my cheek.

Dear God, I am anxious to visit my baby girl. Although she is soon to become a mother, she is still my darling miracle child. It is with much distress I think about her giving birth as I recall the day I gave birth to her. Had it not been for You allowing Your son to use Your powers through him, this day would not have happened. I want to think about Ruth and Deborah, the daughters I lost, but I must not allow my mind to go there and dwell for any length of time. My mind can easily get lost in those unlived memories, but there is too much to be thankful for in the world of the living to dwell in the world of the dead. Father, please guide our path as we travel to Cana tomorrow.

Jesus said to him, "Go; your son lives."
The man believed the word that Jesus spoke to him and started off.
John 4:46-54

Mary Meets Her New Grandbaby and Doctor Luke

If I had only known, I would have left earlier and been here when baby Zachary arrived. But, as usual, I am trying to fit God's plan into mine and He still will not allow it. Someday he is going to give up and let me do something on my time instead of His. I sincerely doubt I will live to see that day.

Sarah and Joel were married exactly the needed amount of time for a baby to develop when their son arrived. Sarah and Joel named their son Zachary, after Joel's father. They did not know Simon and Leah had named their son Zachary Joseph. I now have two grandsons named Zachary. I am pleased because I am fond of that name.

Jesus came to visit Sarah when she gave birth. Sarah said if it had not been for him and the wonderful doctor who came, she would have lost the baby and maybe her own life. I pray she never experiences the sorrow of losing a baby as I have. It is the most devastating thing that can happen—especially, if you carry them full term and their breath will not come when they arrive. I remember the midwife trying her best to breathe her own life into darling Ruth as her tiny little face continued to turn blue. Again, I cannot dwell with that thought. I must think of this new life I see lying in the beautiful handcrafted crib made by a loving, devoted father. Every time I lay baby Zachary in the crib, I see Joseph trying desperately to steady his hands as he engraved the beautiful scroll work along the edges.

A radiant glow emanated from the new mother today as I watched her nurse her son. Sarah's gentle spirit and caring heart is the perfect requirement for the wife and mother God intended women to be. Joel and his family treat her like a queen and now that she has given them their second grandson, I am sure her status has grown even higher. Gabriela delivered a fine young boy exactly one week before Zachary. My heart sings with joy to think of the two young boys growing up together. Cousins are such a blessing for young children. We were always fortunate to have many living close enough to visit.

Sarah told me while Jesus visited a few days earlier, a member of the royal family came to implore him to heal his son who had reached the point of death. She said Jesus simply told the man, "Go because your son lives." The man turned and left. The report came that before he could get home, his servant came running to tell him his son lived.

More people believe every day. Word of Jesus has spread faster than any wildfire in this area. Sarah said there were so many people in Cana looking for Jesus they had little time to visit. That is the bad part about his well-known status. He has no time to visit and talk with his family anymore without the crowds swarming around him.

Sarah said some people still mention their wedding and how the wine barrels were replenished. She said people do not have any idea what happened. Most people think the good wine had been misplaced and found after the other wine had been drunk. At the time, she did not know anything had happened. Joel told her the servants said Jesus had saved them some embarrassment by making some new wine for their guests. She asked me about the incident and I explained it to her the best I could.

Sarah knows Jesus has some miraculous powers, but I am still not sure she understands what I am telling her. I have repeatedly tried to explain the miracle of her birth, but my voice begins to tremble and I cannot finish the entire story. It does not matter if she knows or not. She would believe anything about her brother without realizing a miracle had been performed.

During my visit, the young doctor came to check on what he called 'his miracle baby'. The doctor said he had been hearing stories about Jesus and when he heard he had come back to Cana, he came to see for himself. When Sarah suddenly began having pains, the huge crowd prevented them getting word to the midwife. It is doubtful she could have made it through the crowd in time to help. Joel had seen the doctor nearby and ran to bring him to help with the delivery. The baby came feet first so the doctor had to turn him around to allow him to pass through the birth canal.

Luke, the young doctor, apparently just happened to be at the right place at the right time. Of course, after meeting the young doctor, I know who had a hand in his arrival. Jesus could have helped Sarah, but, for some reason, he felt this young doctor needed to come into our lives. After we sat and talked for awhile I realized the young man is the son of the doctor Luke who had cared for me in Bethlehem when Jesus was born.

He confirmed the story of his father's death which the innkeeper had told Joseph and me. One year while we were in Jerusalem observing the Passover Feast, we went back to Bethlehem to visit the stable and I asked the innkeeper about Dr. Luke. He said when Herod had issued the decree to kill all the male babies two years old and under, the soldiers marched into Dr. Luke's house and tore the baby from his mother's arms. Doctor Luke, trying to save his son, threw himself in front of the baby. The soldier's sword pierced both their bodies and they were left to die. This young Doctor Luke was only four years old when this occurred, but he said he could remember it as if it happened yesterday. His mother had quickly taken the rest of the family and moved to Cana to escape King Herod.

I told him about his father coming to care for me when I had hurt my ankle and cut a gash over my eye while we were living in the stable after Jesus' birth.[9] He looked at me in awe.

"You are the one," he said staring, trying to refresh his memory. "Mother wisely brought father's writings. I have read those many times and often wondered what ever happened to the woman who could play senet and gave birth to the son in that stable. Are you telling me that young baby is Jesus?"

"I am," I replied. "Your father loved to play senet. He taught me so much about the game. I would have gone crazy in that stable all day if he had not come to play the game with me."

"What happened to you?" the doctor asked. "In my father's last note, he said you were going to the temple for the redemption of Jesus and your purification. It seemed you just vanished. I thought the soldiers must have come by shortly after his last visit with you."

"They did," I told him. "After we came back from the temple, three kings from the East came to visit us bringing exquisite gifts. They had the misfortune to be taken to Herod when they had inquired about the birth of a new king. You can imagine how upset Herod became when he heard a new king had been born. He even had two of his own sons killed because he thought they were trying to overthrow his kingdom.

"Herod had implored the kings to return to him to tell him the location of this new baby so he could also worship him. Instead, God placed in their hearts a desire to return home another route. In the middle of the night the wise men left, an angel visited my husband and told him we must leave the country quickly because King Herod looked for the child to kill him. We did not waste any time in leaving. It is a good thing we obeyed the angels command. We heard that at daybreak the next day, King Herod's soldiers roamed through the towns and country around Jerusalem slaying all male children two years old and under. We barely missed that sword."

---

9   *Jesus My Son: Mary's Journal of Jesus' Early Life*, 54

"You mean to tell me Jesus is the reason my father and brother were killed?" the doctor asked puzzled.

I could tell this news greatly disturbed the young man. He could not believe this man, Jesus, with his rebellious message had caused such sorrow so many years ago.

We talked for awhile longer. The young doctor said his mother had never remarried. Few men are willing to take on the responsibility of two young sons and an ailing mother and father. His mother had worked as a servant for some prominent families to earn money to care for her family. One of her masters, Theophilus, had agreed to pay for her children's schooling if they would become doctors. He wanted someone he could trust to care for him in his old age. The mother agreed and Luke and his brother are now prominent doctors in the region. After hearing my story of his father, Luke seemed pleased with the choice of his profession.

He told me he had become very interested in Jesus' teachings. Being a scholar of the prophets, Luke thought this man could indeed be the one Isaiah proclaimed would come and save the world from their sins. He had read the papers his father had written, but had not connected them to Jesus. He could not wait to get home and read them all over again. Now he wanted to know every detail of the birth of this man he feels certain is our Messiah.

Feeling compelled to trust the young man just as I had his father; I told him everything I could remember. I started with the day the angel first visited me, the visit of the shepherds, the visit of the three kings, our flight to Egypt and Jesus' very normal childhood, except for the incident at the temple when he was twelve years old.

Doctor Luke tried so hard to remember everything. He asked if anyone had recorded any of these events. I told him I had written as much as possible with the materials I could find. I explained that whenever my writing materials ran short, more were provided. He asked if he could read my notes. I invited him to come to Nazareth to read the scrolls I have written. He promised he would visit soon. In the meantime, he would keep my story private so as not to cause any harm to my family.

I had not even thought of the possibility of my stories creating danger for my family. Because the Pharisees and leaders are so eager to get to Jesus, they could try to use his family to trick him. Perhaps that is the reason Jesus said he would not recognize us as his mother or brothers.

Doctor Luke seemed so trustworthy, I told him everything. His father, Luke, had also been careful who he sent to the cave to bring us food and changing cloths. If he had not been so generous, I do not know how I would have managed. As Sarah will soon find out, it takes many changing cloths for a newborn baby. Even in Bethlehem, Doctor Luke feared for our lives if too many people knew of the truth of Jesus' birth. He often warned me not to tell anyone unless God had put in my heart a willingness to trust them.

Dear God, help me to be more cautious. Never let me do or say anything that might bring harm to Jesus or the rest of my family. You wanted me to talk to this young doctor since You so mysteriously put him in our lives. I think You have a purpose for him also. Guide me as I speak to people to say only the things You want me to say. It is so easy for me to brag to everyone what I know, but I pray You will give me insight to know the motive of their questions and to answer with the wisdom that only You can give. Pour Your blessings on this young family as they strive to raise their son in the way You would have him grow.

When Jesus saw the crowds, He went up on the mountain;
and after He sat down, His disciples came to Him.
Matthew 5:1-7:29; Luke 6:20-49

Mary Hears of Jesus' Sermon on the Mount

Home feels so good, but what a blessed week I just experienced spending time with Sarah and my new grandson, Zachary. When I told Simon and Leah his name, Simon smiled and said, "Great minds think alike."

I love holding my little grandbabies. Sarah's mother-in-law could not keep her hands off her new grandson. If I had not known differently, I would have thought this to be her first grandchild. It is comforting knowing she is there if Sarah needs someone. I have some amazing stories to write about today.

James and I had a very long talk on the way home. He is gravely concerned for Jesus' well-being. Perhaps my doubt is showing through my brave words, because the more I try to tell him Jesus is being watched over, the more he turns a deaf ear. God will eventually turn James and his brothers to the truth, but I fear what must happen before that time.

Nearly everyone who passes by now has a new story to tell about Jesus' activities. They tell about this man who has drawn thousands to him by his teachings. They said one time there were so many people he went up on a mountain so they could hear. I often wondered how everyone can hear with so many people around. But having been there, I know they can. They say his message is of love and caring. He even called the poor blessed.

They said he talks of fulfilling the Law of the prophets not destroying it, as the scribes and Pharisees think he is. Our laws teach an eye for an eye, he is telling people that if someone offends you, you should turn the other cheek and forgive all sins. And love you enemies! His teaching is to love your neighbor and your enemy. He told them how to pray to a heavenly father without being boisterous as some are. The travelers could not remember all he said, but they were impressed with what they heard. One group said they listened to him speak an entire day.

Another group came by talking about Jesus preaching at Lake Gennesaret. The large crowd forced him to get in a boat and go out a little way from the land in order to preach to them. After he preached, he told the fishermen, who had not caught a fish all day, to put down their fishing nets. They tried to tell him it would be useless, but he insisted. The travelers said the enormous catch nearly broke the net. Some fellow fishermen helped and they both netted so many fish, the boats started to sink. They were laughing because the fishermen did not get to enjoy the fruits of their catch. As soon as they got to shore, they left everything to follow Jesus, but everyone else had a satisfying meal of fish that night.

Could it be because of his message of kindness and love, now people seem to be kinder when they talk about him? Some of those who were laughing at him earlier are now starting to believe his message. They are amazed he has avoided being imprisoned for this length of time because of the way he mocks the voices of authority when it comes to religious matters. The scribes and Pharisees have been known to order death to those they deem blaspheming. Jesus must be sly when it comes to disappearing among the crowd or maybe they are beginning to actually believe his message. I am glad to hear someone say he must have some divine power watching over him or he would already be arrested.

Dear God, I know he is fulfilling the plan You prepared for him since the day of his birth. I think about the innocent little baby I held in my arms. The wonderful, caring, young man he grew up to be, and the devoted son to You he is now. I can only pray that You love him as dearly as I do—with all Your being. With Your almighty power, You must keep him safe from harm.

And they cried out, saying, "What business do we have with each other, Son of God?
Have you come here to torment us before the time?"
Matthew 8:28-34; Mark 5:1-20; Luke 8:26-39

Stories of Jesus' Healing Ability

Tonight I am using the last of my scroll. I wanted to save this little bit in case Jesus came home with some astonishing news. Instead, I am writing words that are almost embarrassing to read. I am having a hard time understanding this latest news. We are getting such strange reports from the travelers. People come by every day with new stories. Jesus is now living in Capernaum and preaching about the kingdom of heaven. The people in Nazareth are still mocking him and laughing behind our backs. How I wish we could help them understand. In my heart I feel it is time to join him and offer help in any way. I have to know if what he is saying is true. Is he still talking about that heavenly kingdom? Where? When? How can I be a part of this kingdom before I die?

Another story being told is about him calming storms. They said the large crowd forced him to go out on a boat so the crowd could hear. When he finished speaking, they set sail across the sea when a tremendous storm arose. People on the bank were terrified for the safety of the men in the small boat amidst the giant waves. All at once the wind stopped blowing and the waters became calm. When the boat came to shore, his disciples were awestruck. He had actually commanded the waves to be silent. How can he do that? I know he possesses some unbelievable powers, but to control nature also? God has power over all nature, but for a man who came from my body to have those same powers is almost too much for my humble, human mind to comprehend.

He also is becoming well-known for his healing powers over all types of sickness. Diseases and sickness of every kind are being wiped away by his touch or even by his command. Even men with the dreaded disease, leprosy, are being made clean. They said a centurion came to Jesus about his paralyzed servant. Jesus healed the servant just by telling the centurion "Go and your servant will be healed." He did not even have to see the man.

All these amazing stories are so heartbreaking to hear from other people. I long to witness the stories myself. How will the world know of these things if they are not recorded? Has God given one of his followers the ability to also record these events? I pray the message will not be forgotten. Although Jesus said he would never recognize us as his mother or brothers again, I can still let him know that we are listening and we care about his safety.

A man came through late this evening saying Jesus drove out all sorts of demons and spirits in the country of the Gadarenes. The man told one story about two men being so demon-possessed, that other men could not walk around them due to their violent nature. Jesus went to them and the demons started talking to him. He then drove the demons into a herd of pigs. The whole herd went crazy and rushed down a steep bank into a lake where they drowned. I can only imagine the terror that gripped all the onlookers. The man said the people of the region pleaded with Jesus to leave the area.

People fear what the Romans may do if they find Jesus among them. The people are so oppressed by our government, they cannot see beyond that tyranny. It amazes me how the strongest people can be diminished to mere weaklings by fear. Even here in Nazareth our once strong leaders are totally dependent on the control of those tyrants. They even say Herod disguises himself as a peasant to mingle among the people to hear what is being said of him. A man hung from a cross outside our village the other day. The story spread that the man invited a stranger into his house for some food. During the conversation the man spoke some unfavorable words about the government. The next day soldiers stormed the man's house and carried him away. The town's people believe the stranger must have been Herod or one of his secret spies. I will have to remind my sons to be carful of the travelers they invite into the shop.

Some people are still saying Jesus is led by the devil. How can men be so dense? Why would the devil want to destroy his own demons? Why is it so hard to understand that Jesus is our Messiah, the son of God? Can they not see his authority by his deeds and the good works he performs?

Travelers coming through tell me stories like this all the time. It surprises me the reaction people have. They believe it is some tall tale or sort of magic trickery. I cannot blame them. Although I know he is capable of the stories I hear, it is still hard for me to believe.

Dear God, I have reached the end of my scroll. I can write no more until I find more material. I may not need a scroll where I am going so I decided to go ahead and use the last little bit. Are the current activities of Your son a part of Your plan? Give me the wisdom to understand his actions. You know I love him no matter what happens, but I believe if I could only talk to him, I could see that all is well. Direct me in what I should do. My other sons think it is dangerous for me to seek him, but my heart tells me I should be close by his side. There is no way I can help if I am far away. The closer I am, the better able for me to attend to any needs he may have. I desire to follow him even if it is from a distance. Direct my path as I plan to search for him, and please, take care of his needs.

Being unable to get to Him (Jesus) because of the
crowd, they removed the roof above Him;
and when they had dug an opening, they let down the
pallet on which the paralytic was lying.
Matthew 9:1-8; Mark 2:1-12; Luke 5:17-26

Jesus Drives out Demons and Friends Tear off a Roof

My heart leaps with joy when I open this fresh scroll from one of the travelers. After he shared our meal, he took out this brand new scroll and handed it to me. "Something tells me you need this a bit more than I do," he said.

My mouth dropped open and my eyes opened wide as I gratefully accepted the scroll. My last entry finished the scroll I had been using and I have been praying for God to replenish my supply. As usual, he provided my need.

Along with the scroll, the traveler brought some exciting stories of Jesus. Apparently, he has given all his chosen followers the authority to drive out demons and baptize people. How amazing that must feel to a mere human.

We last heard he taught in the synagogues in Capernaum amazing everyone with his voice of authority. They say he preached the laws of Moses without all the frills and traditions that our so-called righteous leaders have added. They are giving him the reputation of a lawbreaker when in fact he breaks no laws. He obeys the laws to the letter. They become very upset when he does not pay any attention to the ordinances they have initiated through their teachings.

Some other travelers said demons violently escape from people when Jesus sternly commands them to come out of their bodies. Then he commands the evil spirits not to talk. Is it because the demons know he is truly the Son of God? Why does he not want everyone to know?

The travelers say people are still crowding around him. Even a man of leprosy came up to Jesus and asked if he could make him clean. Jesus simply replied, "I am. Be clean." Immediately, the man became clean. When he left to offer his sacrifices, the priests could not understand how an incurable disease had been cured so quickly.

I wish I could write about all the other stories we are hearing. But there is not enough time or material. I just hope someone close to Jesus is also trying to record all these events so the world will know of these miraculous happenings.

One of the most amazing stories I have heard is the one two travelers were telling today. They said one day Jesus met with the Pharisees and leaders of the law who had come from every village of Galilee and Judea and even Jerusalem. They apparently were interviewing Jesus trying to catch him in a lie so they could charge him and throw him in jail. He must have already performed the healing for this crowd, because they were also listening to him speak.

The man continued to say they were discussing the prophecies of Isaiah; probably like the time the leaders were questioning him when he was twelve years old in the temple. I can still picture that scene in my mind.

The traveler said he saw four men carry a cot up to the top of this house where Jesus and the leaders were holding court. He said suddenly dirt and leaves and clay started falling from the roof until a hole appeared right above Jesus.

When Jesus looked up, a cot with a paralytic lying on it descended from the roof until it rested on the floor directly in front of him. The men had gone to the roof because the large crowd prevented them from getting near Jesus. They must have not been prepared for this crowd because they had used the sashes around their tunics for rope to lower their friend.

What faith those friends must have had. They tore a roof off someone's house to help their paralytic friend. Wonder what the owner of the house thought? What an amazing friendship those men must have had. This is one of the most amazing displays of loyalty I have heard. Jesus must have felt their compassion because the man said Jesus told the paralytic, "Friend, your sins are forgiven you." Because of the faith and determination of a few friends, the paralyzed man became whole. If only we could all so willingly carry the cot of our friends in need. [10]

As you can imagine, Jesus' command caused much distress for the Pharisees and leaders listening to him. How can anyone forgive sins except God? After more discussion, the man said Jesus told the paralytic, "Get up, take your mat and go home."

Jesus knew how the leaders would react. He also knew the great length the friends had gone to receive healing for their sick friend. Jesus did not fear what the Pharisees might think. He had a job to do and he did it. He did not only make the man well, he also forgave his sins to prove to the crowd without

---

10   This idea was inspired during a revival sermon at Minorsville Christian Church in August, 2011.

a doubt some of the heavenly powers he possesses. How can they even think he could do that without his Father's help?

The man said the crowd immediately began glorifying God. He also said they were filled with fear. I can understand those feelings. I have been filled with fear and awe at his powers. Maybe if those Pharisees and leaders who witnessed this deed become believers, they could help persuade their associates. I pray this incident will help Jesus continue preaching his mission.

Dear Lord, my prayer tonight is for friends as faithful as those who went to such a measure to help their invalid friend. How different would this world be if we could be as compassionate for others? I am so glad Jesus helped the man even if he did anger the Pharisees. My dear Lord, I must also thank You for the beautiful scroll You have provided for my work. I know You are pleased with the words I am writing or You would not continue to bless me with the much needed materials. Thank You for the many blessings You pour on my family.

Lazarus Reports to Mary

The words dance from my quill tonight as I write about the visit we had today. Our dear friends Lazarus, Mary, and Maratha came by to tell us the latest of Jesus. While in Jerusalem for the feast, he and his followers stopped by Lazarus' house for a short visit. Martha told me she fixed the party a plentiful meal. I am sure Jesus and his friends appreciated their kindness.

Mary told me through wide-eyed wonderment how they went to Jerusalem with Jesus where they witnessed some miraculous deeds. She said, "Mary, do you remember the pool of Bethsaida we walk by as we travel to the temple? Every time we walked beside it there were always people waiting to get to the pool after an angel of God comes and stirs up the waters. The first person who steps in the pool after the water is stirred is made well. When we were walking with Jesus, a paralyzed man who had sat at the edge of the pool for thirty-eight years caught Jesus' attention.

"Jesus walked by him and asked, 'Do you want to get well?'

"The man replied, 'I have no one to help me into the water. Someone always gets there before me.'

"Then Jesus did the strangest thing, Mary. He looked at the man and said, 'Get up, pick up your pallet and walk.'

"The man immediately did as Jesus said and he could walk. He had not walked for thirty-eight years. Yet, he jumped up and walked just like we do. His legs were not weak from lying on the cot all those years. Mary, your son made his legs strong enough to walk! How glorious is that? How proud you must be of him?"

"I have always been proud of him," I replied. "I just hope Lazarus is telling his brothers this same story. They need to hear from someone they trust."

Mary went on to say this happened on a Sabbath, which did not please the Pharisees. Mary said Jesus said to them, "My Father is always at his work to this very day, and I, too, am working." That, she said, infuriated them. He not only broke the Law of the Sabbath, he also called God his Father, making himself equal with God.

His words, which mocked their teachings, did not rest kindly with the Pharisees. I guess they have accused him of just about everything, but they have never found him guilty of breaking any laws. He may not abide by all their traditions, but I know he knows the law to the letter. I helped teach him. Really, I guess he helped write them. I can hear him reciting many of those laws to the Pharisees when they question him.

Mary could not believe the Pharisees said Jesus broke the law by helping people on the Sabbath. If someone cut themselves and was in danger of bleeding to death, would it be unlawful to save them? Is helping people unlawful? Even on the Sabbath?

In spite of the reaction of the Pharisees, his message continues to be of love and forgiveness. He gives blessings to all people who are humbled and willing to accept them. Mary said the Pharisees nearly jumped up and down in protest when Jesus told the people to look at themselves before they judge others. My dear son, why are you trying so hard to anger them?

We had an abundance of visitors today. As we enjoyed our visit, another family came by talking about the Pharisees getting angry because Jesus picked grain on the Sabbath. He and his friends were on their way to Galilee when the men grew hungry and picked some heads of grain to eat. The Pharisees accused them of doing what is unlawful on the Sabbath.

The first time I heard of Jesus being disrespectful of the Sabbath caused me some confusion. We have always taught our children to hold the Sabbath day holy in honor of our heavenly Father. The scribes and Pharisees have a right to be angry with Jesus breaking that command. But when I heard the whole story, I understood. Doing work on the Sabbath and saving lives on the Sabbath is not the same thing.

With much sadness I told Mary and Martha goodbye as they were in a hurry to finish their trip. All my persuasion could not convince them how badly they needed a good night's rest (or maybe it was how desperately I wanted to continue our conversation).

Dear God, thank You so much for the visit from our dear friends. I know the stories they tell are true. Please guide them safely as they travel back to Jerusalem. I just pray You will watch over Jesus and keep him safe. He is doing so much good for the people, but it must be hard for You to watch and listen to what the Pharisees are saying about his good works. How will the people ever be convinced that the good deeds he performs are from You?

The dead son sat up and began to speak. And Jesus gave him back to his mother.
Luke 7:11-17, 36-50

Mary Receives a Special Visitor

The other day a most-welcome visitor stopped by the shop to visit. Doctor Luke came to read my scrolls in exchange for a new one to continue my work. I accepted the gift and eagerly shared everything I have written. He tells me he is writing the happenings of Jesus for his friend and benefactor, Theophilus. This friend wants to know of every detail of Jesus' life.

Doctor Luke's eyes did not stray from my writings except to listen to the stories of the travelers. I watched with interest his reaction as he read my stories. Every once in a while he would look at me and say "Oh, my!" He had not heard of any of the events except the decree of Herod to kill all the babies under two. He remembers the soldier putting their sword next to him to measure him. That is the way they determined a child's age. If he had not passed the sword test, he also would have been slain.

The writings held his attention until well past the evening meal. He agreed to spend the night so he could finish the scrolls. His praise of the work I have completed over the last thirty years encourages me to continue. Every time I wonder if I am doing the right thing or writing enough to make a difference, my Lord sends precious words of encouragement from an unlikely visitor.

Doctor Luke only got as far as the story where the angel appeared to Joseph and told us to head to Egypt. As more travelers came by telling more stories, Doctor Luke felt compelled to stop reading to listen to their tales.

Before he retired for the night, he asked if I would like to play a game of senet. I nearly cried. I wiped the dust from the game board Joseph had made and set up the pieces. It did not take long for everyone in the house to gather around us. Playing the game reminded me of his father and the hospitality he showed us in Bethlehem. After Doctor Luke barely beat me, Joseph challenged him to a game. I could watch them play all night. I must make sure the game board is available so we can play more often. It is a good distraction from the stories we are hearing.

Perhaps Doctor Luke can return another day to finish reading the other scrolls. I allowed him to read about Joseph doubting my story, but I made him vow he would never repeat or write about the incident. My Lord has shown me that Doctor Luke is trustworthy.

He repeatedly thanked me for the information and assured me that no harm would come to Jesus because of him. I sent a small gift to Zachary and asked Doctor Luke to return anytime. He said we would meet again as he waved goodbye and headed back to Cana.

Jesus appears to be in a different town for every story we hear. Today's travelers said he traveled through the town of Nain where he healed the only son of a widow as the men carried the young man in a coffin. Jesus told the boy to get up and he did. I can just imagine screams of joy from the mother when the young man jumped out of the coffin, and the screams of fear coming from the mourners as they fled.

Judas later asked me if I thought that might be the widow and son he had met on his trip to Jerusalem with the group of young men. He recalled the story of the widow and son whom they had helped in exchange for some refreshment and fresh water. Her son would have been about the age of the young man.

Jesus would also remember Judas' story. I remember Jesus asking Judas all kinds of questions about the circumstances of the woman. Judas did not know much except that they had been alone for some time and the boy had become the household provider. Jesus often became upset when he heard of someone in distress. He always wanted to help, but knew he could not because his Father had not yet given him the authority.

Sometimes some of the stories of Jesus get mixed up with John. They say Jesus tells how John came before him to prepare his way and then he severely criticizes the scribes and Pharisees for rejecting John and putting him in prison. Jesus praises all those who were baptized by John.

It does not seem Jesus is very picky about the people with whom he associates. I have heard the travelers say that he regularly dines with the Pharisees but their meals are often interrupted by people trying to get close to Jesus.

They told one story about a sinful woman who brought an alabaster jar of perfume to the dining table, wet Jesus' feet with her tears and then wiped them with her hair. After she kissed his feet, she poured the expensive perfume on them. The Pharisees were troubled that he let the sinful woman touch him. According to the story, Jesus politely told the Pharisee the woman acknowledged him more than any of the hosts at the supper. This woman must have had a strong yearning to please her Lord.

I have heard there are some women following Jesus now. If this is true, then I should fit in without being noticed. No one has to know I am anything more than another follower. I plan to leave after I visit Elizabeth and my other new granddaughter.

One must be careful how they pray. I asked for a granddaughter and received two. Elizabeth named her daughter Mary after me. It sure does warm a mother's heart to know her daughter thinks enough of her mother to allow their child to carry her name. The hardest part about following Jesus is leaving my precious grandchildren behind. If I could, I would get the boys to build me a cart to carry them right along beside me, but I must be content to carry them in my heart. When I think of all my children, my heart feels as if it could explode from an abundance of pride. I know my Lord tells me I should not be puffed up with pride, but He did not consider children and grandchildren when He made that command.

I wish I could slip off from my family without them knowing I had left. I hope James will go with me and the others will be content to stay here and take care of the business.

We still get many orders for the shop. The other day a traveler came by and commissioned a dozen chairs. The order surprised everyone because we do not often use chairs. Only the wealthy sat in chairs and the young man did not appear to be wealthy. Perhaps they were for someone else. Judas and Joseph finished them the other day and they are beautiful. It would be nice to have chairs for my table. I hope the young man does not come back. Maybe I will be allowed to keep them.

I have been thinking so much about Jesus, I have not taken time to write about any of my other children. I have been cautious about using my scroll to record anything except Jesus' works. Since I have almost a new scroll, maybe it is time to add a little about the rest of my family before I leave. I may not be able to write much where I am going.

Joseph is the only other son who is currently interested in marriage. He and I went to talk to Ettezus' parents a few days ago to contract a betrothal. Since I am leaving for awhile, they can take my room. I know Joseph will want to stay close to home. With his God-given gift and ability for crafting masterpieces, he will never move far from his father's shop. I can also use that as an excuse to follow Jesus. With Ettezus and Leah running the house, I have no worries about the well-being of my sons.

The rest of the boys will probably always stay close by, except for James. I believe when he finally accepts the message of Jesus, James will become one of his most devout followers. I can tell he misses Jesus very much and has wanted to join him for some time now, but is afraid to leave me. With Jesus gone, James feels he must assume the role as head of the house.

James tackles everything with a vengeance. He can perform any one task absolutely perfectly, but ask him to do two things at once and they both fall apart. For some reason God chose to make men very one dimensional. I cannot count how many times I have cooked a meal, cleaned the house, soothed a scraped knee, changed a toddler's dirty cloths all while holding another baby in my arms, and sometimes even entertaining visitors—all at one time. I smile when I see Elizabeth and Leah doing the same thing, but my sons follow in the steps of their father who also could not work and talk at the same time. Thank You Lord for that difference. I cannot imagine how some of their masterpieces would look if they tried to work on multiple pieces. As usual, I have determined God planned each of His creatures perfectly and the sooner one realizes the difference between each one, the happier everyone will be.

Elizabeth will not be happy I am leaving because her precious little girl is very young. She tells me baby Joseph often asks about his Uncle Jesus. Oh, if he only knew.

Dear Lord, help us find Jesus and please let it be the right thing to do. I pray for Your guidance in this matter. My heart yearns to see him and talk to him, but I know his life is now devoted to You. I just want to see for myself that all is well with him. I promise I will not interfere with the mission You have prepared for him. Please keep the rest of my family under Your protective wings.

Now when Jesus heard that John had been taken into
custody, He withdrew into Galilee;
Matthew 4:12; Mark 1:14; Luke 3:19-20

Mary Hears of John's Arrest

I write with such a heavy heart tonight from the disturbing news we have heard. James came running into the house exclaiming John had been imprisoned. King Herod, apparently, does not like being told the truth. The story we were told is that John told Herod the law forbade him to take his brother's wife as his own. From what I have heard about Herod, I am surprised he did not have John put to death. Everyone knows John only publicly spoke the words everyone else speaks in secret. Herod knows John is a righteous and holy man who speaks only the words of the law.

Hopefully, John will remain safe in prison. The story told by one of Herod's servants is that King Herod often calls John to his palace to talk to him. Before the conversation ends, Herod becomes so upset over John's words, he sends him back to prison.

I fear even more for John's safety. He has always been a rebel of sorts and very outspoken. He does not know how to hold back his feelings. If he thinks something, he says it. He does not care who he offends. He is not going to change his story just to make Herod happy. "If it is the truth, it should not hurt" I have heard John say many times. I wonder how long Herod can keep him in prison without a good reason. I am sure John's followers are there daily to check on him. I hope they will be brave enough to demand his release. Herod cannot keep John in prison indefinitely.

I wonder if Jesus knows of his cousin's predicament. He always tried to protect John. I fear he may go visit him and also be thrown in prison. My heart yearns to be with both of them—to help in some way. I cannot just sit here and fret.

Another group of travelers came by today telling that one of Jesus' new followers is a tax collector named Levi. I am beginning to wonder if all this tumult is beginning to affect his mind. Why a tax collector? They said he even had dinner at his house. He is deliberately associating with sinners. What is wrong with him? He knows how sinful tax collectors are? Why would he want to associate with the likes of them when he has his pick of good righteous men? I must go see what is going on in his mind. It is time for me to leave this house and do whatever I can to help him. The boys can take care of things here and it appears Jesus needs me badly.

Dear God, please help me find Jesus. I know he can explain everything. I must see for myself what everyone is talking about. I beg for John's safety. May he and Jesus and their followers abide safely under the cover of Your always protective out-stretched wings.

John sent them to the Lord, saying, "Are You the Expected
One, or do we look for someone else?"
Matthew 11:2-19; Luke 7:18-35
See, I will send my messenger, who will prepare the way before me.
Then suddenly the Lord you are seeking will come to his temple;
Malachi 3:1

Mary is Told of John's Inquiry

I feel I could sing like the nightingales tonight after talking to a woman named Lydia who stopped at the shop today with her family. Talking to someone who has insight into Jesus' life lifts such a burden from my soul. Their journey stretched from Bethany to Magdala to visit a daughter who had moved from their home to join her new husband. We soon realized we had something in common when I told her about Sarah moving to Cana. She knew Lazarus, Mary and Martha, and remembered our big family often going to visit them at Passover.

She said Lazarus had not been feeling very well. I hope our dear friend has recovered his good health. I miss our visits. I wonder what he thinks about Jesus' latest actions. Our last trip to observe Passover passed so quickly we did not have time to visit any of our old friends. Our lives have become very busy with the new grandbabies and the increase in work at the shop.

Lydia's version of the story detailed so much more than what the men usually tell. I felt comfortable enough talking to her to tell her my story. Her eyes grew wild with excitement when I told her I am the teacher's mother. She looked at me for a brief moment and then hugged me as our tears ran together. "I can only imagine what you must be going through," she said wiping her cheeks.

She proceeded in great detail to tell the latest story she had witnessed herself. I am so thankful and comforted for a new friend and this enlightening news.

She reported that Jesus sent his twelve to different cities while he preached by himself. As usual, a huge crowd gathered. The crowd had grown so large; everyone tried to get closer to hear Jesus. Lydia said the people were amazed because every word he says is clearly heard by everyone there. She also confirmed the story that some women had joined his chosen men and were now following Jesus. Perhaps I could discreetly join that group of women.

Lydia said the crowd sat and listened to Jesus when some other disciples came and started questioning Jesus. Lydia said the disciples followed John before, but since his imprisonment, they had been drifting, looking for some guidance. She heard one of them ask Jesus, "Are you the Expected One, or shall we look for someone else?"

It surprised me because John knows Jesus is the Expected One. He baptized him and saw the dove. How can his followers even think to question if Jesus is really the Expected One?

Jesus understood and explained their inquiry. He told the men to go and report to John the deeds they had witnessed. The men saw the blind receive sight, the lepers healed, the lame walk, the deaf hear, and the dead rise. Unlike our religious leaders of today, Jesus preaches his gospel to the poor as well as the wealthy. He blesses those who do not take offense at him.

To help confirm his story, he quoted the scripture the prophets wrote about John being the Messenger who would prepare the way for him. Then Jesus explained that he has no motive for doing these things except to glorify God and fulfill His plan. Although people are not going to accept him, he will continue to do everything he can to prove to the people that he is the Son of God.

I listened to Lydia repeat that whole conversation. It is difficult for me to understand, but when I think about it, John must be wondering why he is in prison if Jesus is the one sent by God. If he is supposed to prepare the way for Jesus, why is he not free to do so? John must think something has gone wrong with the original plan. Jesus is not performing any of the deeds we expected from our Messiah. He can do all these miraculous things, but yet he allows his messenger to be put in prison. I must say I have a hard time believing this is part of God's great plan. From where John is watching, it is reasonable to wonder if Jesus really is the person John thought him to be. I know I have written this before, but it is still hard for me to believe and I have always known!

The rest of Lydia's party prepared to leave so we said our heart-felt goodbye. I am grateful for the comfort of her story. It is good to know there is a woman who shares my views and my worries about my son.

Dear God, thank You for sending Lydia into my life when I desperately needed this news of Jesus. Please forgive me when I do not understand. You have to realize how difficult it is for me to watch what is happening to John and know Jesus wants so badly to do something for him. I earnestly pray for John's release. It must be agonizing for him to stay in prison when he hears of the things Jesus is doing. I know John feels he should be helping Jesus. John's experience has given him the knowledge of Jesus' identity, but God, only You can give him the wisdom to understand.

When His own people heard of this, they went out to take custody of Him;
for they were saying, "He has lost His senses."
Matthew 12:46-50; Mark 3:31-35; Luke 8:19-21

Mary Tells Her Sons She is Going to Visit Jesus

Today I had a frank talk with my sons. I told them the time had come for me to find their brother. Their reaction shocked me. They all wanted to go with me, but not for the reason I would hope. I want to go to hear more of his message, but they want to go because they think he has lost his mind or has been possessed by some demon. The stories they hear from the travelers have them scared for Jesus' safety. They know the Pharisees, if given a chance, will kill Jesus for blasphemy. They want to bring him home, using force if necessary. Their words left me speechless. I have some doubts about the stories we have heard, but I did not realize they were as adamant in their disbelief of him.

Now I am really concerned. They know he did some powerful things when they were growing up, but they never considered those things miracles. They saw him change the water to wine. How can Simon not believe after seeing the healing of Silas' eyes? They know he drove out the demons from a man in the synagogue when he last came here. They know, and yet they still doubt. How can he ever convince anyone of his powers? Even James, who I thought would never doubt his brother, agrees with them. Their concern is not selfish; it is for Jesus' safety.

Since our people have been looking for a Messiah for such a long time, I thought they would be eager to believe Jesus' story. But everyone expects an Elijah or another prophet to be that long-awaited Messiah. No one ever expected our Messiah to come from a humble family living in the midst of Nazareth. Everyone expected him to come in a blaze of glory, saving all the righteous and slaying all the sinners. Instead, he is eating with the sinners, even choosing them to follow him, and contradicting the righteous. He associates with the sinners more than he does with the honorable. Where is this "throne of David" he is supposed to rule—the promise I received from Gabriel?

As distraught as I am with my sons, I cannot blame them for their disbelief. I have some myself. How can I help anyone believe with the uncertainty that exists in my mind?

Our plan is to leave in a few days to begin a search for their brother. Joseph must finish a few jobs in the carpentry shop and I must invite Elizabeth and my grandchildren over for one last feast.

Jesus should not be hard to find. We will look for the crowd and follow the stories. Along the way I will attempt to talk some sense into the boys and again persuade them to believe my story of Jesus' true identity. I have told them the story before, but God has not opened their hearts to accept the truth. What can I do to convince them? They think I am trying to give Jesus credibility. Why would they think I would make up such an unbelievable story? As much as they all know I would never lie, they also know I would do anything to protect my children. They think I am fabricating the truth to help Jesus.

I must take this new scroll with me. It is important to keep writing about the events I witness. The world must know the things Jesus is doing and the reactions of the people, even from his own family. Maybe his family's disbelief will help others understand.

Dear God, I pray for the words to convince my sons that their brother is Your son. You are the one who has given him this message of love he is teaching and the power to perform the miraculous deeds we have witnessed and heard about. As contradictory as it may seem, his message is a wonderful story of salvation. It is almost too hard for them to comprehend this new gift of salvation freely offered to those who believe in You. How can we be saved without the blood of the sacrifices? What blood, my dear God, is going to wash away our sins?

Having been prompted by her mother (Herodias),
she said, "Give me here on a platter the head of John the Baptist."
Matthew 14:1-12; Mark 6:14-29; Luke 9:7-9

Mary Hears John Has Been Beheaded

My dear journal, I can hardly write these words tonight. My hand trembles as sorrow floods my soul over the news we just received. Cousin John has been beheaded. Oh, that evil King Herod! I would not want to be in his sandals when the judgment day comes. John wronged no one. King Herod did not like John's condemnation of Herod taking his brother's wife, but, my dear Lord, everyone in the area said the same thing—only they said it silently. Everyone knew the king had his brother killed so he could marry his wife. No one likes to be reminded of their evil deeds.

The story told by the travelers is that Herod's stepdaughter danced for him at his birthday party. Apparently, she has the gift of her mother to entice men to yield to her desires. She must have greatly pleased Herod because he promised her any gift she desired. The girl already possesses every material thing available. When Herod asked her what she desired, he probably expected her to say some marvelous, lavish gift or even one of the handsome soldiers as her personal servant.

It is believed that her mother persuaded her to request the head of John on a platter. I cannot even imagine someone being so evil and heartless. Who would want to see a head on a platter? I am so glad Elizabeth and Zechariah have already left this earth. How hard it would be to hear your son had died in this manner. My heart is breaking today for them. I can only imagine how heartbroken Jesus must feel. I wish he could come home to allow his family to console him.

This is the last straw. His brothers and I are leaving early tomorrow to find him. They may have to delay some of their jobs in the shop, but I am leaving—with or without them. If following him at a distance is as close as I can get, I will be content to do so. Just knowing I am there may offer some encouragement for him. His brothers do not fully understand Jesus' message yet, but I trust their believing will come with time. I wish I could say with all certainty that I believe all his message is correct, but I do have my doubts. After this news today, I have even more doubt.

If John came to prepare the way for Jesus, how could God let John die in such a manner? Is his job over? Had John done all he could? If so, what does this mean for Jesus? Surely, God would not allow his son to die in such a hideous manner.

I feel good about leaving as long as someone is here to watch the house. Simon and Leah are not going anywhere with those little bundles of joy they have. Joseph and Judas told me they finished the job they had started so they can leave for a few days. James will go and stay as long as I do. Elizabeth, Amos, Joseph, Jesus, and baby Mary came to visit yesterday so I have had a good measure of my precious babies to last for some time.

I cannot help but wonder why God would allow someone as devoted as John to die in such a manner. John never showed pain or fear. He did not fear death because he knew he had a better place in heaven. But what could be gained by such a horrendous death? It does not seem a fitting death for someone as special to God as I know John must have been.

Death comes in many forms and for many reasons. But John did not get killed because of his preaching. His death came because he spoke the truth. He died as a result of Herod's game. The world is full of evil people and John died at the hands of the cruelest of the cruel.

With the crowds engulfing Jesus, he will not have time to properly grieve. He never has an opportunity to be alone. At least with the crowd no one will be able to capture him or throw him in prison for his teaching as they did John. It would take some very brave soldiers to try to arrest him. From what I have heard, the crowds almost worship the ground on which he walks. They treat him as a god. I believe his followers would go to great lengths to protect him.

He will not be too hard to find. All I have to do is follow the stories the travelers are constantly reporting and then look for the large crowds. He will be there talking to them and healing all their diseases. I hope he knows how very proud I am of him. If I must be proud in silence, so be it. I do not need everyone to know who I am. I only wish I knew who I am, and why, and who Jesus really is, and what will be the outcome of this experience. My mind has become so confused with this latest news.

Dear God, please console Jesus at this time. You know how he loved his cousin John. This news will devastate him. I pray You will also comfort his followers who knew John. I truly believe everything is a part of Your plan, but I have a hard time understanding. Forgive me when my doubt overcomes my belief. I know with certainty the source of Jesus' powers, but I feel so powerless at this time.

Someone said to Him, "Behold, Your mother and Your brothers
are standing outside seeking to speak to You."
Matthew 12:46-50; Mark 3:31-35; Luke 8:19-21

Jesus Denies Knowing
Mary and His Brothers

Luckily, the stars and moon have provided ample light for my quill tonight. When I am under the stars, I often wonder if they still talk to my precious Sarah as they did during her childhood. I wonder what they would tell her tonight. As long as they provide enough bright light for me to write the events of the day, I am happy.

Judas, Joseph and I are anxiously waiting in a secluded spot under a big tree or I would not be able to write anything. We are waiting for James and, hopefully, Jesus. Surely, James has not caused Jesus any harm since we last saw them.

Early this morning my heart filled with love and sorrow as Sydney Katherine's breath brushed my cheeks when I kissed her goodbye. Zachary Joseph was too busy eating to acknowledge my goodbye kisses. Those kisses must last through this trying time. James, Joseph, Judas and I waved as Simon and Leah, holding their precious children, watched from the doorway, a blanket of worry hovering over all of us.

The bright sunrays directed our feet along the dusty path as we headed east to see if we could find Jesus and his group of followers. Luckily, he had been spotted in Nazareth a few days before. I hoped he would stop to visit while Elizabeth and her family were there, but he has told me it might be dangerous for him to acknowledge us as family. He would never put any of us in danger.

We caught up with Jesus in a synagogue at Tiberias. We tried to get close to him by telling the people we were his mother and brothers, but not many believed us. After some friendly persuasion, some people finally moved enough to clear a narrow path for us. We inched our way to the door and told the guards that Jesus' mother and brothers had arrived. I expected to at least be given the right to enter the room. When the news reached Jesus that his mother and brothers were outside, his reply pierced my very soul.

"Who is my mother and who is my brother?" He said pointing around the room. "Here are my mother and my brothers. For whosoever does the will of my Father in heaven is my brother and sister and mother."

Jesus told me this would happen, but I could not understand how he could completely forget the times we have shared or our love for him. My tears were gathering, waiting for the freedom to escape...until I caught the corner of his eye. He moved closer so I could see him and he smiled that knowing smile I have seen so many times before. Like the one he smiled when he placed a breathing Sarah in my arms. My disappointment and anger immediately subsided. I did not understand, but that is unimportant. I have known since the day of his birth that something like this would happen. I did not expect the rejection to be so difficult, but, again, I have the feeling that Simeon's sword has barely touched the surface of my pain.

I had not considered how his brothers would react until I heard James exclaim, "Mother! He has disowned you. Do you think Jesus is in his right mind?"

I tried to turn him around and disappear into the crowd to explain that Jesus had to do what he did. The task would not be easy, but I knew God would give me the right words.

"No, Mother!" James said, pulling away from my grip. "I am getting to the bottom of this nonsense. I will have a talk with that disrespectful brother of mine." He disappeared into the crowd with Judas and Joseph following him.

"Take her away from here," I heard James yell at Judas and Joseph. With a scowl, they returned to usher me out of the meeting place.

We moved away from the crowd and found this secluded place to wait for James to return. I need some rest, but rest does not come to a worried mind.

The crowd finally dissipated, and we waited...and we waited...and we are still waiting. We do not know where either one of them are, but I suspect they are together, having the talk they have needed for some time. We decided to stay here for the night, so I am writing while the boys slumber restlessly. I know sleep will not be my friend tonight.

I do not fear for the crowd seeing me write as I once did, especially since they are so preoccupied with the day's events. I do not think they would even notice.

Dear God, please direct my sons as they work out the problems You have allowed to surface between them. James thinks he is right in what he does. He is only trying to protect me and Jesus. Jesus has told me that his followers are now his family. I know he is doing what he must do, but that thought does not make it any easier for a mother. His words today were more for the benefit of the crowd than they were for us. The people need to know how much he loves them. He considers them his brothers and his sisters, his family. I know Jesus still loves all of us deeply. He just cannot acknowledge us at this time. My prayer is for our hearts to be opened for the understanding we need.

James, a bond-servant of God and of the Lord Jesus Christ,
James 1:1

James Becomes a Believer

I am writing with a little lighter heart today. Judas, Joseph and I spent last night in a secluded spot under a tree. After Jesus quit preaching, many of the people left to go home. Later I watched as a group of Roman soldiers rode through the crowd. I assumed they were looking for Jesus, but no one would give up his location. We also were waiting to see Jesus and find James. There were not many words spoken the entire night.

Thankfully, God directed me to pack some ink and papyrus to bring on the trip. Writing came easily after everyone fell asleep. My writing helps ease the worry I feel for Jesus and now for James.

We spent most of the day waiting for James and Jesus to return. The area still had some stragglers who had come to hear Jesus speak or who had brought their sick for him to heal. We had almost decided to start back home, when we saw James' silhouette walking across the field. He had not slept nor was he ready to go home. James assured his brothers that Jesus had not lost his mind as they had suspected. He told them they had talked long into the night and Jesus had proven to be sane. Jesus had not meant to be disrespectful when he had denied knowing who his mother and brothers were yesterday, but he could not acknowledge us in the midst of the crowd.

"He knew the people would overcome us with their desire to know more about him. It would have been dangerous for you," James said with a gentle smile I have not seen from him before. James knew his brothers were still livid over yesterday and wanted to assure them Jesus thought only of our safety.

James and I finally persuaded Judas and Joseph to return home while we stayed to be with Jesus. As they were getting ready to leave, Jesus appeared to apologize and explain his actions.

"I am sorry for the pain I caused you," Jesus said with his damp eyes glistening. "I could not take a chance on someone causing you harm. You know in my heart you will always be my family. Nothing can take that away."

The memory of their loving hugs has erased the look of doubt yesterday morning and the look of anger last night. I feared I might never see them embrace again when we left the house. Joseph and Judas hugged me goodbye then left to return home.

Jesus looked at me and said, "Are you not going with them?"

I knew I might have a battle on my hands so I quickly pleaded with my heavenly Father to give me the right words. "Jesus, I have not seen my sister, Salome, in many years. Since we are close to her home, I have decided to visit for a little while. I am sure you will welcome your brother and me in your group for a short time. No one will recognize either James or me. I promise to stay in the back and not cause you any problems," I said half pleading with him.

He smiled, grabbed my shoulders and gently kissed my forehead. "Thank you, mother," he said. "I cannot deny you this simple request. If it were not for a mother's love, where would this world be?" He turned and walked away as James held my shoulders to provide support.

James eased me over to some stones and sat me down. "Mother, how long have you known?" James asked and immediately answered. "I guess since you gave birth to him you have known all his life. This is what you have been trying to tell us, is it not?"

I smiled and nodded my head, "I tried to tell you, but you were not receptive to my words. I dismissed your disbelief thinking God had not opened your heart to comprehend. I learned a long time ago not to rush God's plan. I have known Jesus would be leaving some day, but I always thought it would have happened much sooner. Now, I know why God chose to wait until now to reveal the secret to you. He needed Jesus to publicly acknowledge his believers as his new family. He is the Savior of all believers. His family is now those who believe his word as he said yesterday. I am surprised he waited so long, but it is not my place to determine the time. I have tried before to rush God's plan and it just does not work."

"I know," James said with a sparkle in his eyes. "Jesus talked to me all night last night. I do not think he sleeps. His twelve followers had no trouble falling asleep, but Jesus wanted to stay awake, so we talked. We were camped right over there," he said, pointing to a large clump of trees just beyond where his brothers and I had stayed. "He saw you and Joseph and Judas. I wanted to come over and get you to join our group, but Jesus said you were safer where you were. I will not question his decision anymore for around midnight last night a group of Roman soldiers rode through looking for Jesus. All the people started gathering around until the soldiers finally gave up and left. He is not worried mother. I feared for his life, but he did not worry."

"Son, you have to realize there is a much higher power watching over his every move. His heavenly Father placed Jesus on this earth for a reason. When it is time for that reason to be known, we will all know the truth. Until that time, I only know how the angel Gabriel promised that my son would receive a great kingdom to rule over the throne of David. I have been waiting for over thirty-two years for that kingdom. I think we have experienced its beginning."

"Mother, Jesus said he planned to make it possible for all of us to enter his kingdom. He said our Father prepared the perfect sacrifice to be offered for our sins. It pained him to talk about it. I fear what must happen to him before that kingdom is established."

"What do you mean?" I asked grabbing his arm as pent-up emotions began to surface. "Must he be the sacrifice that will atone for our sins? How can my God do that to his own son? James, please tell me that is not what you are saying?"

James hugged me tightly as he whispered, "Mother, I am afraid that is what Jesus is saying."

James held me as I cried until there were no more tears. From that moment we both became believers of Jesus' message. We knew he would be offered as the perfect sacrifice. We do not know the exact meaning of the words or how or when, but we fear it may happen soon.

We decided to follow him from a distance until we reached Salome's house. I will stay there for awhile and James will continue with Jesus. We agreed we are where we need to be, but we also know we must keep our distance to allow Jesus to do the work he came to earth to accomplish.

Dear God, thank You for finally giving me the comprehension I have longed for these last thirty-two years. I understand why I could not know any earlier. The pain I feel I must endure while watching him complete his earthly assignment is more than anyone should have to endure in a lifetime. I pray for comfort and the wisdom that only You can give. Please keep my family within Your abiding presence. Today, I hope the door unlocked to Judas and Joseph's heart. They will provide the key to unlock Simon's. I have no doubts that You will reveal to them what You revealed to James.

Jesus answered, "Truly, truly, I say to you, unless one is born of water
and the Spirit he cannot enter into the kingdom of God."
John 3:5

Mary and James are Baptized

Today is one of those days when lifetime memories are made. James came to me early this morning and said, "Mother, Jesus is going to the water to baptize the people. I am going in the water with him. I feel in my heart this is what we must do."

"My dear son," I replied nearly jumping for joy. "I have wanted to do this for some time. I could not sleep last night thinking about our conversation with Jesus. This will make him so happy."

"Do you know what it is for, mother?" James asked.

"It is for the salvation which brings eternal life," I replied. "I know Jesus is my son. I also know he is the Christ, the son of the living God. I want to obey the command of baptism just like Jesus did," I told him.

"I will go tell him," James said, rushing over to the crowd where Jesus stood. Jesus turned and looked at me with the smile I have grown to know and love.

Late yesterday I met some of the other women who have been following Jesus. There is another Mary who is the mother of James and Joses. A woman named Joanna, the wife of Cuza, the manager of Herod's household who left everything to follow Jesus. Suzanna is the only other name I remember. I have not yet heard her story. I know these women are wealthy by the clothes they wear and their manner which indicates they once enjoyed pleasures of the rich. Now they are content to follow their Messiah as humbly as the rest of us.

Then there is Mary Magdalene. I do not know all her story, but from what I can piece together, Jesus drove seven demons from her before she began following him. Hopefully, I will have a chance to learn of her strong faith.

James motioned for me to join him. We walked to the water with the others and the crowd that had gathered. Mary Magdalene, Joanna, and the other Mary came to stand beside me.

Jesus took my hand and led me into the water, while James followed. Jesus leaned over to whisper in my ear, "Dear Mother," then he looked to heaven and said in a loud voice, "I now baptize you in the name of my heavenly

Father." I felt my heart would burst with the joy of the presence of my new life. Oh, what a glorious salvation I received.

Dear Lord, as I write tonight, my mind is so full of praise for You and Your son. The baptism by Your son is one of the most memorable events I will ever experience. Thank You for the new friends I have found. I feel we will share many memorable moments together. All the women, especially Mary Magdalene, are so thankful for the new life Your son has given them. I praise You with all my heart.

As he (Jesus) walked along, he saw Levi son of Alphaeus
sitting in the tax collector's booth.
"Follow Me," Jesus told him, and Levi got up and followed him.
Matthew 9:9-13; Mark 2:13-17; Luke 5:27-32

Jesus Causes Problems with the Pharisees

What an awesome God I serve. After James and I were baptized, Jesus' chosen men spent the rest of the day baptizing and healing those who came from surrounding villages. I am not sure how Jesus plans to establish his kingdom, but I do not see how they can cause any harm to the Roman government if he expects to use the mild-mannered men he has chosen to follow him.

The only ones who are capable of any kind of rebellion are Simon or Judas Iscariot. They both were members of the Zealot sect of Jewish rebel fighters who refused to pay tribute to the pagan Romans. Once the military caused their rebellion to fail, the members continued to roam the hillsides looking for followers to help join a revolt to overthrow the government. They probably thought Jesus planned to create another rebellious movement. I have a feeling they will be surprised and perhaps disappointed with his message.

All of Jesus' followers have an average appearance and most of them appear to be somewhat educated. I do not think any of them except maybe Bartholomew received much of a structured education. I have the impression Jesus did not chose them for their mind. He must have looked at their heart and saw the same gentle spirit God saw in King David when He chose the young boy to be king.

The one named Thaddeus is gifted with a beautiful voice. I heard him singing a tune this morning as we walked to the baptism. After we were baptized, he sang a joyful praise song to his Lord. In a few minutes everyone joined him as the beautiful voices lifted to our heavenly Father. I know He sang right along with us. Even my screechy voice sounded decent mingled with the rest of the people.

When we started out again this morning, I joined the women following from a distance, while James worked his way up closer to the front. With the clothing we wear, I can discreetly hide among this group. It is difficult to tell one woman from another. Certainly, James will be welcomed by Jesus' other followers.

I made an awesome discovery today. Everyone calls him Levi, but I know him as Matthew. I just realized the tax collector Jesus chose as his follower is indeed his cousin Matthew, the son of Alpheus who is Joseph's brother. I remember how upset I became when I first heard Jesus had chosen a tax collector and had even gone to eat with him. I have always heard tax collectors were cheaters and sinners. Maybe I should not jump to conclusions and throw everyone of a particular occupation in the same basket. Even in the most sinful occupations, good people can be found.

I had not seen Matthew since his family joined us for a Passover feast many years ago. I think Jesus may have been around seven. The family used to come by quite often when they lived in Nazareth, but shortly after Elizabeth's birth, the family moved to Tiberias on the Sea of Galilee to care for ailing parents.

Joseph never said, but I suspected they were Joseph's parents. I remember his parents moving shortly after we came back from Egypt and never coming back to visit our family. Joseph refused to say anything bad about them, but I think they were angry with Joseph for marrying an adulteress when they realized I had been with child before we married. When we returned from Egypt, not many people knew or questioned the day of Jesus' birth. Joseph must have told them I gave birth the day we arrived in Bethlehem. They could not forgive their son for marrying an adulterous woman. Pride can sometimes be a very strange, deceiving friend.

Alpheus sometimes came by after the move as he traveled to Jerusalem, but Joseph's parents never returned. I assumed they had become too ill. I silently wondered why Joseph never went to see them. He kept busy with our big family so I knew he had an excuse. I did not want to burden him with anymore guilt so I never mentioned it. Maybe their story held a different explanation than I thought.

When I introduced myself to Matthew as his Aunt Mary, his eyes popped wide with excitement. Matthew remembered his father talking about a brother Joseph, but he had not made the connection with Jesus' father. He had been only nine or ten on their last visit. He explained that after Alpheus' death, he became a tax collector to care for their family. Out of the corner of my eye, I could see Jesus watching us. He knew Matthew and I would discover this connection. Wonder what he has planned for us?

We could not talk much longer because the crowds started gathering again. Jesus is really causing problems among the Pharisees and the leaders of the Law. It is just a matter of time until they grow weary of his popularity. I cringe when I think of what might happen, because Jesus preaches only brotherly love and he lives it completely. His message is so contradictory of their teachings. We never taught him to be a fighter, but now I sometimes wish I had taught him more about protecting himself. None of his followers carry swords or any means of protection. I think Peter may be the only one who carries a sword of some kind because I have seen something glisten in the sun when he walks.

I want to get mad at the scribes and Pharisees when they look at Jesus with such contempt or start whispering behind his back, but he does not seem to mind. He always has an answer for their inquiries. Today they asked Jesus about a sign. When he turned around and called them a wicked and adulterous generation, they flew into a rage. I have never seen so much huffing and puffing. I also think that is the angriest I have seen Jesus.

He told them they look to the birds for signs, but they cannot see the signs he places right in front of them. He told them about the sign of Jonah. We have all heard the story of the prophet Jonah running away from God and being stored in the belly of a huge fish for three days until the fish spewed him out of his mouth onto dry land. In fact, I am sure I told Jesus that story. So he has not completely forgotten my teachings. I remember him wanting to hear the story over and over until I nearly screamed. I am not sure if Jonah has anything to do with his kingdom, but I fear I may soon learn.

Then Jesus told how the Son of Man is going to be in the heart of the earth for three days and three nights. Is he talking about himself? Is he going to enter in the heart of a great fish as Jonah did? I gave birth to him but did not conceive his seed from an earthly man so why does he call himself the Son of Man? He talks about the Queen of the South rising at judgment and coming to listen to Solomon's wisdom. And now he says there is one coming that is greater than Solomon. Is there someone who is greater than Jesus? I wish he would take the time to explain his words to his mother. But he will not talk to me or even acknowledge that I am his mother in front of people. I am in the dark as much as anyone. I have always known he is something very special and my belief has been reinforced many times.

I plan to stay around and follow Jesus until I understand more of what the future holds. Although he does not acknowledge me in public, I will never forget or stop loving him. I have known from the very beginning we would have some difficult times, but he is still my son and I will always have a very special place for him.

Dear God, today I have experienced a complete range of emotions. Of all the people who have witnessed him today, I am the one who should experience only rejoicing. For I alone know who that Son of Man really is. I must try to put my worries aside and start believing what I know to be the truth. Jesus is our Messiah who has come to save us. James and I have accepted this message through our baptism. I must have patience to allow Your hand to guide me through the times of doubt. Thank You, Lord, for listening.

"Only in his hometown and in his own house is a prophet without honor."
Matthew 13:1-52; Mark 4:1-34; Luke 8:4-18
I will open my mouth in a parable; I will utter dark sayings of old,
Psalm 78:2

Jesus Speaks in Parables

My treasure box and beautiful scroll welcomed me as I sat down to write this entry. It is so good to finally spend a night in my warm comfortable home. James and I hurried to prepare what we thought would be a feast for Jesus and his followers, but, as usual, we were wrong. James and I decided not to tell his brothers and sisters about our baptism until Jesus arrived. We wanted him to be able to share the good news. Now we will wait a few more days to see if he comes home.

What a celebration we enjoyed. Elizabeth brought her three children to spend some time with us. Sydney Katherine, who is trying to walk, adores her Aunt Elizabeth. My heart melted when those precious little hands reached up to crawl in my lap so I could tell her a bedtime story as Joseph did for our children.

Our last few days of following Jesus have been eventful. One day the huge crowd forced Jesus to board a boat so the people could see him. The crowds are amazed by his stories and parables. I heard one of the disciples ask him why he spoke in parables. He explained they were easier for the people to understand since he uses actions of farmers and fishermen—things that are familiar to the people.

I am thankful Jesus had time to stay with his uncles on their farm and in their fishing boats as a child. His life experiences have helped him with his teaching. Most of the people who come to hear him have had those same experiences.[11] Since people do not have knowledge of the secrets of the kingdom of heaven as the disciples have, they cannot grasp the true meanings of his message. To get his point across, he often quotes and explains scripture the prophets have written.

I would like to take credit for his knowledge of the prophets, but all my teaching barely touches the surface of what he knows. I believe he must have been around when the prophets foretold the future. He not only quotes the

---

11   The inspiration for this idea came during a Wednesday night study session at Capital City Christian Church in June, 2011.

prophet's words, but he knows exactly how each prophecy fits the situation. That is hard for even the most learned Pharisee to explain. As everyone knows, it is not an easy task to interpret the sayings of some of those wise old men. And yet he seems to comprehend every word.

After he told the crowd some parables, someone said he had gone back home to Nazareth. Forgetting my good intentions to visit Salome, I hurried to welcome him and his friends and fix them a feast. I knew they must have been starving. It worries me they never seem to eat on a regular basis. I have heard him say, "Man cannot live by bread alone, but by every word that precedes out of his father's mouth." Still, their bodies need nourishment. Jesus looks so frail at times.

Leah, Elizabeth, and I hurriedly prepared the meal and patiently waited, but Jesus did not come home. A neighbor came by to tell us Jesus visited the synagogue amazing the people with his teaching. When they recognized him as the carpenter's son from Nazareth, they took offense at him. Jesus did not stay long and he did not perform the amazing miracles as he has elsewhere.

I hoped he could impress everyone with his abilities. After his first encounter in the synagogue last year, I am surprised he returned. I guess you never give up on your home people. If only they could see what I have seen and know what I know, they would believe. Instead, they choose to mock and scorn him. As he left, someone heard him make a comment about only in his hometown and in his own house is a prophet without honor. His heart must break thinking some of his own brothers still may not believe him. Of course, Sarah and Elizabeth adore their brother so much, they would believe anything he says.

It is hard for the boys to believe that someone they played with and grew up with could have such powers. I have seen his deeds, yet I understand how hard it is for them to believe. I know he is capable of anything his Father allows him to do.

I still cannot understand why God allowed John to be murdered so early in Jesus' ministry. I know John could explain all this to me with his incomparable knowledge of the prophets. Why did God not allow him to stay and prepare the way for Jesus? It appears there is still much to do.

I know it is not for me to question anything, but I just wish I understood better. I miss my dear friend Elizabeth. I miss the visits and the talks we shared. I can hear her telling me to have faith that God will arrange things in His time and not mine. She knew of my lack of patience when it comes to my son's kingdom that Gabriel promised. I often wish I could be more like my dear friend. She did not worry. She could always look at someone's heart instead of their outward appearance and know if that person truly served God.

Often when Elizabeth and Zechariah would bring John for a visit, a neighbor would drop by to see them. Elizabeth always warned me to watch my tongue around this one particular neighbor who could not keep any of my words to herself. Every time I would go to the well for water, the lady would follow to tell me all the news of the neighborhood before I could complete one sentence of conversation. If I could only speak to Elizabeth today, she would ease my fears concerning Jesus.

Dear God, why must it be so hard for people to understand Your son's powers and his message. Even seeing, they do not believe. Although his teachings may seem strange to us, I know there is a special reason for every action he does. You have hardened the people's hearts and closed their eyes. Must it be, so he can use them to fulfill his mission? After James and I talked to his brothers some still doubt his message. Help them understand and believe. Also, help my doubts to disappear. Even knowing, I am unable to convince my children. Give me the strength and patience to continue this journey.

And there are also many other things which Jesus did,
which if they were written in detail,
I suppose that even the world itself would not contain the books that would be written.
John 21:25

Miracle of the Baby and Matthew's Writing

This morning James and I arose early to return to Jesus. His brothers are so angry he did not come home for a visit. James talked till he turned blue in the face, but he cannot convince them of his brother's message. The truth of the salvation Jesus offers is something each one must discover himself. Only God can soften a heart to be receptive to His son's words. When I explained how dangerous it would be for us if Jesus did come home, they scoffed at the idea. My heart aches to see their disbelief. I only pray someday God will see fit to soften their hearts so they will believe.

James and I finally caught up with the crowd. Because of our fast pace, I had grown very tired. I found a comfortable place to rest as James moved closer to the front.

An incident today compelled me to miss my little Sydney Katherine. I yearn to be home to hold and snuggle her. All day Jesus healed the people who sought his service. Many have problems and come for deliverance of an illness, but many are just curious. Word spreads quickly when he is around.

A young girl, ready to give birth, sought Jesus today with concern for the health of her unborn child. The baby had been very active until a few days ago, when, suddenly, it had become very still. I remembered the birth of Ruth and felt the pain and the concern of the young mother-to-be for her first child. Like me, she had barely passed childhood.

Ignoring the pleading from her parents, she had come to seek the power of Jesus, but the large crowd prevented her from getting close. Jesus must have seen her distress, because he walked straight toward her from the midst of the people. The people in the crowd gasped as Jesus took his long narrow fingers and wrapped them over the girls bulging belly. Men do not normally touch the belly of an expectant woman—especially in public. I remember the smile on Joseph's face when I placed his hand on my expectant belly, so he could feel Jesus practicing his jumping jacks. After that day, every time Joseph came into the house, he would wrap his hands around my belly to feel the movement. The babies must have sensed his warm hands, because they always started performing for him.

The concerned look on Jesus' face subsided as he asked his heavenly father to bring life back to the child of this womb. The girl stood with her eyes full of hope and her face full of fear. Finally, Jesus smiled, as she burst out crying and exclaimed, "He moved. I felt him move again. Oh, thank you, my Lord." The Pharisees were taken aback at the actions of Jesus, but even more so at the praise of the young girl and her mention of Lord. She had committed blasphemy.

Jesus looked at the young girl with delight as he said, "This child is not the result of your sin, but the sin of a very cruel and callous man. I can tell you, that man will not awaken from his sleep in the morning."

More than one of the Pharisees gasped at Jesus' statement. It will be interesting to see how long a man can live without going to sleep. I have to smile at the fear that must be gripping the guilty party in his final day.

Jesus continued, "In a short time you will deliver a healthy baby boy. He will be great among the people and many will look up to him for guidance and hope during otherwise dreary times. His leadership will be comforting for many. Take good care of him. Go and live in peace."

Many of the Pharisees immediately began condemning Jesus for touching someone who had been considered to be an adulteress. "She should be stoned," I heard one of them say. "How dare her parents let her appear in public?" But one in the group remained noticeably silent.

I understood the parents concern and admired the courage of the young girl to face the crowd in search of her Savior. She risked her life for the well-being of her unborn child. Apparently, she had been hiding for many months or else the "righteous" leaders of the town would have stoned her.

The Pharisees would not dare harm her now. They completely ignored the blasphemy charge. It will be interesting to hear them explain the death of the guilty party tomorrow. Everyone in the crowd today will know the real story. No matter how confident one becomes in hiding his sin, God will eventually expose the truth.

I could relate to the young girl's feelings. Her situation reminded me of the fear I had when I thought Joseph might have me stoned. As the young mother-to-be disappeared into the crowd, I silently wondered who this leader might be that Jesus had foretold and if I would live to see it happen.

While Jesus continued his healing, some of the women and his followers went to rest under a shade tree. Following Jesus is a very tiring, but fulfilling job. I saw Matthew take out a scroll and begin writing, so I went to sit beside him. I had seen him do this before and wondered what he wrote. In many of the towns we enter, Matthew goes off by himself and searches for writing material and a quiet place to write. Being a former tax collector, he knows a lot of the people in this area and has access to things we do not. I have seen him write about the miracles Jesus performs. After Jesus preached on the mountain, Matthew wrote for days. Taking a seat beside him, I inquired of his writing.

"Oh, just taking care of some business," he replied without looking up. "I know it is necessary to record what Jesus is doing for the world to believe he really is our Savior. I am afraid this will not happen if I do not record the stories. I feel that is one of the reasons Jesus chose me. Why else would he choose a tax collector? I did not realize at the time that Jesus is my cousin. I am just trying to live worthy of the special assignment Jesus has chosen for me. Did you ever wonder why you were chosen? I have seen you writing also."

I took out a few of the special scrolls I keep with me. "I think you will find these very interesting," I said handing them to him. I watched the delight in his face as he read about the angel's visit and the birth. He read with amazement about the events that took place in that cave that was used as a stable. He could not believe Jesus and John had interacted at such an early age. It amazes me that Matthew had never met Cousin John. I thought they would have at least crossed paths at our house during one of the Passover feasts. He only knew him through the stories of Andrew and John and the few others that had followed John before following Jesus.

When he read the story of the death of the two year old boys, he stood up and exclaimed, "I remember this! I was four or five when this happened. I had blocked it out of my memory until now. Oh, what a horrible time! My mother feared Herod would change his mind and come after the older boys. Anytime a soldier came to the house, mother would hide me."

Matthew told about one of their neighbors having a one year old son. One day, while the child nursed, a soldier stormed through their door and ripped the baby from the mother's bosom. The mother followed the soldier outside screaming and grabbing his garments, begging him to stop. Outside the soldier dropped the baby to the ground, drew his sword and ran it all the way through the tiny body. The baby lay on the ground in a pool of blood as the mother picked up the lifeless body and held it tightly. It took all the women of the village to pry him loose.

The mother, covered with blood, walked into the house and never came out again. Matthew remembered his mother taking over food and trying to force the woman to eat, but she only sat there staring at the crib. She never spoke or ate again. She soon starved to death. The husband somehow blamed his wife and left. No one ever saw him again.

How terrible that time must have been. My heart aches every time I think of what happened because of my son, and know that had it not been for the warning from the angel, my son would have been among those slain.

We talked for some time. Matthew said he remembered seeing some scrolls his father kept under his sleeping cot. He often wondered what they were, but he had never gotten them out or read them.

"When I go home I am going to see what stories they may hold. Mother thought they were letters from his brother Joseph or something Alpheus had written about his brother, but she had never read them either. Now I cannot wait to see those stories," he said.

"They are probably stories Joseph told Alpheus when he was too distraught to talk to anyone else. I know Alpheus knew as much about Joseph's story as anyone does," I said thinking that the world may learn of Joseph's disbelief of my story after all. I hope the people do not view his doubt unfavorably. He only did what any other betrothed man would have done.

Now that Matthew and I are sharing this bond, we will discuss many of our stories. My heart dances with joy to know that he also will be writing of Jesus' good works. He already has a number of the miracles committed to paper. I wondered how the events would be recorded that took place before I joined them. It does not surprise me that God has provided an answer.

Dear Lord, thank You for the gift of a fellow scribe. I am delighted You guided Jesus to that sinful tax collector, Levi. Did You plan to teach me a lesson? I have judged every tax collector by the sins of a few. Why are people so eager to jump to conclusions based solely on rumors? Thank You for choosing Matthew to ensure everything You want to be remembered will be recorded. I can only assume You want the people to know the entire story of the birth—even of Joseph's doubt. The people will be grateful for the truth. Guide our words, Father, as we attempt to make Jesus' life believable for everyone. I can only imagine how hard it will be for someone to read this and believe the words. Give us the innocence needed to fully accept what we now believe.

"In a short time you will deliver a healthy baby boy."

For she was saying to herself, "If I only touch His garment, I will get well."
Matthew 9:18-26; Mark 5:21-43; Luke 8:40-56

Jesus Heals Jarius' Daughter and the Woman with an Issue of Blood

It is with a glad heart I am writing tonight about some wonderful events of the past few days. In some of my earlier writings it seemed my mind focused on only sad events. I much prefer writing about the happy things. The events of today can only be described as awesome.

As we followed Jesus, one of the synagogue rulers came to ask him to heal his twelve year old daughter. The request surprised everyone since very few of the rulers believe in his work. Walking to the ruler's house, Jesus, enclosed by his usual crowd, suddenly stopped. Everyone packed around him so close, I stayed behind for fear I might be trampled. I saw Jesus say something and heard his disciples laughing. Then they started walking again. After a few minutes a woman came out of the crowd beaming with delight. I knew something had happened. I finally got close enough to inquire of the reason for her excitement. Words gushed from her mouth like a fountain.

After a few minutes, she calmed down enough for me to understand her story. "I only touched the hem of his garment," she said.

I knew immediately.

"And he knew," she added. "He knew, and I am well."

"What do you mean, you are well?" I asked.

"I have had a bleeding disorder for over twelve years," she explained. "My life has been one of constant torment. I have not been able to perform any duties or have a family or do anything. More importantly, I could not worship in my beautiful temple. And now, by a simple touch of his cloak, the bleeding has stopped."

I asked her to tell me more.

"I saw him walking and I knew in my heart if I could only touch him, I would be healed. I struggled to get through the crowd pressing in on him. Finally, I reached out and barely touched the hem of his cloak. Immediately, the bleeding stopped, and so did the teacher.

"'Who touched me?' he asked looking around at the crowd.

"His followers laughed and said it could have been anyone in the crowd since they were packed together like peas in a pod. There were so many people trying to get to him.

"'No,' he told them. 'Someone touched me because I felt the power leave my body.'

"I fell down, terrified that he would be angry. I declared in front of everyone why I had touched him and how I am healed. The teacher told me, 'Daughter your faith has made you well; go in peace'.

"I am so happy," she said nearly dancing through her words. "I cannot wait to do something, anything right now!" She stopped and became somber for a minute and then added, "I did not touch him. I only touched his cloak. His power is not released by his touch. I did not have to touch him. I only had to believe he could heal me."

I am careful not to mention my relationship with Jesus if there is a crowd around, but listening to her miracle, my pride overcame me and I told her I knew he had miraculous powers because that man is my son. Her happiness abruptly turned into confusion as she asked me how a man born of an earthly woman could have such powers.

"I thought he is the Son of God," she said with a confused look.

Then the people started gathering around us because of the woman's reaction. Some were even laughing and calling me a liar. For a brief moment I again feared for my safety. The people soon dispersed as most of them walked on to catch up with Jesus. No one believed me. Not even the woman who experienced Jesus' healing power. She could not comprehend the fact that Jesus could be born of an earthly mother when he possesses such miraculous powers.

Maybe I have learned my lesson this time. I think from now on I will not mention who I am in front of a huge crowd. Jesus has told me that more than once. When will I learn it is not important for these people to know who I am? They only need to know who Jesus is. Someday people may look at my life and think good of me, but for now, I must remain anonymous. Jesus knew I could possibly be in danger if the people learned of my identity. Again, I realized he is thinking of my safety even though I think he is ignoring me. Bless his heart. He is still my very special son.

While we were talking, a servant of the ruler rushed through the crowd and told him not to bother the teacher anymore because his daughter had died.

From my position in the back of the crowd, I could hear the man wail and Jesus tell him, "Do not be afraid. Only believe." Then he took a few of his disciples and went to the ruler's house. I did not follow, but the story soon got back to us that the family and friends grieved loudly as the group approached. Jesus simply walked into the room and told the girl to get up. She stood up and started walking around. I think Jesus captured many more believers with his work today. If they do not believe after witnessing this awesome deed, there is no hope for them. I, too, have learned a valuable lesson. I will brag silently.

Dear God, thank You for such a special caring son. Even though He belongs to You now, I know he still deeply cares for me. I pray I will be able to see his concern for me in the things I do and that he will remain that caring son forever. Help me to be at peace with everything he is doing, and to brag silently.

She Only Touched His Cloak

She struggled to get near him.
Just a little bit closer.
There He is. I see Him.

She crawled through the crowd.
If I can only touch Him,
His power will heal me.

She felt His power emanating.
This area is drenched
with a powerful energy.

She spotted an opening.
Stretch just a wee bit farther.
Reach out to Him.

She barely touched the tip of His cloak.
My trembling body
feels the power.

She became whole.
I am healed.
My bleeding stopped.

She did not escape notice.
Oh, my, He knows.
Among this crowd He felt my touch.

"Who touched me?" He asked.
"Anyone could have," they replied.
"No, someone's faith touched me."

She trembled with despair.
Please do not be angry with me.
I knew Your touch could heal me.

She received His blessing.
"Daughter, your faith has made you well:
go in peace and be healed of your affliction"

Grow near and feel the energy.
Touch His garment and become whole.
Abide in His presence and receive His gift.

*The Father loves the Son and has placed everything in his
hands. Whoever believes in the Son has eternal life,
but whoever rejects the Son will not see life, for God's wrath remains on him."
John 3:35-36*

Mary Has a Private
Conversation with her Son

Tonight Jesus is finally giving his followers a rest after healing Jairus' daughter. Within a few minutes they were all sleeping like babies. Jesus' women followers have always been invited to stay in someone's house for the night, but last night we stayed outside with the men. I thought Jairus would invite us to his house, but his excitement over his daughter being revived from the world of the dead filled his mind. Jesus left so quickly after the healing; Jairus did not really have a chance to offer an invitation to stay.

The night sky overflowed with such bright stars and moon last night, I could write about all the events of yesterday. I am so glad for this opportunity to write this entry again tonight. I need to record the private talk I had with Jesus after everyone else fell asleep.

Last night, as usual, Jesus moved to a secluded area to have his daily talk with his Father. As soon as I finished writing my entry I slipped over and stood behind him just to listen to his wonderful heartfelt prayer.

"Mother, would you like to come and sit with me?" he asked without turning around.

"I am so sorry to disrupt your talk with your Father," I replied. "I have missed listening to your prayers. Thank you for allowing me this time."

"Mother, you will never disrupt me. I have missed our talks also, but after the incident today with the poor woman with the bleeding disorder, you should know why I cannot acknowledge you in front of the crowd.

"Oh, did you see that?" I inquired as my cheeks turned a little pink.

"Your time will come," he continued. "But I am afraid you will not be here to see it. In the future, people will honor you above all women. Some will even place your worth above mine. My Father will allow that through the Word He inspires. He gives each of us a mind with which to think and interpret all of His divinely inspired writings.

"Father wants His children to search through His words and interpret them as best they can. He knows there will be multiple interpretations, but He gives each of us the ability to find the truth. You only need to search with an open heart as well as an open mind. When the truth is found, His Word will be complete. Nothing will be left out. When He places that last period on His written Word, all the instructions anyone needs to receive His divine gift of salvation will be contained within.

"Mother, what I am telling you may sound foreign, but when my words are completed and read, people will understand what I am saying."

"Jesus," I whispered, "I am trying so hard to understand your message. Your brothers have also struggled with the understanding. The first time they came with me, they intended to find you because they thought you had gone crazy. They had planned to force you to go home. If you had not convinced James, you would be sitting at home bound to your favorite tree. They were that convinced you had lost your mind. Why must it be so hard? Will your heavenly Father ever soften their hearts so they can understand and believe?"

"Oh, yes, Mother," Jesus said as a smile crossed his lips, "but it will come in His time and not yours."

"I am greatly familiar with His schedule," I said with a raised eyebrow. "Do you know how long I have been trying to improve on that schedule?"

"Oh, probably over thirty-two years now," Jesus said with a smile. "I would think you would learn some patience by now."

We laughed and chatted a little longer before I drifted off into a peaceful slumber. It is amazing what good sleep medicine a simple conversation with our Messiah can be. It is much better to be open and talk than to allow problems to build up until they almost cause you to explode. His words will provide answers to any dilemma we may face. When I awoke this morning, Jesus had disappeared.

My great and awesome God, Our son is coming home to You. For some reason You have chosen to keep his mission a secret. Although I have accepted his message and his baptism, You have not enlightened my mind to all the glories of his teaching. I envy his followers who have that insight, but I am starting to sense there is at least one who has not grasped the full picture. May our hearts be softened and our minds be open to the message Your son is teaching.

But Jesus said to them, "They do not need to go away; you give them something to eat!"
Matthew 14:15-21; Mark 6:35-44; Luke 9:12-17; John 6:5-14

Jesus Feeds Five Thousand

What a delight to be able to write this story and share this miracle with the world. I know this one will be repeated for many years.

We stopped last night to rest near the beautiful city of Bethsaida along the Northeastern shore of Galilee. Its reputation for having abundant fish is evident with the number of fishing boats lining the banks. This morning the crowd was so huge, Jesus had to go to the top of a mound so everyone could see him. Taking a few minutes to enjoy the beautiful scenery, I sat on a rock far behind the crowd to enjoy a sip of water. I have never seen as many people so anxious to hear someone speak. Suddenly a young women ran up beside me yelling, "Jarad! Jared, where are you?" as she frantically searched the crowd.

Sensing the concern in her voice, I touched her arm and asked if I could be of some help.

"My son is lost," she explained, still scanning the crowd for the boy she could not find.

I asked her to sit down beside me so I could help watch for him.

"Look at that," she said, anxiously waving her hands at the crowd. "Who knows what could happen to a young boy in the midst of all that."

Understanding her concern, I calmly asked if she had searched along the shore for him.

"Yes, I quickly walked the shores, but when I saw this crowd, I knew he would be right in the midst of them. He is a normal curious nine year old boy. Can you imagine a young boy not wanting to see what is going on with this crowd? I know he is right there up front listening to that man they call Jesus. He has been curious about him for some time now. I have tried my best to turn his interest to something else, but that is all he wants to talk about."

Remembering the time I lost Jesus when he stayed behind at the temple, I knew the distress going through the woman's mind.

Needing to relieve her concerns, I offered her a sip of water and asked about her family as we sat there scanning the crowd for any sign of the young boy.

"My husband died a few years ago at the hands of the Roman soldiers who were trying to take one of our neighbor's daughters as payment for his overdue taxes. My husband and neighbor tried to save the daughter when a group of soldiers came by and trampled both of them. They lay in the streets dying because no one could help them without incurring the wrath of the soldiers. My son, then seven, tried to reach them, but the soldiers forced him back. The men were dead by the time the soldiers left. We could do nothing.

"I have had to raise my son by myself. No kinsman redeemer exists, but I do not wish to remarry anyway. My son has become my provider. He left this morning to go fishing for some food. I gave him five small loaves and two fish I had preserved for his meal. I did not realize that man named Jesus planned to come through here today with all his followers, or I would never have sent Jared out knowing the crowds that man draws."

Intrigued by her story, I sat listening intently when a young boy came running up to us.

"Mother, where are you? What has happened to you?" he asked. "That man named Jesus told me my mother sat with his mother over here on the rocks. He said you were looking for me," the boy said, quizzically eyeing us.

"Mother, look! Look what Jesus did with my lunch," he continued as he presented a basket of bread and fish to her. "You would not believe it, Mother! The most amazing thing just happened. Did you see what Jesus did? Did you get here in time to see it? Did you eat from my lunch" he said, jumping around like a frog.

"What are you talking about, son? You only had enough food for yourself. How could I eat of your lunch? Where did this basket of food come from?" the Mother asked looking at me with a 'what a wild imagination' look.

"He gave it to me, Mother. That man named Jesus gave it to me."

We both listened as the young boy told his story.

"While I fished this morning, this huge crowd came from nowhere. Jesus stood at the front of the crowd. He walked up to the top of the mountain to face the people and talk to them. I had to stop fishing, Mother, to see what happened. I finally snaked my way up through all those men and got real close to Jesus. For once, I was glad to be small.

"He talked for some time, Mother. Everyone lost track of time. The most beautiful words poured from his mouth. He talked about how blessed the humble, meek and poor people are. He said we should love everyone—even our enemies. Mother, does that mean I should love those evil Roman soldiers? I wanted to listen to him. I could not leave, Mother. I am sorry if I made you worry, but I just could not leave."

"Do not worry, my son. Just tell me what happened next," the mother said.

"Then one of his followers asked him how he planned to feed all these people. They had all sat there for such a long time, the hour was too late to purchase any food. One of the men voiced concern that some of the weak might not be able to make it home without some nourishment.

"I heard Jesus tell his men to feed the people. They only laughed and asked how they were supposed to get enough money to feed such a crowd.

"The man named Andrew told Jesus a young boy had five loaves and two fishes. He said it with a laugh as he continued, 'What is that going to do for these thousands of people. That is not even enough for you, much less the five thousand men gathered here'.

"Then the man came and asked me if I would like to talk to Jesus. I was not a bit scared, Mother. I was thrilled to talk to him. Jesus asked if he could borrow my lunch to feed these people. I gave it to him. I had no doubt he could feed the people. I knew he could. He took my food and asked his heavenly Father's blessing. I have never seen anything like it. When he started breaking my bread and dividing my fish, the most amazing thing happened. The fish grew, the bread grew, and it just kept getting bigger and bigger. The more he broke, the more it grew. He passed the food around to everyone here. Look at this crowd," he said, waving his arms to encompass the entire area. "He fed all these people with my lunch! It was a sight to behold. I am amazed at what he did. I saw it all, Mother. It was not a dream."

The boy finally ran out of words. His mother just stood there and stared at me.

"He is right," I told her. "That man named Jesus is my son and your Messiah. Through his heavenly Father he is able to perform miracles such as you have just witnessed."

"Oh, bless you, dear woman. You have given us new hope. Look at my son. His spirit is renewed," the woman said, hugging me.

They picked up their basket of leftover food and headed home as the boy continually waved his hands while retelling his story. I turned to continue my quest of finding Jesus only to be faced by a crowd of curious women.

"Are you truly the mother of that man named Jesus?" they asked.

"Yes, I am," I replied arching my shoulders back and standing a little taller...for a brief instant.

"How can that be?" one of the women asked belligerently. "How can he be your son and also the Son of God as he claims? Did you take a visit to heaven and unite with God?" she asked.

I heard all the questions, but had no time to answer as the women began to press around me again. Backing up to the rock, I listened to all their rude remarks. As my eyes began to moisten, the crowd parted and Jesus walked through them.

"Come, Mother," he said taking my hand and leading me away from the crowd of women, who were shaking their heads and whispering to each other.

We walked in silence for awhile trying to escape the crowd.

"Do you still not understand?" he asked, with that simple smile.

"Yes," I replied with sadness. "I do understand why I can no longer be known as your mother. But you told the boy and he told us. I did not intend for all the other women to hear. You have told me many times of the danger I would be in if the crowds knew. I promise I will try to be more careful."

"You have rightly spoken. Goodbye, Mother," he whispered, as he gently kissed my forehead. "Always know, no matter what happens; I love you with a special part of my heart."

I watched as he walked on to the head of the crowd to lead his followers.

Mary Magdalene, Mary and Joanna raced up beside me. "Come on," they said. "Where have you been? We have been looking for you for some time. Jesus is over there. Let us catch up with him. He may want to introduce you to this crowd. After all you are his mother! We are so glad you have come to join us."

"No," I replied, pulling back from the eager group. "I have told my son goodbye. I think I will stay back here for awhile as long as the crowd is here. He has much work to do. Besides, the crowd does not need to know the identity of his mother. They only need to know his heavenly Father."

I stood in silence for some time watching the crowd disperse and Jesus and his followers board one of the boats to sail to the other side toward Gennesaret. The women raced ahead, but waited at the edge of the water for me to join them.

My dear, heavenly Father of my son, thank You for allowing Jesus to teach me a valuable lesson today. I often wondered why he chose to completely ignore me in his teachings. Now I have been a witness to the danger he is keeping from me. People see and know Jesus performs miracles, but they will never accept the fact that his birth came from someone like me. I understand the consequences of such knowledge. May You help me hide my identity as I follow him from a distance. As any mother, I am as proud of him as I can possibly be, but I must be proud from a distance and in secret.

"Mother, look what that man named Jesus did with my lunch."

Now Jesus was asking His disciples, "Who do people say the Son of Man is?"
Matthew 16

Jesus Questions His Disciples

This morning I stood on a hill overlooking Magdala. The beautiful scene of this fishing village nestled on the edge of the Sea of Galilee took away my breath. From my view, I could see the small synagogue, the well where all the women were gathering to draw their daily supply of water, and many, many fishing boats. This visit caused distress for Mary Magdalene who once lived in this town. She still remembers the torment of the demons that possessed her before Jesus cleansed them.

She told me a little of her story, but I do not think I can record the turmoil she experienced. Young women are often forced to perform hideous acts for the pleasure of men, but when women have no control over their bodies and wantonly seek that gratification, the outcome is unbelievable. The deeds sought by the demons that possessed Mary Magdalene's body cannot be described in my journal. I am afraid I must pass that story to someone else. I felt pity for the woman as she recalled her experiences. She knows that if Jesus can cleanse her body and make it white as snow, there is hope for anyone.

The men of this town have learned the craft of preserving their tiny fish through a salting process. Had the young boy not had those two tiny fish the other day, I wonder how Jesus would have managed to feed all those people? Would the deed have been as miraculous if he had produced the fish from nowhere? He wanted the people to know the fish were real. He had taken a plain ordinary bit of food and used it to his glory. How awesome is his power?

Wherever we go now there is always a group of Pharisees and Sadducees in the crowd, but I do not think they are following because they believe his message. One day they asked him to show them a sign from heaven. I could not help but think, "Does he have to knock you in the head for you to see what you are seeing. If all these miracles are not signs from God, what are they?"

He patiently answered them and said they can discern the face of the sky with the redness of the sky, but they cannot discern the sign of the times. He told this group just as he told the other one. He said no sign would be given except the sign of Jonah. I wonder what that story has to do with Jesus' kingdom. I hope I have a chance to ask him that question during our next talk.

We left Magdala and headed toward Caesarea Philippi. Walking by the large springs feeding the Jordan, Jesus turned to his disciples and said, "Who do men say that I, the Son of man, am?"

Standing at the foot of Mount Herman, I could see the wall of niches where idols of every god imaginable were placed. Listening to his followers give him all sorts of answers, I thought how ironic that we are standing among representations of some of the most worshipped and evil gods known to man as this simple earthly being stands tall, as the greatest God of them all. Listening to their answers of John the Baptist, Elijah, Jeremiah or one of the other prophets, Jesus finally turned to them and asked, "But who do you say that I am?"

Simon Peter eagerly answered, "You are the Christ, the Son of the living God."

From a distance, I listened in silence, but I almost wanted to shout, "Hey! How about me? He is my son, too. I raised him. I nursed him. I nurtured him. I tucked him to sleep at night. I soothed him when he hurt. I fed and clothed him. What about me?" But I knew I could not say a word. I eagerly give God the glory for this remarkable child.

Jesus turned to Peter and said he was blessed because his Father in heaven had revealed that answer to him. He also said that Peter's statement would be the rock on which he would build his church. *Church? What is his church? What has happened to his kingdom?*

Then he told Peter he would give him the keys of the kingdom of heaven. I can only assume that is where his kingdom will be established…and Peter has the key. Peter holds the keys to the kingdom of heaven.

Dear God, I can only pray that our son will establish a kingdom in the beautiful heavens where we will all gather for Your blessings. Forgive me when I sometimes crave the glory of being his mother. I am so proud of him, but I also know of the danger of being recognized. You have put words in his heart that are foreign to his followers. He speaks of things in the future as if we will be a part of it. I pray I am doing the right thing by following him and recording the things I see and hear. Someday when people read my writings, I hope this church and kingdom of heaven will mean something to them.

Then Jesus was led up by the Spirit into the wilderness to be tempted by the devil.
Matthew 4:1-11; Mark 1:12-13; Luke 4:1-13
For He will give His angels charge concerning you.
Psalm 92:11

Mary Discusses the Forty Days of Temptation with Matthew

It has been a few days since I have written because of our travels. Every day we walk a while until a crowd gathers and Jesus stops to preach or perform miraculous healings. Jesus healed the people today while the rest of us rested under the shade. It is very interesting how differently the twelve accept Jesus' early life. John does not even want to talk about the miraculous birth.

Although I have told all of them some things about the events leading up to the birth and many of the events that took place in that little cave, Matthew is the only one who really shows any interest. John feels the only thing important about Jesus' life happened after the baptism when his heavenly Father in the form of the dove acknowledged Jesus as His son. To John, God appointed Jesus as our Messiah that day.

John believes Jesus' life before that event is not relevant to his teachings of today. John is one of the few who have been with Jesus since the very beginning of his ministry. He knows firsthand about the miracles and the many lessons Jesus has delivered. My hope is for him to feel compelled some day to write them down, so the world will know of the ones where Matthew and I were not present. His version will definitely be the most accurate of Jesus' early ministry.

At first, Andrew and Peter were followers of John while he baptized the crowds that came to him. They saw the dove land on Jesus and the heavens open for God to speak to his son. They did not know of Jesus' temptation. They thought he had gone home for a brief period to prepare his ministry. They just know they were fishing one day and Jesus appeared and said "Follow me." And they did so without question.

Matthew on the other hand is extremely interested in Jesus' early life. Is it because he comes from the same lineage as Joseph? Since Joseph and Matthew's father were brothers, they have a lot in common.

I have told Matthew about the miraculous birth, but I have not told anyone about the miracles Jesus preformed for his family. They have seen enough of his miracles to know for certain that he is the real thing. The miracles he performed for our family are private matters. I do not think I want anyone else writing about them. I want them to remain with our family.

The first miracle Jesus performed for the benefit of his followers occurred when he turned the water into wine at Sarah's wedding. Matthew is amazed at all the events that so completely fulfill prophecy. He is an educated man and has studied most of the prophets. He and Jesus have some very interesting discussions—especially, now that he knows the whole story.

Matthew delighted in the story of Jesus' temptation when I told him the other day. He said he had often wondered how the world would accept someone who had not gone through the same trials men do. He said Jesus keeps telling us we can endure anything as long as we have the Holy Spirit with us. Knowing that Jesus did endure the temptation of the devil makes his story much more acceptable.

We talked about the Holy Spirit who helped Jesus through those forty trying days in the wilderness is the same one who visits us when we call for Him. What an awesome thought. Can we possibly be as important to our heavenly Father as Jesus? We will face many trials and temptations, but none will compare to the temptations Jesus faced during his time spent with Satan those forty days in the wilderness. If God can get His son through that, think what He can do for us. A glorious peace overcomes me when I think of that comforting thought.

Dear Lord, thank You again for Matthew and all the other followers You have so wisely given Jesus. Some of them may not have been wise choices, but I know You have a reason for every one of them. Help Matthew and me write and preserve what You think the world needs to know. Give us the wisdom to know the difference.

*The disciples said to Him, "Where would we get so many loaves
in this desolate place to satisfy such a large crowd?"*
Matthew 15:32-39; Mark 8:1-9

Jesus Feeds Four Thousand

I am fortunate to be able to spend a few days with my dear Aunt Lydia who lives in a seaport city on the Sea of Galilee. Jesus told me this would be a good time to visit, while he preached around the region close to the sea. After a few days rest, I packed my few writing materials and left Aunt Lydia's early this morning. She voiced her concern to see me heading off by myself. With a hug and kiss on the forehead, I assured her fear no longer entered my mind. It is very early in the morning, but I need to write about the event I just witnessed. When I need to write, God always provides the brightest night sky. There is so much light, it looks like God spread a blanket of stars above us.

As I neared the location of Jesus, the crowd looked similar to the stars. It looked like God had spread a blanket of people to listen to His son. Like everyone else, I listened so intently I lost track of time. My heart ached when he told the crowd John now resided in a much better place. He offered hope as he told the people if they believed his message, they too would inherit this marvelous heaven. Everyone sat and listened for hours. As evening approached, some in the crowd began to get hungry, but not enough to leave.

Just as Jesus did when he fed the 5,000 before, he blessed the few fish and loaves of bread Andrew had gathered from the crowd. Everyone ate until they were full. I wonder if this meal came from a young boy similar to Jared. That young man beamed with pride when Jesus used his lunch to feed all those people. This time he sent out his disciples to gather the leftovers which amounted to seven full large baskets. After we ate, Jesus dismissed the crowd to their home. I do believe if he did not dismiss them, they would have sat there forever and listened to him speak. The crowds seem to become mesmerized by his voice. So do I. When he speaks, all the distractions around me disappear. I hear nothing but his voice.

The twelve went to the water to search for a boat to take them to the other side of the lake. Jesus said he would join them tomorrow morning with the women. He slipped to the top of the mountainside to talk to his heavenly Father as we fell asleep on the ground with rocks for our pillows. As I write I think how uncomfortable we should be, but no one ever complains of our surroundings. We are happy to be where we are. God has blessed us with more than we could ever imagine. We do not even think about complaining. I soon drifted off to a pleasant slumber.

Around the fourth watch, a howling wind awakened me. I watched as the light of the moon shone on the turbulent sea tossed by the contrary winds. Out in the distance I could see what looked like the speck of a boat being thrown from wave to wave as if it were one of the balls of the young boys.

As I surveyed the scene, fear engulfed my frozen body. I searched the surroundings to see if Jesus or James or any of his followers had joined us. They were not there. They must have found a boat to take them across the sea. Were they in that tiny speck facing the menace of the angry waters? Could Jesus be with them? Knowing he could calm the turbulent waters, I stood to search for him. A lightning bolt flashed and I saw Jesus walking toward the raging water. I could not help but notice the calm where we were sleeping. The howling of the wind did not even awaken anyone else.

Just as I started to shout for Jesus, he entered the walkway formed by the raging waves on either side of him. The turbulent waves did not calm down. *What is he doing? He is going to be swallowed up by those giant waves.*

As I watched, Jesus started out across the water, walking to the boat. Yes, he walked on the water! I could hear the fear in the voices of the men in the boat as they called to him. I could not tell if they were more afraid of the storm-tossed sea or the sight of a man walking through the turbulence of the giant waves. I should not have been able to hear Jesus, but as clearly as if he were standing right beside me, I heard him say, "Be of good cheer; it is I. Be not afraid."

I looked around to see if anyone else had heard. I do not know how (yes, I do), but everyone else slept through the whole incident. I, alone witnessed this miraculous happening. Standing up to get a better view from the moonlight, I saw one of the men in the boat try to walk out to meet Jesus. The man walked for a short distance until the waves became more boisterous. My heart sank along with the man in the water.

When he spoke, I recognized Peter's voice. Again, it appeared he stood beside me as he said, "Lord, save me."

The wind carried Jesus' voice so clearly to me as I heard him say, "Oh thou of little faith, wherefore didst thou doubt? Peter, you must keep your eyes on me."

He reached out and took Peter's hand and pulled him out of the water. I watched as they walked hand in hand to the boat. They entered the boat, as the wind immediately calmed and the waves ceased. Mary Magdalene awoke and asked what happened.

"Oh, Jesus is teaching his followers a lesson in faith," I said. Mary Magdalene turned over and I reached for my precious journal. I am so glad the winds have ceased and the moon provides enough light for me to write this entry. The boat is drifting out of sight on the glass like surface of the once turbulent sea. I thank God for the powers He has given His son.

Dear God, if Jesus can challenge the power of a storm tossed sea, what can he do for us? You have lifted me through the many storms of my life. To think that Jesus has experienced those same storms firsthand is reassuring. He knows the leap of faith Peter displayed when he left the boat to walk on the water. He also showed Peter and all his followers the consequences of taking their eyes off Him. Had Peter only kept his eyes focused on the peace of Your presence, he would have completed his journey on top of the water. As the angel Gabriel reminded me when I questioned Your ability to plant the seed of the Holy Spirit in a virgin, I know from experience that "Nothing is impossible with God."

"Peter to keep your head above water, you must keep your eyes on me."

And He was saying to them, "Do you not yet understand?"
Matthew 16:5-12; Mark 8:14-21
Now hear this, O foolish and senseless people, who have eyes but do not see;
who have ears but do not hear.
Jeremiah 5:21;

Jesus is Angry With his Twelve

These long days are beginning to take a toll even on Jesus. Today I saw the first hint of Jesus' patience beginning to wear a little thin. It is a good thing he sees our hearts and knows we are good people, because he must be getting tired of our lack of understanding.

I saw his twelve put him to the test today. They all seem to think his miracles are for other people and not them. I used to feel that way, but the more I follow and listen to him, I know I have just as much right to his powers as the sick and lame. His power is so much more than his healing ability. If we only believe in what he can do, we can move mountains. Those mountains of worry we sometimes hide behind, can all disappear with one simple prayer and leap of faith. Will I, or his believers, ever realize this awesome revelation?

When Jesus and I have our evening talks whenever possible, he assures me he will provide all our needs. Even sleeping outside on the ground, we are comfortable. Jesus always manages to find a comfortable spot for us to lay our head. We have never gone hungry. From nowhere we have always gotten food when we needed it.

Jesus' followers have witnessed him feed 5,000 people with five loaves and two fishes and 4,000 with seven loaves and a few fish. Yet, they are still concerned from where the bread will come for their meal.

Philip and Andrew were telling me that Jesus and his followers got in a boat going to Dalmanutha. They had planned to stay for a while, but the Pharisees, still seeking a sign of his powers, came out and began to argue with Jesus. Philip told me he sighed deeply and said, "Why does this generation seek for a sign? Truly I say to you, no sign will be given to this generation."

Andrew added they again embarked and went away to the other side. He said Thomas nearly panicked because he had forgotten to bring food. They only had one loaf for the entire crew. When Thomas said something to Jesus about the lack of provisions, Jesus quizzed him about all he had just seen and asked, "Are you that dense? Do you know what I am capable of doing? How many people do you think I can feed with one loaf? Do not worry. We are not going to starve!" he added.

Philip said Jesus even compared them to the Pharisees who still doubt his work after all they have seen. No one else mentioned the food or said they were hungry. He said they would starve before they questioned Jesus again.

I think Jesus grows impatient when people expect to continually receive their needs without working for them. Through his teachings, he has taught that man has a responsibility to take care of himself. Jesus may be trying to teach us another lesson. We cannot depend on him for everything. He can do whatever he wants, but he expects us to do what we can. Although his gifts may be freely given, they should not replace our ability to do for ourselves.

I have some relatives who live near Dalmanutha. I will try to visit a few days with them while we are so close. My mother's family came from there originally and I know she still has some sisters or nieces in the area. I plan to look for them and stay with them to let my tired old bones rejuvenate from this tiring journey following Jesus. Mary Magdalene should be joining us again in a few days. She appeared delighted for the time to stop and visit with her family when we traveled through Magdala. Everyone is so happy about the cleansing of her body from those dreadful demons and about her decision to follow Jesus.

Dear God, thank You for giving me some quite time with Jesus. When we are alone he is still the baby boy I nurtured. He confides in me his thoughts and hopes for the things he knows needs to be done. He never wearies from healing the sick and helping people. His only fear is that there are so many of them they may interfere with his real mission on earth. He tells me of his kingdom and how beautiful it is. How I will join him there someday, but first I must suffer just as he must. I try not to worry or act concerned. I do not want him to know how deeply terrified I am of the things he talks about. Help me, Lord, to mature in his wisdom and gain comfort from his peace.

His Chosen Twelve

When I glance around
and see His chosen twelve,
my smile cannot be contained.

Average appearance
Average knowledge
Average men with loving hearts
adoring the Savior who walks among them.

Is He to establish a kingdom
with this mild-mannered twelve?
Each one is unique
in their love for their Master,
but different in so many ways.

Peter, the outspoken one,
a natural leader of men,
a stumbling block with unending faith.
He will fight to the end
but will hide through his lies.
Upon his revealed confession rests
the foundation of the church.
"You are the Christ,
the Son of the living God."
Could it be any simpler?

Andrew, from Bethsaida,
brother of Peter,
a fisherman of fish by trade,
a true fisher of men by design.
Originally followed John.
Gathers non-Jews to be followers.
Defends the temple.
Expresses doubt of the new message,
but always persists.

John, son of thunder
and an ambitious mother.
Recorder of events.
Writer of letters.
Always in the company of Christ
as the one He loved.

James, John's brother,
short tempered,
ready to call down fire from heaven.
Save the Lord.
Destroy the people.
Ambitious to a fault.

Phillip, from Bethsaida,
friend of Andrew and Peter.
Called out Nathaniel.
Often tested.
Brings others.
Eager to study the facts,
analyze the situation,
spread the word.

Nathaniel, from Cana,
opinionated and prejudiced,
"Can anything good come from Nazareth?"
Big thinker under the fig tree
alone with his dreams.

Matthew, hated tax collector,
beloved cousin
from Joseph's lineage.
Changed follower.
Wrote all the truth
even though unfavorable.
Recorder of Jesus' earthly walk.

Thaddeaus, steady and strong,
perseverer of mysteries,
questions of end times.
Abiding Love for his Master.
Obedient follower.

James the Less,
slinking in the background
never in the limelight.
Faithful and true
without show.
Always there for support,
but never a lead role.

Thomas, the Twin,
doubter of words.
Show me the facts.
Let me see the truth and I will believe.
Should his doubt be condemned or praised?

Simon, the Zealot,
member of Jewish sect
of rebel fighters.
Save the world,
destroy the Roman rule,
overthrow the government.
Hot headed
fanatical follower.
Is Jesus a probable partner
to fulfill his dreams.

Judas Iscariot, treasurer,
but above all, betrayer.
Faith never reaches his soul.
Faith of the flesh cannot withstand
temptations of the world.
Sold his soul for a few pieces of silver.
When insides poured out,
his heart could not be found.
But God used him to fulfill His plan.
Great honor for such a man.

Jesus' chosen twelve, on the outside,
such a peculiar group of men,
but God looked on the inside,
such a beautiful group of men.
Jesus loves their hearts of service.

Jesus' chosen children,
Can He love us any less?
Our hearts are made to serve Him
joyfully with open arms.
He wants to bless us
with an abundance of love.
As His children we claim a right
to all His blessings.

Average appearance,
Average knowledge,
Average children with loving hearts,
Adoring the Savior who walks among us.
When I look around and
see His chosen children,
my smile cannot be contained.
He loves us as much as His twelve.

When they had crossed over, they came to land at Gennesaret. And they implored Him
that they might just touch the fringe of His cloak; and as many as touched it were cured.
Matthew 14:34-36; Mark 6:53-56
Because this people draw near with their words and honor me with their lip service,
but they remove their hearts far from me, and their reverence
for me consists of tradition learned by rote,
Isaiah 29:13

Jesus Heals the Clean and Unclean at Gennesaret

If Rebekah had not joined our group I would not be writing tonight. With her funds, she secured a boat to carry the group of women to Gennesaret this morning. There are still many others waiting to be carried over to this side. Rebekah willfully offered the ship's master more than the required amount. Apparently, she must be quite wealthy.

By the time we arrived, we were forced to take our usual place in the back of the crowd, but it does not matter where we sat. Everyone in the crowd hears as if Jesus is standing right beside them. The other women and I are content to follow close behind so as not to distract Jesus from his work. We do not stray too far because we do not want to miss any of his miraculous teachings.

The way he continues to stir up controversy, he may need my help. If I had known thirty-two years ago that the kingdom the angel Gabriel promised me would result in the happenings of today, would I have been so willing to accept the call? This is definitely not what I expected from our Messiah, but like everyone else, I really did not know what to expect. His kingdom does not appear to be like David's or Solomon's as Gabriel told me. His mission now is to heal the sick and preach a message of love to as many as will accept it.

Everyone began talking about his miracles as soon as we reached the land. People are coming from far distances merely to touch his garments. I have never seen such an array of varying emotions. People were crying tears of happiness while others were struggling with pain to touch him. He did not heal by saying anything today. He only walked slowly along and let people touch his robe. My heart swelled with pride.

The festive attitude disappeared when some Pharisees and leaders of the law came and broke through the crowd to approach him. The leaders asked why he and his followers transgress the tradition of the elders by not washing their hands before they eat bread.

With words of wisdom, Jesus responded to their questioning. He told them the ceremonial cleansing they do with washing their hands does not make them any cleaner. Using a few dabs of water for their required cleansing ceremony cannot remove the dirt. They wash only to impress the people. He asked the Pharisees why they transgress the commandment of God with their traditions.

Jesus quoted Isaiah and said to them, "Rightly did Isaiah foretell of you hypocrites. You neglect the commandment of God, and hold to the tradition of men. You worship with your lips instead of your hearts. Your doctrines are more from the instructions of men then they are from the Laws of Moses."

Even his disciples were worried after that confrontation. I heard Philip whisper to Nathaniel as they shared a nervous laugh, "He actually called those hypocrites, hypocrites."

He turned to the crowds and started teaching again. He said men were not made unclean by what goes into their mouth but by what comes out of it. The food we eat may make us sick at times, but eating with unwashed hands cannot make us unclean. Only the words that come from our mouth can make us unclean. I have witnessed some filthy-mouthed men who indeed had dirtied their souls. I remember the men who came upon Jesus and me while we were sitting at the entrance of the cave in Bethlehem. They were making fun of the lowly shepherds proclaiming they had seen the miraculous virgin birth of our Savior.[12] The hearts of those people were as hardened to the truth as the men today.

Jesus went on to say that if a blind man leads a blind man both will fall into a pit. Then Peter (it is always Peter), asked him to explain. Jesus looked at him and said, "Are you still so dull?"

Strong, bold Peter seemed to sink into a shell. Jesus politely told him, "Wake up and think for yourself!" He then explained how what we put in our body through our mouth is eliminated by our bodies and does no harm. But what comes out of the mouth comes from the heart and evil thoughts such as murder, adultery, theft, lies, slander, sexual immorality indeed can make one unclean, but eating with unwashed hands cannot make one unclean.[13]

Everyone understood Jesus' simple explanation. As Jesus withdrew to the region of Tyre and Sidon, the people, with uplifted spirits, started to go home.

---

12 *Jesus My Son: Mary's Journal of Jesus' Early Life*, 49.
13 The inspiration for this entry came from Barry Farris at Oakland Christian Church in 2010.

I watched with silent pride. My pride quietly turned to fear as I heard the Pharisees grumbling and complaining about his actions and discussing among themselves what they could do. It did not sound good and I fear terribly for his safety as he continues his teaching. His kingdom must be coming soon or else he may be put to death before it even begins. I am fearful, but I know his Father will care for him. I hope something will soon happen.

Dear God, I hope You were as proud of Your son today as I. Although our son is one and the same, I am sure we have different measures for success and pride. The Pharisees think he is going against Your teaching. His message is different from anything we have ever heard, but have we been hearing the message as You intended us to hear it? Have the scribes and Pharisees led us astray by their personal interpretations of the original message? Will the same thing happen to Jesus' message? Dear, Lord, I pray his message will last until the end of time. My soul grieves to think that all he has taught the people can be undone by one false teacher.

He fell on his face and implored Jesus saying, "Lord, if
You are willing, You can make me clean."
Matthew 8:2-4; Mark 1:40-45; Luke 5:12-16

Mary Talks to the Leper

I write tonight with a renewed faith of the power of my son. Not that I needed it, but sometimes my heart is filled with joy from some of the miracles Jesus performs. The women and I followed close behind the crowd when a man came up to us proclaiming the power of the one called Jesus. I had not seen the miracle Jesus performed so I ran back to talk to the man.

"Can you tell me what the man Jesus did for you?" I asked cautiously, afraid to reveal my relationship with Jesus. That is one lesson I have learned.

"Woman, it is the most wonderful thing he is doing. He healed my leprosy. Before I saw him you would not be standing that close to me. Infection oozed from my skin due to the sores. He spoke and my leprosy left immediately.

"But, I have to say, his healing possessed no more power than the fact that he touched me. Before he healed me, he touched me. Do you realize how long it has been since someone actually touched me? The fact that he willingly touched my leprous skin is more powerful than any miracle he performed."

"Can you tell me more?" I begged.

"Yes," he began. "The sores of leprosy covered my body. I have had the skin disease ever since I can remember. No one would come near me. I have not seen my parents for most of my life. When I saw Jesus, I fell on my face and said to him, 'Lord, if You are willing, You can make me clean.'

"Then it happened. He touched me. He stretched out his hand and touched me as he said, 'I am willing; be cleansed'."

I listened in awe at the man's story. A simple touch, how healing can it possibly be? Do we often ignore those who need our touch so badly? Do we realize what our simple touch can do? How glorious would it be if we could share the power our Father has given us in our touch? There have been so many times I have watched people suffer when I knew I could help them with an embrace or some type of action to let them know I care. Could we possibly have those same powers of healing? Jesus told his followers they have his power. Do we posses it also?

Is our love so unconditional that we could perform the simplest healings of the mind just by showing someone we care?

"Is that all he said," I asked, eager to hear more.

"No. He ordered me to tell no one, which I am afraid I have failed miserably. I could not help myself. People have seen me and are amazed. They wanted to know where my leprosy had gone. I could not lie. The healing is such a great thing. Why does he not want me to tell?" he asked not expecting me to have an answer.

"As powerful as he is, he must still respect the Law of Moses," he reflected.

"Why do you say that?" I asked.

"Because he told me, 'Go and show yourself to the priest and make an offering for your cleansing, just as Moses commanded, as a testimony to them.' I am on my way to the priest, but the crowds have prevented me getting there. Everyone wants to see my clean white skin. Some are still afraid to touch me."

He paused and asked. "Do you want to touch me? Here, feel my soft skin."

I reached out and touched the now clean hand of the once oozing skin of a lifetime leper. His simple smile offered more than any monetary reward Jesus could have given him.

He headed toward the priest as I made my way back to the other women. Thinking of the gift of the simple touch, my heart feels a little warmer. How much courage did it take for the leper to even be here to talk to Jesus? How many people looked at him with scorn and fear before my precious son touched him and made him whole?

Dear Lord, my heart is warmed tonight from this experience. I saw the unconditional love of Your son for the one who expressed such courage in his actions. Does it sometimes take some action on our part before Your son can reach out and touch us? Must we also recognize him as Your son in order to receive his blessings? May the priests accept the man's offering and allow him to rejoice in the gift he received because of his belief? Thank You for the son who is willing to touch the sins of a lifetime and provide healing to those who believe he can.[14]

---

14   Credit must go to Tod Schwingel, Sebring Christian Church in Sebring, FL., whose sermon, January 9, 2011, inspired this entry.

Then Jesus said to her, "O woman, your faith is great;
it shall be done for you as you wish."
Matthew 15:21-28; Mark 7:24-30

Jesus Travels to Tyre and Sidon

My body feels like I have been lounging in those pools of Siloam known for their rejuvenating powers. My cousin, Abigail, who lives in Tyre, provided her house for a good rest for my tired aching body. I also have had the opportunity to write more of the things I have witnessed. So much is happening I have to write them as soon as I can or I cannot keep up with everything. Memories seem to escape much more quickly. Everyone is asleep while I sit outside to again take advantage of the blanket of stars God has spread above me. I hope when my words are found they will not be too poorly written for someone to read.

As we neared the coasts of Tyre and Sidon, a Canaanite woman came and cried out to Jesus, "Lord, Son of David, have mercy on me!" I immediately cringed when she called him the son of David. They know who he is and his earthly lineage. If only they could comprehend the heavenly side of the lineage.

As she pleaded with Jesus to free her daughter who had been grievously vexed with a devil, Philip asked Jesus to send her away because she cried out so loudly. Jesus told Philip he came to help those who cry out in need. They are the lost sheep of Israel.

By that time the woman knelt before Jesus and cried out, "Lord, help me!" Jesus said something about dogs eating the children's bread. The woman's reply must have pleased Jesus because he answered her saying, "Woman, you have great faith. Your request is granted."

As the men moved on, I sought the woman to speak to her as she praised Jesus. I asked if Jesus had talked to her and she replied, "He not only talked to me. He healed my daughter. My servant just rushed to me and said my daughter had regained her health."

"How wonderful," I exclaimed. "Why did Jesus question you?"

"You realize I am a Canaanite woman. I am not a Jew as most of Jesus' followers. I told Jesus I only wanted a small portion of the great gift he has given the Jews.

"I told him, 'Even dogs eat the crumbs that fall from the table.' Apparently, he appreciated my faith because he replied that because of my faith my wish had been granted."

"Yes, he is here to spread his greatness to all people—not just the Jews," I confirmed for the woman.

"What a blessing that greatness is," the woman said walking away.

Later someone came by to report the woman's daughter had been healed at the very hour Jesus had told her she would be. What great faith that Canaanite woman must have possessed to approach Jesus on behalf of her daughter. I wonder if the woman's faith had not been so strong, would Jesus still have healed the young girl? Is it possible for our children to suffer because of our lack of faith? That is a question I want to ask Jesus when we have our next talk.

We then headed for the Sea of Galilee. Jesus and all the followers went up on a mountainside and sat down. Again the crowds swarmed around him. There is no such thing as rest for him. The people marveled as the mute spoke, the crippled walked and the blind received their sight. He did this for three solid days!

Finally he dismissed the crowd and got in a boat to go across the sea.

The other women and I waited for another boat to come and take us to the other side. Thankfully, another woman who has sufficient money to secure a boat has joined our travels. God has always provided someone to fulfill our needs.

Before the new women realize I am Jesus' mother, they often ask about my children. I smile and say they are all doing very well and are trying to keep out of trouble. If they only knew! When someone asks, I cannot help but wonder what my children and grandchildren are doing. I miss all the children and the grandbabies very much. I pray I will soon be able to return home for a short visit, but I cannot leave Jesus now. I am not sure I can trust him to behave himself. Of course, I do not think my presence is going to make much of a difference.

Dear Lord, I pray Jesus can continue his healing of the sick and freeing those who are demon-possessed. I could never grow tired of watching the joy on the faces of those he has made whole. The changes he has made to so many lives will long be remembered as generations pass down these miraculous stories. Thank You for allowing me to be a witness to many of these blessed events.

When He (Jesus) had said this, He spat on the ground,
and made clay of the spittle, and applied the clay to his (blind man) eyes,
John 9

Jesus Heals a Blind Man with Spittle

I am thankful for the opportunity to record the miracle Jesus performed on this Sabbath. We all rejoiced for the blind man who received his sight, but I felt sorry for the oppression he endured from the leaders.

As we walked to the temple, a blind man began to approach us. Thomas asked Jesus, "Teacher, who sinned, this man or his parents, that he was born blind?"

Jesus replied, "Neither, this man nor his parents sinned but this happened so that the works of God might be displayed in his life. As long as it is day, we must do the work of Him who sent me. Night is coming, when no one can work. While I am in the world, I am the light of the world."

Then, instead of touching the man's eyes to heal them like he has done for everyone else, Jesus spit on the ground and made clay of the spittle to put on the man's eyes. Then Jesus told the man to go wash in the pool of Siloam. Why would he make the man go to the water? What did he see in the man's heart that was different than all the others he had healed? Did someone in the crowd need more than a gift of healing? Did Jesus want to show us how his gifts must be earned by some, but given freely to others? Another question to add to my list the next time we have a few minutes alone.

The people were shocked that the man could see. As we continued walking through the elaborate portico of Solomon, some men brought the once-blind man before the Pharisees. I heard them ask the man how he had received his sight.

The man told them, "The teacher put mud on my eyes and I washed it off and now I see."

The Pharisees began to mumble among themselves and said, "This man is not from God, for he does not keep the Sabbath."

Another one asked, "Maybe so, but how can a sinner do such miraculous signs?"

The group of leaders became divided in their belief so they asked the blind man, "What do you have to say about him, since he opened your eyes?"

The man simply replied, "He is a prophet."

Still not believing the man, the leaders sent for the man's parents to testify that the blind man was indeed their son who had been blind since birth. The parents said they did give birth to this man and he had been blind from birth. Then the Pharisees asked them how their son could now see.

Fearing what the Pharisees might think of their answer, they replied, "We know he is our son and he had been born blind, but we do not know how he received his sight." Then they added, "He is of age. Ask him."

"Humm," I thought, "smart answer." The parents knew the Jews had declared that if any man confessed that Jesus is the Christ, that man should be put out of the synagogue. They had done nothing wrong and did not want to be banned from visiting their place of worship.

The Pharisees again summoned the blind man and said, "Give glory to God. We know this man is a sinner." Oh, those poor blind Pharisees. Do they not realize this man and God are the same person? How can someone with their knowledge and ability to see so clearly be so blind?

The man replied, "Whether he is a sinner or not, I do not know. The one thing I do know. I was blind but now I see!"

The Pharisees would not give up. They again asked him, "What did he do? How did he open your eyes?"

Finally the man said, "I told you and you did not listen. Why do you need to know? Do you want to become his disciple, too?"

At that, the leaders hurled insults at the man and replied, "You are this fellow's disciple! We are disciples of Moses! We know God spoke to Moses, but as for this fellow, we do not even know where he comes from."

The man smiled and shook his head, "Now that is remarkable! You do not know where he comes from, yet he opened my eyes. We know God does not listen to sinners. He listens to the godly man who does his will. Nobody has ever heard of opening the eyes of a man born blind. If this man were not from God, he could do nothing,"

I do not even think Jesus has ever made them so mad. "You were steeped in sin at birth," they screamed at him, "how dare you lecture us!"

Then they threw him out of the synagogue. I desperately wanted to go to the man's defense, but knowing that would only cause more trouble, I chose to tell Jesus instead. Jesus found the man and asked him, "Do you believe in the Son of Man?"

That poor blind man, I am sure he did not expect this joyous occasion to cause so much grief for himself or his parents. He looked at Jesus and said, "Who is he, sir? Tell me so I may believe in him."

Jesus took his hand and said, "You have now seen him; in fact, he is the one speaking with you."

The man bowed down and said, "Lord, I believe."

Jesus' replied for the man and the Pharisees who had gathered, "For judgment I have come into this world, so the blind will see and those who see will become blind."

The Pharisees asked, "What? Are we blind, too?"

Jesus turned to them and said with a sad look, "If you were blind, you would not be guilty of sin; but now that you claim you can see, your guilt remains."

Jesus talked to them so much more, but I cannot remember or write it all. I only know at the end of his speech, the Jews were much divided. Some were saying Jesus was demon-possessed and raving mad, while others said his words were not the sayings of one possessed by demons. Demons are not able to open a person's eyes. At this point, I believe some of the Pharisees would trade their soul for an opportunity to arrest Jesus and others would give their soul for an opportunity to talk freely with him.

While Jesus and his followers rested for a brief spell, I saw the man's parents lurking in the background. When I approached them, they almost ran. They could not suppress their joy, but were very cautious to talk to me. I know I should have learned my lesson by now, but I felt safe to tell them Jesus is my son. Their fear of the leaders seeing them talking to one of Jesus' followers subsided a bit as they told their story.

They had used all of their earnings trying to heal their son. They had even chosen not to have any more children for fear they would also be blind. For his entire life, their son had been ridiculed and mocked by the other children. Even the Pharisees had suggested they keep him out of the synagogue to prevent him from creating a disturbance. They said they had brought him today hoping for the miracle they received.

Like everyone else, they do not understand why the leaders are not rejoicing over this healing. They asked me, "How can our leaders not understand these miracles are from God? The leaders have no one in their kingdom capable of performing the acts they have seen today. I feared for our lives when they began questioning us. If we had told them what we believe, they would have thrown us out of the synagogue, too. Why should something this joyous cause so much confusion?"

I wish I could have given them a better answer, but I could only shake my head along with them. My heart grows heavy when I think of the fear existing in our worship today. If people are worshipping because of fear, are they really worshipping? People want so badly to receive the message Jesus is teaching. His different message of love, compassion, and understanding is so welcomed by the people.

Dear heavenly Father, please help the Pharisees see through their blindness. What a brighter world this could be if the hardened hearts of those who call themselves Your servants could somehow be penetrated by Jesus' message. The blindness of those who can see is so much worse than the blindness of those who cannot.

Jesus said to them, "The Son of Man is going to be delivered into the hands of men; and they will kill Him, and He will be raised on the third day."
Matthew 17:22-23; Mark 9:30-32; Luke 9:43-45

Jesus Tells of His Upcoming Death

Journal, I really do not want to share with you tonight the happenings of today, but feel it is important to record this particular event. As usual, the older women take a little longer to travel than the young men. By the time we joined the younger crowd in Galilee, Jesus had taken his twelve special followers to a private place for a discussion. No one from the crowd knew exactly what had happened, but I feel he is again talking about his death.

How can his heavenly Father establish a kingdom if His son is going to die? The angel told me he would have a kingdom that would never end. He is to rule over David and the house of Jacob. He is thirty-three years old and I can see no sign of that happening. He has many followers, but he is not attracting the bold and daring. Most of his followers are very meek and humble. I have never heard of a kingdom being established with meekness. My heavenly Father has again chosen to test my patience and force me to play the waiting game.

When they returned, Matthew discussed their meeting. The details of his prediction this time really frighten me. Matthew said he told them the Son of Man will be betrayed to the chief priests and leaders of the law. They will condemn him to death and will hand him over to the Gentiles who will mock him, spit on him, flag him and eventually kill him. But three days later, he says he will rise and his mission on earth will be complete. Matthew told me they did not fully understand his words, but none had the courage to ask him to explain.

What can this death be? Surely, God is not going to allow His only son to die at the hands of such misguided people. How can this happen if he is going to save the Jews and all the believers? Have I missed the direction God has led me. Heaven forbid, that I have not followed God's plan as he directed.

My Lord, forgive me if I have strayed and missed some of the promises You have given me. My desire is to be Your humble servant and completely do Your will. May Your hand be with me and show me the direction You would have me go. My heart grieves at the words he is now saying. Death? After only thirty-three years on this earth? Has this journey we traveled been all in vain?

He rebuked Peter and said, "Get behind me, Satan;
for you are not setting your mind on God's interests, but man's."
Matthew 16:21-26; Mark 8:31-38; Luke 9:22-25

Jesus Predicts His Death

My quill is shaking as I write this entry tonight. The concern for his kingdom I had the last time I wrote has turned into intense fear from the message he now speaks. I cannot bear to listen to his words.

Every time Jesus talks to his disciples he tells them he must go to Jerusalem and suffer many things at the hands of the elders, priests and leaders of the law. Oh, Simeon, I wish I knew more about that sword you said would pierce my heart. I fear the few times I have already felt the tip of the sting of that sword is nothing compared to what may be in store for me based on the words Jesus is now saying.

Today he again said he must be killed and on the third day be raised to life. How can this be? How can God allow this to happen? Why would God give him to me for thirty-three years just to allow him to be killed? What about his kingdom? What is this talk of being raised in three days? Is he going to raise himself from death like he did the widow's son? Must this happen before his kingdom can be established?

I wanted to shout "No! No! This cannot happen!" I am glad I did not.

When Peter began to rebuke him, Jesus turned to his followers and said to Peter, "Get behind me, Satan! You do not have in mind the things of God, but the things of men."

He called his beloved follower, Peter, a stumbling block. I am so glad I questioned in silence.

Will those who are standing with him not taste death before we see the Son of Man coming in his kingdom as he said? I have this uneasy feeling the kingdom I have expected these many years may not be recognized on this earth as I originally thought. When he talks about his kingdom being established after his death, I wonder what he is saying. His message is so foreign to me now.

His words are drenched with a sense of urgency. He wants us to understand so badly, but God has still not chosen to open our minds with the ability to comprehend. James is beginning to worry me. When Jesus talks, James looks sad and subdued. The cloud of despair that looms over him, tells me he may have reached the understanding God has not yet chosen to give me.

Jesus also said something else I did not understand. He said he would come in his father's glory with his angels and he would reward each person with what he has done. What could this reward be? What is he talking about? He has no money or possessions. How does he expect to give out rewards? I must add that to my list.

It is late and we have had a very trying day. Thank God, I have found another cousin to stay with tonight. I really do believe God is directing me to these people so I can freely write the events of the day. I am glad because that means he is still content with the work I am doing.

This cousin, Mutua, has heard all about Jesus and declares he is mad. She told me I should be very careful because children like him often turn on their parents and do terrible things. I bit my tongue and thanked her for the well-intentioned advice. I wish I could convince her Jesus is the real Messiah and if she only believed his message, she too would receive this reward he has been talking about. She just laughs, but the cot feels good, so I am very thankful.

Dear Lord, I do not understand the complete blindness of the people. Although sometimes I feel I am blinder than any of the others. As long as I have been traveling with him, I should be able to understand the message he is teaching. The true meaning still escapes my thinking. Thank You for always taking care of my needs. When I have been so weary and felt as if I could not go another day, You have provided a comfortable night's rest for me. I have never told Jesus I am tired, but he just seems to know and directs me to a house where I am always welcomed. I am also thankful for this chance to write, although I am not openly displaying my work. I do not think Cousin Mutua would approve of my writing anymore than the men do. Why Jesus has directed me to this house of a nonbeliever I do not understand. I am assuming he has a reason.

Get Behind Me, Satan

My desire for his safety
overrides my thinking.
He is my son by nature,
but God's son by Spirit.

I want to shout, "No. This cannot happen."
Why must he suffer and be killed?
How can he rise on the third day?
Can the dead raise the dead?

I have walked His earthly life with Him
expecting the throne of David,
a glorious mansion with servants and maids,
luxury at my fingertips.

What reward will we receive
from His Father's glory?
When will my Lord chose
to open my mind to comprehend?

Satan has blocked my heart from understanding.
I have become a stumbling block,
sitting my mind on the interest of man,
ignoring God's plan.

Listen to the words He speaks.
As strange as they may seem,
they are simple and true.

Take up your cross and follow Him.
Do not be ashamed to declare His words.
Lose your life to save it.
Gain the world and forfeit your life.

I feel Simeon's sword piercing my heart.
My son's foreign message haunts my very soul.
The cost, I fear, may be paid by this son
I have loved for thirty-three years.

Get behind me, Satan!
So I can believe through my blindness.
To see clearly the promised kingdom.
To want the reward no matter the cost.

He was transfigured before them; and His face shone like the
sun, and His garments became as white as light.
A voice out of the cloud said, "This is My beloved Son,
with whom I am well-pleased; listen to Him!"
Matthew 17:1-13; Mark 9:2-13; Luke 9:28-36; Isaiah 42:1

Mary Hears of the Transfiguration

Oh, my! What a wonderful thing a good week's sleep is! I rested at Mutua's house for seven days. That is the longest I have stayed in one place for some time. I am thankful for this break in our trip so I can write about the last day of my visit with Cousin Mutua. All week I expected Jesus to stop and visit to, hopefully, talk some sense into my hardheaded cousin. It grieved my soul to think that Jesus had studied her heart and knew she would not believe him. Before he finally did come, I did not believe she would be receptive to his message. After his visit, I think her mind may have been opened. At least he gave her something to think about.

I enjoyed the comfortable cot and pleasant memories shared of our family. As the week wore on, I fear my welcome may have wore thin. Mutua has such a different lifestyle than I am used to living. When she introduced me to her guests as the mother of the man roaming the countryside healing people, I did not often receive a warm reception.

Yesterday, someone came to visit, and, as usual, the conversation turned to the healings Jesus performs. A smile spread across my face, but Cousin Mutua only looked at me and raised her eyebrows.

Later someone came by and said Jesus had taken a few of his disciples and had gone up on top of a high mountain. While they were there, a big bright cloud appeared over the mountaintop. We saw the frightening cloud in the midst of the otherwise bright, sunny day, but could not hear any turbulence in the sky. The visitor said his followers would not tell what happened up on the mountain. I wonder what secret Jesus might have told them. When I saw the cloud, I thought about the cloud God sent before Moses and the Israelites when he ushered them out of Egypt.

I think this house must be a favorite gathering place of people, or a better name may be gossip center. It is almost as busy as the community well. Seems like everyone who comes by has a different story to tell. One talked about Jesus' healings and how his disciples could not heal this one boy who had enormous seizures. He had bruises and cuts all over his body where the demons had thrown him into the fire and water.

The woman told how Jesus rebuked his special followers and told them that if they only had enough faith, they could even move a mountain. Everyone in the house laughed when they thought about mere men having those powers. It is strange how they do not believe Jesus' message, yet they recognize his special powers. How can anyone believe he has a special ability without accepting his message? I cringe when Mutua glances at me pitifully as she laughs. I wish I could convince her to listen to Jesus with her heart instead of her ears; or just to open her ears and really hear the message. Like so many others, she listens, but she does not hear.

The more I hear and the more I see, the more I know this promised kingdom is close to being established. I fear those who do not accept Jesus' message will experience terrible times. For this household, I feel I have stayed long enough. I am thankful for the rest, but their unwillingness to believe has shadowed my visit.

As the last gossiper told us Jesus and his followers were preparing to move on the way to Galilee, Mary Magdalene came running through the door. "Come, Mary," she said with urgency. "The crowd is moving on to Galilee. Jesus slipped away from them, but they said the followers had started that way. I am going to gather the other women. We will meet you at the end of town."

I collected my things, including my journal, and bid my cousins farewell. I did not want to get too far behind the crowd.

As I walked out the door, Jesus met me. "Hello Mother," he said. "Have you had a good visit?"

I wanted to tell him everything, but I only replied, "I am thankful for the rest."

"Dear Mother, it is not in you to say anything bad about someone, is it?" he said, as he walked into the room where Mutua and two of her fellow gossipers were sitting. Their expressions looked as if they had just swallowed a frog.

"Well, hello Jesus. Come in and tell us some of your latest miracles you have been performing." One of the women said with a slight smirk.

"Leave him alone," Mutua said. "He is my guest. Come Jesus, sit and talk to your aunt for a while."

"Aunt Mutua, I just wanted to thank you for giving my mother a much needed rest," Jesus said, as he embraced the woman. Then he took his finger and gently touched her lips. He turned around to the other ladies and curtly said, "Good day, ladies. I hope you will enjoy the solitude of the rest of your visit."

We walked out of the house as Mutua tried to speak, but her lips were sealed. The other women could only stare in disbelief.

"Do you think she will believe now?" I asked Jesus as we walked down the path.

"Oh, yes, Mother. She believes. But not what you want her to believe," he said.

I looked back at the house and waved as Mutua stood with her lips closed and her arms flinging aimlessly. Her friends could do nothing but stare.

"She has been very kind to me," I said to Jesus.

"Yes, Mother. I will fix her…in a short while. Let us give her just a little more time of silence. Maybe she will realize how nice it sounds."

He took my arm and escorted me down the road toward Mary Magdalene and the other women. I cannot remember Jesus laughing as hard as he did when he turned around and waved at his Aunt Mutua. I never looked back again. I sure hope he did not forget to open her lips. Maybe I should ask him. I guess Jesus dislikes the gossip as much as I do.

Dear Lord, give me the words to persuade people I have contacted that Jesus preaches only the message You give him. The Law of Moses may need a fresh interpretation. I am convinced You would not allow Your son to say things that would contradict the laws that Moses gave the people through You. Just as my stories may be different from others that will be written, give people an open mind to accept these words You have placed in my heart. I pray for safety as we continue this journey. Thank You for allowing Jesus a little humor in this tense time of his journey. His heartfelt laugh warmed my heart.

Jesus answered and said, "You unbelieving and perverted
generation, how long shall I be with you?
How long shall I put up with you? Bring him here to me."
Matthew 17:14-22; Mark 9:14-29; Luke 9:37-43

Disciples Could Not Heal the Epileptic Boy

Tonight as we rested, the followers discussed the events of the week I had visited Mutua. It is nice of them to try to keep me updated. At first I hesitated to show them my writings, but God finally allowed me to tell them about my work. They were more surprised that I could write than they were of what I wrote. They seemed grateful these awesome events are being recorded. Now they try to keep me updated when something happens that I have not witnessed. They enjoyed a good laugh at Jesus' miracle with his Aunt Mutua. I certainly hope she is back to normal. Maybe she became a believer of his word. How can she experience what Jesus did and still not believe his message?

They told me about a man who had brought his son to the disciples. The son had been possessed since birth by a spirit that had robbed his speech. The spirit threw him on the ground, caused him to foam at the mouth, grind his teeth and become very rigid. The disciples had tried to drive out the demon but they could not. Thomas laughed when he said Jesus called them an unbelieving and perverted generation because by now they should be able to do anything.

After most of the men had drifted off to sleep, James filled in some of the details. I am so glad James has seen all these miracles so he can tell his brothers. Perhaps he will lead them to believe Jesus' message. They may not admire James as they do Jesus, but they do respect his opinion.

James said the father approached Jesus and said, "If you could do anything, please take pity and help my son."

Jesus asked the man, "If I can? All things are possible to him who believes."

James said the man immediately cried out, "I do believe; help my unbelief."

Then Jesus rebuked the evil spirit and said, "You deaf and mute spirit, I command you, come out of him and do not enter him again."

The demon came out so violently the boy became like a corpse and everyone thought he died. Jesus took his hand and raised him up. The elated father and son hurried home to tell the mother.

When we first sat down to rest, I heard the disciples ask Jesus why they were not able to drive out the evil spirit, but I did not understand why they were asking. I heard Jesus tell them, "Because of the littleness of your faith. For truly, if you had faith the size of a mustard seed, you would be able to move that mountain. But this kind of spirit cannot come out by anything but prayer and fasting."

Evidently Mutua's friends were right about what they heard, I thought.

Does that mean there are different levels of demons? Are there demons that only the most devout followers will be able to drive out? If Jesus gave his followers their power, how does anyone receive the power necessary to confront these particular demons? Can any earthly person possess that much faith? I guess some require an extra level of prayer and fasting.

As I watch him perform these miracles, I am proud and yet my heart is sad for him. He never complains about what little he has. There are plenty of invitations for dinner since everyone is so interested in interrogating him, but he does not care if he eats or sleeps. Wherever he goes there is usually enough food prepared for every one of his followers, which has grown to quite a large number.

I can feel the excitement in the air when he walks into a town. His reputation has spread throughout the area. People run home and come back with sick children or parents or friends. They all struggle to touch Jesus. He is patient as he speaks to every one of them. He knows why they are here and he tries his best to satisfy their needs.

It is such a wonderful feeling watching the sick being healed. They are so very thankful. The last one of the day is as overwhelming as the first. At the end of the day, everyone is emotionally drained. I am so glad to be a part of this miraculous journey.

I wish more of his brothers and sisters could see him in action. I worry for all of their disbelief. I pray each day that the word Jesus preaches will reach their heart and they will respond as they should.

I probably need to go home and check on them, but I cannot right now. There is urgency in Jesus' teaching and I feel I need to be here for the climax of this venture. He is a king. He will have a kingdom, but I fear that mansion is one that only a few will ever enter. My understanding only creates more fears of what is to come.

Mary Bailey

Dear God, I know he has the power to do anything he wants to do. I just pray he can continue to help the people. It is overwhelming to see the happiness on the faces of the ones he heals. I pray You will allow him to continue the good work he has started. I know his kingdom is waiting. I just wish I more fully understood Your plan.

Mary Visits her Sister, Salome

What a blessing to be able to sit down and write again tonight. Jesus' stories about being betrayed into the hands of man have my spirit dragging the ground. Since we are now in Capernaum, I decided to finally make that visit with Salome I planned from the first day I asked Jesus to allow me to join his group of followers. I am surprised he has not reminded me of my initial excuse for being here.

We have roamed the countryside for some time now. Although we were in Capernaum before, I did not want to take the time to visit for fear I would miss some of Jesus' message. Today I knew I needed to talk to my sister for a spiritual uplifting. She has always been able to give my spirit a boost when I am down. I have not seen her for a long time—much too long for sisters to be separated.

What a glorious greeting! No matter how long you have been apart or how far away you have been, sisters always welcome you with outstretched arms. After the initial hugs and tears, it seemed we saw each other only yesterday. We had so much catching up to do. She is as worried about Jesus as his brothers are. I finally told her everything; even about the miraculous birth.

"Why did you not tell me sooner?" she asked with amazement in her voice. "How could you have kept this fabulous secret from me for so long?"

"Think about it," I replied. "I know how impatient you are. We would not have had a minute's peace if you had known that my son, Jesus, is our Messiah. You would not have believed me anyway! I can see you rolling those dark brown eyes until they were white as snow at my news. I was only fourteen years old. Mother and Father believed, but they knew Joseph had also been visited by an angel."

"You are right. I am not sure I believe you now and I have seen with my own dark brown eyes what Jesus is capable of doing," she said, rolling her eyes. "I saw the crowd when Jesus healed so many sick people in Capernaum. I tried to reach him, but there were too many people and he vanished."

"Do not feel bad," I smiled at her. "I would not have believed you either."

We talked and laughed into the night. I did not get to bed as early as I had hoped, but the cot provided a restful night's sleep. Salome is also worried about her sons. They gave up everything to follow Jesus. Salome said James and John told her Jesus and John were preaching and they must find out more of their message. They left their fishing boat one day when Jesus came by and invited them to join him. She said their father roared like thunder when he heard the news. He still has not fully embraced the message of Jesus and John, or the fact that his sons eagerly left a lucrative business to follow them. I suspect he may be more upset that they did not ask his permission first.

My dear Lord, thank You so much for sisters. You created a bond between sisters that years of time cannot loosen. The friendship we share is more than just being two women born from the same parents. All those years we were apart, I still thought of her often as I know she did me. What an uplifting visit we have shared. My soul has been revived enough to allow me to hear the words Jesus is now telling us about things that must happen. Thank You for the strength that comes from sisters.

*"go to the sea and throw in a hook, and take the first fish
that comes up; and when you open its mouth,
you will find a shekel. Take that and give it to them (tax collectors) for you and Me."
Matthew 17:24-27*

Peter Retrieves a Coin from a Fish's Mouth

Saddened but happy to rejoin Jesus and James and my other friends, I prepared to leave Salome's house. I hugged her goodbye and promised to stop when we come by this way again. To my delight, she smiled and grabbed a small bag of clothes she had packed.

"You do not really think I am going to let you leave here knowing that something, heaven knows what, is about to happen to my favorite nephew. If he is going to inherit a kingdom, I want to be there to see," she said hugging me.

Emotion flooded my soul at her offer, but I assured her it was not necessary. I reminded her of the children and grandchildren who depend on her support at times.

"Ridiculous," she scorned, "and how many children and grandchildren have you left behind? It will do them good to be alone for awhile. Come on, let us go." Walking out the door, she grabbed my arm and skipped along the pathway dragging me behind.

My step grew a little lighter with my sister by my side. I think now I can face anything knowing I have a shoulder to lean on. Thank You again, Lord, for sisters.

We had a delightful conversation walking along the shore of the sea. Then I spotted Peter fishing alone which was very strange. They have been traveling in a group for so long; I thought they had lost their individual identities.

Peter threw out a line and immediately caught a good size fish. Salome and I watched as Peter opened the fish's mouth to take out the line and found a shekel in it. He acted as if he expected the coin to be there—as if that happens all the time. How did he know that coin would be in that fish's mouth? I had to catch up to hear the story. He took the coin with him as he threw the fish back in the water.

"I see things like this all the time," I told Salome as she shook her head in amazement.

"Now do you believe?" I asked as we ran to keep up with Peter to see what he would do with the coin. Matthew met Peter when he returned with the coin. Since Matthew is a tax collector, perhaps he wanted to talk to Peter about a tax payment. I saw Peter waving his hands as he talked to Matthew. I know Matthew is writing his version of these stories so I hope Peter told him what happened.

Peter took the coin and gave it to the tax collectors. I do not know why Jesus felt compelled to pay the taxes. When he gains his kingdom, I assume people will be paying taxes to him. I whispered to Salome that he must be trying to stay on the good side of the government, or maybe he is just trying to stay out of trouble.

Jesus' actions create more questions. Why did he pay tribute for only two of them? What will the others do? If Jesus could put a coin in a fish's mouth, why would he not make enough for all twelve of them? That is another question I must ask. I hope when his kingdom is established, he will have time to visit and talk to me. Thankfully, I have a chance to write all these questions so I will not forget to ask him.

Dear Lord, thank You again for my companion. The days will be much easier with my sister by my side. I pray Salome's faith will grow stronger as we walk together. Guide us toward the truth of what we must believe from the message Jesus is teaching.

*"See that you do not despise one of these little ones, for
I say to you that their angels in heaven
continually see the face of My Father who is in heaven.
Matthew 18:1-35; Mark 9:33-50; Luke 9:46-48*

Jesus Compares the Greatest to Little Children

Salome and I followed far behind the crowd today. She is seriously thinking about the things she sees. We sat by the sea to wait for Jesus to quit teaching and the crowd to disperse. A woman with a small child came and sat beside us.

"Did you hear the man named Jesus today?" she asked.

We smiled and told her we could not get close enough today, but we had heard him before. As I talked to her, it struck me that his voice had not reached all the way to the back of the crowd as it usually does. Normally, I would have heard every word he spoke from where I followed. I wondered why until I heard the woman's story.

"Jesus was so charming today," she said pointing to her child. "He took my boy, Jacob, and used him as an example. Jesus said everyone must become like Jacob to enter into the kingdom of heaven. Those like my little Jacob will be the greatest in his kingdom. His words touched my heart when he said the face of the angel who watches over my child beholds the face of his heavenly Father every day. What a reassuring thought that is."

The young mother again praised Jesus as she picked up her son and hugged him while walking away.

I sat there and let her words sink deep into my mind. *The face of the angel who watches over our children constantly beholds the face of our heavenly Father.* I have always thought God must have special angels to watch over little children otherwise half of them would never reach the age of three. Today Jesus confirmed my thought.

Standing to continue on our way, I saw the few rays of remaining sunlight glisten on Salome's damp cheek. "He truly is the son of God," she said. I nodded my head as she continued, "Why did you not tell me sooner? I have been blind for so many years."

Reaching for her hand to help her stand, I replied, "There is no way I could have convinced you like that innocent young mother and her child did today. Welcome home," I said giving her a hug.

By the time we reached the others, the crowd had gone. When we approached the followers, Salome said, "Where is Jesus? I desire to be baptized."

The twelve cheered as John came forward. "Here Mother," he said. "May I do the honors?" They hugged as everyone followed them to the water. What a wonderful sight to behold a son baptizing his mother in the bright blue water of the sea. We all rejoiced over the one whose heart was softened today by the story of a young child.

Salome and I walked away to find some dry clothes while the men gathered around the campfire. When we returned, the twelve were discussing some things Jesus had said today.

"What did he mean when he said offenses must come even to the little ones?" Philip asked Andrew.

"I am not sure," Andrew replied, "But woe unto them! He said it would be better to cut off one of your limbs or pluck out one of your eyes if it offends you, than to have both of them cast into hell fire. When the judgment day comes, I do not want to be one of those offenders who harm the little children."

"Nor I," said Thomas, "but I think Jesus came to search out and save that one out of a hundred who goes astray. He said there would be more rejoicing over saving the one who had gone astray than all the others who are saved."

"I guess the story about being merciful to your brother over repayment of debts hit home with me," Andrew chimed in. "Jesus said our heavenly Father would be very unforgiving to those who do not forgive their brothers from their heart. Ok, Peter, I forgive you for not paying me back that drachma you borrowed ten years ago."

"You do not have a good memory, my brother," Peter joked, "I paid you back double, triple and even seven times more than that over the years. Think back how I bailed you out of all those messes."

"All that forgiveness may be grand," Judas chimed in, "but how can anyone ever make a living if you keep forgiving everyone's debt. When people find that out, they will flock around you like vultures. It would not be long till you did not have anything left."

"Oh, Judas, you are always concerned about the money. Is our treasury running so low it is constantly on your mind?" Nathaniel asked.

Salome and I exchanged glances as everyone grew quiet and began to prepare for the night. I have noticed lately how Judas acts defensively about some of Jesus' messages. Most of the followers will sit and talk to me of their families and the jobs they left to follow Jesus, but Judas avoids me as if I have leprosy. Jesus must have had a good reason to choose him. He does not have the gentle spirit I see in most of the others, but he *can* count money and does keep the treasury close to him. There have been a few times when I thought he counted a little too well, but that is not my concern. I guess if God only chose people with good special qualities, I would not be here writing about my son, the Son of God. Whew, it has been a long, tiring day.

We are sleeping outside again under the stars. Salome could not believe we sleep outside so much. Girls were not allowed to do that when we were home. I remember our brother Judas often going to the roof of the house to sleep under the stars, but we were not allowed. What would Mother think if she could only see us now?

Dear God, this has been such a good day. Thank You for the enlightenment of Salome. I know she now believes. I think she will be by my side for some time. She wants to hear the message of her nephew as much as I do. I also ask that You would touch the hardness of Judas' heart. Soften his heart that he may have the gentle spirit of the others who were chosen.

"And I say to you, whoever divorces his wife, except for immorality,
and marries another woman commits adultery."
Matthew 19:1-15; Mark 10:1-12
"For this reason a man shall leave his father and mother and be joined to his wife,
and the two shall become one flesh."
Genesis 2:23-25

Disciples Discuss Jesus' Teachings

My days are much brighter now that Salome has joined us. I forgot the hard time I had when I first began following Jesus. Unaccustomed to all the walking, I thought my legs would fall off that first week. Poor Salome, she is experiencing the same pain. I have teased her about her laziness and sitting home holding those babies too much.

We went to the region of Judea today. The crowds were as large as they have ever been and the healing as miraculous as ever. Of course, the Pharisees all came with their constant questions trying to trick Jesus with some crazy interpretation of the law.

Some I think are sincere, but most are only to test or trick him. The test today concerned divorce. Moses gave a man a certificate of divorce allowing a man to send his wife away. Jesus teaches that God united men and women in marriage and there should not be divorce except through marital deceitfulness.

My heart still grows heavy when I remember how Joseph thought I had been unfaithful. I remember running to him with the exciting news of conceiving the seed for our Messiah when the Holy Spirit overshadowed me. What should have been the happiest day of my life became the saddest when I realized Joseph doubted my story when he turned away. He thought I had committed adultery and conceived a child. Now I understand how God planned Joseph's disbelief in order for me to escape to Elizabeth's. During that visit I learned all I could from her birthing experience, but at the time his reaction shattered all my dreams.

God has some mysterious ways of preparing us for the experiences He has planned for us. I have learned to realize that every trial we encounter has the purpose of developing our character so we will be able to complete the assignment God has prepared for us.

Thaddeus asked if the better choice would be for a man not to marry and stay single. Jesus said only some men whom God have given a special calling were able to remain single. God created men human and as such have certain desires for women. Men should satisfy those natural, God-given needs. Joseph had desires. He would never have been happy staying single. Although he loved God, he still had those earthly desires of which I am glad. I miss his tender touch so much.

Joseph would have been proud of Jesus. In his last words, he requested me to keep a careful eye on our special child. We both knew which child he spoke of, but I think each of the other children thought he spoke of them. Joseph always treated the children equally. I wish I could ask Jesus about Joseph's salvation since he died before Jesus' kingdom.

My dear Lord, we have lived by the Law of Moses for so long. Forgive those who find it difficult to think that Jesus' new laws contradict Your earlier teachings. The Laws of Moses are so ingrained in our mind; we cannot easily accept a different plan even if it is from You. Help us understand and accept the new message of love Jesus teaches.

*"Martha, Martha, you are worried and bothered about so
many things; but only one thing is necessary,
for Mary has chosen the good part, which shall not be taken away from her."*
Luke 10:38-42

Jesus Visits Lazarus

What a wonderful rest I am having. This stop provides a great opportunity to catch up on my writing. Today we arrived at the home of our dear friends Lazarus, Mary and Martha. They welcomed every one of Jesus' followers into their home. The men have reclined for the night and I am happy as a lark writing in my journal.

When we first arrived, Martha busied herself with the preparations for a glorious feast while everyone else reclined at the table. Salome and I helped Martha, but she thought her sister should be helping also. Martha went to Jesus and asked him to tell Mary to help prepare the meal.

Jesus looked kindly at her and told her not to worry about so many things. He said Mary had chosen well by listening to him instead of busying herself with the preparations. Martha could benefit from relaxing more herself. The work will always be there to do, but he would not always be there to talk to them.

Martha turned around and went back into the kitchen to work with Salome and me. I could tell her anger brewed inside like a boiling pot. I went over to her and said, "Martha, I know you think this meal is the most important thing you can do for Jesus, but he has never concerned himself with much food. You would not believe the meals he has given us with very little preparation. We have never gone asleep hungry.

"Sometimes we all place importance on things that only cause us a lot of worry. I know you want everything to be grand, and you want Jesus to be pleased with your work. Believe me, he is. He knows how much you work to make everything nice for Mary and Lazarus, but today you have company. He wants you to enjoy his company. We would all be fine with bread and honey. We do not require a lot."

"I just want everything to be nice for our dear friend, Jesus. Lazarus has not been feeling well and I can already tell this visit from Jesus has uplifted his spirits. I want him to have the best I can offer," Martha said, at the brink of crying.

"That is an honorable wish," I told her. "Jesus is not saying your desire is wrong. But Mary does not feel the same way. Sometimes we think others share our views just because that is what we want. You must let Mary participate in the pleasure of listening to Jesus while she can. Salome and I will help you. We can prepare something worthy of your dear friend. Come on. Let us get to work."

It did not take any time to have a wonderful meal prepared for everyone to enjoy. Salome and I even talked Martha into sitting down to eat with us. The compliments she received made all the work worthwhile.

Martha's servant's heart will not allow her to relax if there is work to be done. She will never know the meaning of enjoying the fruits of her labor because she must always have something to do. She reminds me of my Leah. I hope she and Simon are enjoying their little Sydney Katherine and Zachary Joseph. What would I give to feel their warm breath on my cheek.

On our way here today Jesus stopped to talk to more little children. He loves to have them gather around him as he speaks. Parents ask him to place his hands on them and pray for their safety. His disciples became a little agitated, but he smiled and continued doing what he wanted to do. According to him, the kingdom of heaven belongs to such as the little children.

Before we arrived here today, Jesus appointed seventy other men to go in pairs ahead of him to every city along the way to notify the people of Jesus' pending visit. His voice quivered as he explained how there were so many people but so few willing to harvest them. His eyes moistened as he said he sent them out as lambs among wolves. Is Jesus saying the people will devour the ones who preach in his name?

My dear Lord, I thank You for the hospitality of Mary and Martha. Their house has always been a haven of rest for us. I pray You will help Martha understand the importance of things in life other than the material things we so often covet. The things of this world are nothing compared to the gift Your son will give us if we only believe. Help us all Father with our unbelief.

"Again I say to you, it is easier for a camel to go through the eye of a needle
than for a rich man to enter the kingdom of God."
Matthew 19:13-30; Mark 10:17-31

Mary Talks to the Wife of
the Rich Young Ruler

As we left the house of our dear friends, Martha handed me a fresh scroll. When I wrote an entry at their house, she commented that I had used nearly all of the papyrus. Her generosity inspires me to write more.

We left their house and headed to Jerusalem. Along the way, James the Less asked Jesus to show him how to pray the way John taught his disciples to pray and as Jesus prays.

Jesus began by telling them there is a certain way to pray. First, they should not be like the hypocritical Pharisees when they stand on a platform in the midst of the courtyard and shout their prayers for everyone to hear. They should seek solitude so they can have a private conversation with their Lord. Prayers should be directed to the Lord and not to an audience.

Then, he said the words of the prayer should come from the heart and not from the head. Just repeating a lot of words does not make a good prayer. If your petition to God is not from the heart, the prayer is a waste of time.

Next, he recited the wonderful prayer he had written for his graduation from the synagogue.[15] The words were so beautiful; I committed them to memory many years ago. Just in case someone reads this portion of my journal without reading my other one, I will repeat it.

> *Our Father which art in heaven*
> *Hallowed be thy name.*
> *Your kingdom come*
> *Your will be done*
> *On earth as it is in heaven*
> *Give us each day our daily bread.*
> *And forgive us our sins,*
> *As we forgive those who sin against us,*
> *Lead us not into temptation,*
> *But deliver us from evil*
> *For thine is the kingdom and the power and the glory forever.*
> *Amen*

---

15   *Jesus My Son: Mary's Journal of Jesus' Early Life*, 155.

We stopped walking and took time to learn the prayer from Jesus. Many committed it to their memory. Jesus said all prayers should be modeled after this one. What a wonderful way to talk with our heavenly Father.

He further explained how every prayer should begin by giving our heavenly Father the respect he deserves by identifying his authority and kingdom. Next, our prayers should recognize the power of God's will over our wishes on earth just as they are in His kingdom in heaven.

We should also ask God to give us only what we need. The Israelites were given everything they needed when they left Egypt, but they still grumbled. They asked for things they wanted, not the things they needed. They paid greatly for their selfish attitude. If we learn to ask properly, God will give us all our daily needs and all the blessings he wants to pour out on us. But we never seem to be satisfied with just our daily needs. There is always a quest for more.

The next part of the prayer is probably the hardest to obey. We always ask God to forgive our sins, but we forget that He wants us to forgive our neighbors before He will even think about forgiving us. We must also forgive our enemies—that is the hard part. It is really hard to forgive someone who has caused us pain and suffering. I hope this request does not include the Roman soldiers who appear to delight in the torture they cause us.

We should ask God to keep us from the temptations of this world that constantly call us to join in and participate in the sinful deeds. Just as God delivered His people in their time of slavery, He will also deliver us from the evil if we only ask.

All prayers should end giving God acknowledgement of all power and glory. God will accept any prayers that follow this simple model above any that are loud and showy as those of the Pharisees.

As we continued along the road, Jesus led his followers while Salome and I stopped to rest. A young woman came by and sat beside us. From the fragrant odor wafting from her presence, I could tell she lived a life of luxury.

She eagerly began a conversation. "We are looking for the man they call Jesus," she said. "My husband and I are seeking to gain his favor. We have obeyed all the laws and want to have a part of this eternal life of which Jesus preaches."

I felt happy for her until her husband came from the crowd hanging his head sorrowfully. She jumped up and followed him as Salome and I made our way closer to hear Jesus speak.

Thomas whispered to me, "Jesus told the rich young ruler that he must sell his possessions and give to the poor to receive his treasures in heaven."

Sorrow quickly overshadowed my happiness for the rich man who at that moment seemed so very poor. Jesus' next statement astonished and surprised everyone. He said, "It is easier for a camel to go through the eye of a needle than for a rich man to enter the kingdom of God."

The disciples were disturbed about his words until Jesus explained that anyone who gives up houses, family and other possessions to follow him will receive a hundred times as much and will also inherit eternal life. It is difficult for those who have become used to a luxurious way of life to give up their amenities.

God wants His children to live a good life, but He also wants them to share with those who are not capable of earning that life themselves. God has said that if a man can work, he should work and support himself. He also said that if a man who is able to work does not, he should not eat. God does not expect His children to support those who are able but unwilling to support themselves.

I wonder how many who hear Jesus' message really understand what he is saying. What does he mean when he says the last will be first and the first will be last? Sometimes we hear with open ears, but our minds are closed to understanding the words. Jesus told a story that no one, including myself, understood about the worker who hired men to work all day, half a day, and just a few hours. At the end of the day he paid them all the same. Is that fair? I do not know, but Jesus believed it to be true.

Dear Lord, the love of money consumed the young ruler today. Can he not see the diminutive value of his wealth when compared to the value of his soul? What must the rich do to enter Your glorious presence? Is it the money itself or the love of the money that destroys so many souls? Is the value of Your gift the same to those who have known it for one hour as it is to those who have known it for a lifetime? I have so many questions I need to ask Jesus. I pray You will provide a few moments for me to talk to him.

"Is it not lawful for me to do what I wish with what is my own?
Or is your eye envious because I am generous?
So the last shall be first, and the first last."
Matthew 20:1-15

Jesus Explains the Value of Heaven

I am diligently trying to write the stories I hear, but it is impossible. I pray Mathew can fill the blanks with his stories. Every time I run out of papyrus or ink, Matthew comes to me with a fresh supply. Sometimes he tells me where I can find some more supplies, and often a place to spend the night.

It is the middle of the day and Salome and I are visiting the home with a believing husband and wife who have three daughters. Matthew told me they would welcome our visit. Her husband had been a fellow tax collector with Matthew. They had heard Jesus and the man had chosen to give up his job and follow him. Matthew knew the woman would not think my ability to write to be odd. She and Salome are talking now as I write.

I have pondered one of Jesus' teachings a few days now. He compared his kingdom to a landowner who had hired some workers early in the day and then hired some in the middle of the day and then hired some an hour before the end of the work day. They had all agreed to work for a denarius.

At the end of the day, when they all came to be paid, the landowner paid each of them a denarius as they had agreed. I did not understand the story at first, because if I had started early and bore the burden and scorching heat all day, I would have expected more pay than the man who only worked a short period of time. Those who were hired last were overpaid. I did not understand this one. Even though they all agreed to work for a denarius, those who worked only one hour did not deserve the full payment.

As I write this, I think I may have gained enlightenment. Jesus is comparing his kingdom to the reward of the workers. It does not matter how long someone has followed Jesus. The reward of his kingdom is the same whether we have followed for a lifetime or for a day. The reward does not change. The glories of his kingdom cannot get any better for someone who has worked all his life or only for a short period of time. The only difference is how wonderful and blessed the life will be for the one who has always followed our Lord. To live a lifetime serving Jesus offers its own reward. Those who only live for him a short period of time are missing out on the joy and peace known only to those who believe.

Dear Lord, thank You for the understanding of the complicated but simple parable. I can only imagine how great Your kingdom is for those who accept it. The value cannot increase or decrease by something we do. We cannot buy a better spot or work harder to receive a better place than our brother. It is available to everyone at the same price. Do I dare ask what that price may be?

Then the mother of the sons of Zebedee came to Jesus with her sons,
bowing down and making a request of Him.
Matthew 20:20-28; Mark 10:35-45

Salome's Ambition for Her Sons

I am thankful for this small reprieve from our walking to give me a few moments to write about an uncomfortable moment caused by my sometimes overzealous sister. My cheeks turn red with embarrassment as I write this. I love my sister dearly, but she does not comprehend the meaning of Jesus' message. I heard her encourage James and John to ask Jesus for a seat beside him in his kingdom. Jesus loves his cousins and has a special place for them in his heart, but all the other men have given up just as much to follow him. Why would Salome think her sons should receive special treatment?

As they reclined this afternoon, Salome and her sons approached Jesus and made their request. I think Jesus must have been expecting them, because he stared at them a few moments before he smiled and said, "You really do not know what you are asking. Do you think you are able to drink the cup I am about to drink?"

They said they were, but my all-knowing son thought differently.

"You shall drink of my cup," he said, "but to sit on my right or on my left is not something I can grant. My Father has already prepared that place for whomever He has chosen."

Apparently, the other men reclining did not think much of the bold request. A few minutes later, Jesus called them all together to talk to them. He talked about the leaders of the Gentiles applauding their position and exercising complete authority over the people. But as his followers, they do not have that same position of authority. Instead, they should consider themselves as servants of the people. In his kingdom those who want to be first must first become a slave of all.

He added, "For even the Son of Man did not come to be served, but to serve, and to give His life a ransom for many."

Salome returned with her chin tucked in her neck. She did not dare make eye contact with me. She knew I would not approve of her even thinking that Jesus would show her sons special treatment. However, I cannot fault her for being a normal mother. We all want more for our children. If I could, I would request a seat for every one of his brothers and sisters to be at his right and left hand in his kingdom. There is only one problem. Unless they change their attitude, I am not sure many of them will even want a seat in his kingdom.

Father, can you tell me how he is giving his life a ransom for many? How will he establish his kingdom if his life must be given as payment? My understanding is clouded by the pain I sometimes feel when he talks about what the future may hold for him.

My dear Lord, when he calls himself the Son of Man, what is he thinking? Is this his way of recognizing me as an earthly parent? Is he trying, in his own way, to give Joseph and me the credit for those thirty years we served as his parents? Now, when I stop to think about the last thirty-three years, I know what an honor You gave me. Joseph and I were privileged to have that precious time with Your son. You chose to make Jesus human so he could know our emotions. He too has experienced everything we have experienced. But, Simeon's sword continues to pierce my very soul with each glimpse of his future through his own prophecies.

Now Jesus loved Martha and her sister and Lazarus...Jesus wept.
John 11:1-44

Jesus Resurrects Lazarus

A few days earlier I dreaded the thought of writing another sad story. Today, my deep sorrow turned to unbelievable joy by one command from my son. We walked back across the Jordan to where John the Baptist had preached and baptized. As Jesus talked to the crowd of believers following behind him, a messenger came to say that Lazarus, his dear friend, had become deathly sick. Jesus said his friend would not die, but God's son would be glorified in his sickness. Although he loves Lazarus, Mary and Martha, he did not hasten to go to them. He stayed and preached for three more days before he headed toward Bethany. I had become a little annoyed at his delay. I knew the sisters must be going through intense turmoil.

Jesus' disciples tried to get him to reconsider his path since the Jews in Jerusalem had attempted to stone him. Jesus said he must go and awaken his friend, Lazarus, from his deep sleep. The men said that if Lazarus only slept he did not need Jesus' assistance. His disciples did not understand he talked about Lazarus' death. Jesus finally very plainly told them "Lazarus is dead and for your sake I am glad I was not there. Maybe now you will believe."

Finally, Thomas suggested that if Jesus had in mind to go, they should all go with him so at least he would not die alone.

By the time Jesus got to Bethany, Lazarus had already been in the tomb for four days. I did not understand the delay since we had only been a short walk away. Martha ran to meet Jesus and told him that if he had been here, Lazarus would not have died.

"Your brother will rise again," Jesus told Martha.

"I know he will rise at the resurrection but I also know if you had been here, Jesus, he would not have died," Martha said.

Jesus told her, "I am the resurrection and the life. Whoever believes on me will not die."

Martha said, "I believe you are the Christ, the Son of God, who has come into the world."

She wept as she left to get Mary. When Mary reached Jesus, she fell at his feet, and weeping bitterly said, "My Lord, if you had been here Lazarus would not have died."

Seeing her weeping, Jesus became deeply moved and also wept. I think that is the first time any of his followers had seen him cry. I had seen him cry as a young child, but not since he had begun his preaching. He shed tears when he could not breathe life into Ruth's body. He also cried when Joseph died. He adored his earthly father and knew the sacrifice Joseph made for him. I also saw him cry from joy when his heavenly Father did allow Sarah to receive the breath of life from him. I will never forget the tears that slid down his face the day his beloved dog, Blackie, died. Burial plots for birds, donkeys, dogs—all kinds of strays surrounded our home.

When we arrived at the tomb, Jesus told them to take away the stone. But Martha said, "My Lord, he has been there for four days. He stinketh."

Jesus looked at her and said, "Do as I told you to do."

Martha reluctantly ordered the servants to remove the stone. When it had been removed, Jesus looked up and prayed to his Father so all could hear him and they would believe.

Then he called out in a loud voice, "Lazarus, come out!"

An icy chill engulfed everyone as they froze, afraid to breathe. Suddenly Lazarus came out of the tomb, still wrapped with strips of linen and cloths around his face. Everyone gasped as if they had seen a ghost! We truly did see a dead man come alive and walk. Jesus told them to take off his grave clothes and let him go.

An overwhelming shout of elation rose from the crowd. The sisters smothered their brother with tears of joy. I wonder what would have happened if Jesus had not called Lazarus by name? If Jesus had simply said "Come out," would all the dead have risen?[16]

Many of the people, who were not already believers, became believers. Some of them could not wait to inform the Pharisees of the miracle they had witnessed. Word came to us that they immediately convened a council with the Sanhedrin to discuss the miracles Jesus performed. They expressed concern over letting Jesus continue his work. Their fear, that the Romans would come and take away their temple and destroy their nation, influenced their discussion.

A woman who knew Joanna told us Caiaphas, a high official, had said in the meeting that it would be better for one man to die for the people than

---

16 The inspiration for this entry came from a sermon by Scott Johnson at Oakland Christian Church in Stamping Ground, Ky.

the whole nation perish. Of course, Caiaphas had prophesied earlier that Jesus would die for the Jewish nation and would gather together the scattered children of God to make them strong. He has had a personal agenda for some time to devise a plot to take Jesus' life.

Jesus is no longer able to move around publicly. He and his followers withdrew to Ephraim near the desert while I stayed the night with Mary and Martha to write this entry.

Everyone looked for Jesus in the temple, for it was the time for Passover. The Pharisees had given orders to report any sightings of Jesus so they could arrest him. I believe they have intentions to kill him because of his ability to influence the people.

Dear Lord, what an awesome miracle You allowed Your son to perform. I now understand the reason for his delay in coming to see our dear friend. This miracle not only helped many believe, but also revealed a human side of Your son. When Jesus cried, people knew he dearly loved his friend. Because of the people's belief, he has been forced to go into hiding. How long must he remain there? Is it possible You would allow his life to be taken by the high priests? I fear for his life and what may happen to his followers including his brother, James.

And Jesus said to him, "Go; your faith has made you well."
Immediately he regained his sight and began following Him on the road.
Matthew 20:29-34; Mark 10:46-52; Luke 18:35-43

Jesus Restores Sight to Blind Bartimaeus

Dear journal, what am I going to do with my son? It does not appear Jesus will remain in hiding. He does not know fear with his Father watching over him. How easy it is for us to forget how that same Father watches over us. I could learn a valuable lesson from my son.

I am blessed to be able to write this important entry tonight. After Jesus visited Lazarus, we headed toward Jericho. Jesus attracts people like a magnet, drawing anyone within walking distance scrambling for the nearest position to him. I sometimes fear there will be a riot among those eagerly seeking to move closer. The scribes and Pharisees would welcome that chance to charge him with disorderly conduct.

At one point along the path, two blind men began shouting at him, "Lord, Son of David, have mercy on us!"

The people in the crowd sternly told them to be quiet, but they cried out even more. One of the men was Bartimaeus, a blind beggar. Most of the blind men become beggars to support themselves. There are few jobs available for someone who cannot see. If people did not generously give alms, most of the blind would starve to death.

Someone said the two men had been blind because of an accident. Their families had deserted them and they had been living alone on the streets for many years. Hopefully, today will give them a better chance on life.

Jesus told Andrew to call the blind men closer to him. He cried out to them, "Take courage. Stand up! He is calling for you."

I can only imagine the excitement going through those poor men as they struggled to stand up. Andrew took their hands and led them to Jesus.

Jesus stopped and asked them, "What do you want me to do for you?"

They cried out, "Lord, we want our eyes to be opened."

I could tell Jesus had pity for them, like he did Silas, Leah's father. Jesus looked at them for a brief moment as if he could view the pain they had suffered their entire life. Moved with compassion, Jesus only touched their eyes this time and said, "Go. Your faith has made you well." Immediately, they received their sight and began following Jesus on the road. I still wonder why Jesus made that one blind man wash in the pool of Siloam, while he has only touched the others to perform the same healing.

We have had many long days, and I am growing tired. I appreciate how all the disciples try to make the women comfortable. They understand Jesus does not have time to visit with me, but every once in a while they will come by to make sure I am doing well. I know Jesus has asked them to watch out for the women.

The only one I am suspicious of is Judas. He is a shrewd man and is constantly counting what little money they have. We have no means to make money so we live on what people voluntarily give. We are often invited into their houses, but there are so many of us now. Fortunately, I have many relatives in the area who have prepared a cot for me, but the men are very content to sleep outside wherever Jesus is staying. They are completely devoted to following him.

My prayer tonight, dear Lord, is that we can all boast the same faith of the blind men. If only we can gain the wisdom to understand Jesus' words, we will all receive the gifts he has for us. Whether it is sight to the blind, or a place in his kingdom, these are all gifts that only those who have faith can receive. Dear Lord, help us to have such faith.

*The scribes and Pharisees brought a woman caught in adultery
and having set her in the center of the court, they said to Him,
"Teacher, this woman has been caught in adultery, in the very act...
John 7:53-8:11*

Jesus Writes on the Ground

Oh, how I still love visiting the beautiful temple. The first trip I made after Joseph's death caused me great distress. I recalled the day of Jesus' Redemption Ceremony when we encountered Simeon who predicted that a sword would pierce my soul, and Anna with her praise for the one who had come to redeem her people. I also remember when Jesus turned twelve and we lost him on our trip to celebrate Passover. We finally found him three days later conversing with the leaders in the midst of the temple. All those memories flashed before my eyes when I again stepped inside, but the overwhelming beauty quickly eased away the sadness. I have so many fond memories of this beautiful place of worship.

Salome, Mary Magdalene and I admired the sculpted relief of the city of Susa on the Gate Beautiful as we walked to the court of women. We started to climb the fifteen steps to observe the splendor of the huge Nicanor Gate when I looked around and saw Jesus stooped down writing on the ground while a woman stood beside him. He stood up and said something to the woman and she left. Jesus then proceeded into the court of men. I wanted to know more so I walked over to the woman.

"Were you talking to Jesus a minute ago?" I asked.

"Yes," she replied. "Do you know him? He is so wonderful. He saved me today from being stoned for adultery."

"How did he do that," I wanted to know.

"They caught me in the act," the woman said bowing her head. "I am so embarrassed, but my husband is an abusive man. He has no love for me, only lust—the same lust he has for all the other women who roam the streets. He chooses to be cruel even in the bed. I longed for a gentle man to give me some comfort. The priest in the synagogue who teaches my son noticed my bruises and took compassion on my plight. He consoled my cries of sadness as I confided in him the brutal life at home. I had no problem falling in love with this kind, gentle man. It did not take long until our feelings for each other could not be contained."

By this time all the women had gathered around us to hear the woman's story.

"The Pharisees followed me today and caught us in the very act. It seemed they had been waiting to catch me. They took me to that man Jesus, and asked him about the command in the Law of Moses that an adulteress should be stoned. Jesus stooped down and with his finger wrote on the ground. He completely ignored them. After they asked a few times, Jesus stood up and said to them, 'He that is without sin among you, let him first cast a stone at her.' I shrugged and closed my eyes anticipating the stones as Jesus again stooped down to write on the ground. I do not know what happened, but when I again opened my eyes, everyone had left except Jesus."

"They must have had a guilty conscience," Mary Magdalene chimed. "What did he write on the ground?" she asked.

"I am not sure. I have never been taught to read the written word. I only know Jesus stood up and asked me 'Woman, where are those that accuse you? Hath no man condemned you?'

"I answered, 'No man, Lord.' Then Jesus told me that neither did he. He told me to go and sin no more. I am relieved, but I fear what my husband will do if I return home. He had to hear the news and I know he will beat me. I cannot leave the man. I am stuck in that hopeless situation."

Feeling sorrow for the young woman, I reassured her that Jesus knew of her dilemma and would not allow her to be given any more than she could endure.

The girl left the temple to return to her family. I wonder what the future holds for her. Today she gained pardon of a sin that is nothing compared to the torment she must be going through at home.

Mary Magdalene and Salome walked over to where Jesus stood to see if they could determine what Jesus wrote. The people had already trampled the area until all that were left were a few marks.

"I think he wrote a bunch of sins that he knew the men had committed," Mary Magdalene said. "Look, here is an "l" and a "u". I believe he wrote lust."

"Here is a "gr". That must have been greed," Salome said pointing to some marks. I joined the women to see, but I could not distinguish any words.

"You are just guessing," I told them as we continued toward the steps. "I think Jesus is the only one who will ever know the facts of that story." [17]

17   The inspiration for this idea came during a revival sermon at Peaks Mill Christian Church in August, 2011. Suggestions were also submitted by Cora Schwingel and Linda Roten.

Dear Lord, I pray You will help the young woman. I do not ask You to condone her actions, but I do plead for her freedom from a life that is riddled with abuse. Father, the Laws of Moses leave no room for interpretation. Do the actions of the abusive husband justify the committed sin? I think not, but do You really want us to live our lives in such misery? Is there no Law that can help the woman? Will Jesus' message give her a new outlook on life and some peace?

Zaccheus said, *"and if I have defrauded anyone of*
anything, I will give back four times as much."
Luke 19:1-10
And he shall make restitution in full for his wrong and add to it
one-fifth of it, and give it to him whom he has wronged.
Numbers 5:6-7

Jesus Talks to Zaccheus

We have met some of the strangest people on this journey. Salome and I were debating whether we should ask Jesus about the writings on the ground the other day, when we looked up and saw a wee little man sitting in the top of a sycamore tree. Apparently he wanted a good view of Jesus.

We were amazed when Jesus stopped at the tree and looked up and said to the man, "Zaccheus, hurry and come down, for today I must stay at your house."

Salome and I just stared at each other as Zaccheus scurried down the tree. He jumped around with excitement as Jesus and all of his followers followed him to his house. There Zaccheus had his servants prepare a feast fit for a king with enough for everyone to eat and be satisfied.

Salome and I went to help with the preparation and to find out some news of this man with such unbridled belief. We were surprised to find out from the servants that Zaccheus is a tax collector. From the décor of his house and the feast he had prepared, we knew he had to be a fairly wealthy man. Did this tax collector earn his wealth by cheating those in his district when he collected their taxes? A tax collector could charge any amount they wanted for taxes as long as they received enough to pay the Roman government. They were allowed to keep everything collected above the required amount. Even passersby could be charged for items if the tax collector needed the money to meet the amount set by the government for his district. Needless to say, tax collectors are not popular people. Their word is nearly as untrustworthy as the word of the shepherds. Neither can be called to testify in a court of law as a valid witness.

We heard the people grumbling about Jesus going to be a guest of the man who cheats the people. Apparently they had experienced Zaccheus' peculiar way of measuring the worth of their items to be taxed.

Jesus and Zaccheus discussed many things regarding the taxes and the rulers who demanded the huge amount of monies. We could hear Jesus talking about the plan of salvation available to all who will accept it, but first, one must right the wrongs they have committed.

Zaccheus thought a while and said to Jesus, "Behold, Lord, half of my possessions I will give to the poor, and if I have defrauded anyone of anything, I will give back four times as much as demanded by the Law of Moses."

What a happy little man Zaccheus became, especially when Jesus said to him, "Today salvation has come to this house, because you, too, are a son of Abraham. For the Son of Man has come to save the lost." Jesus knew Zaccheus realized his need for the salvation offered by Jesus. If only the educated could be so smart.

Our spirits are always lifted high when we experience the salvation of one who has gone astray. Zaccheus learned the value of God's forgiveness today. His desire to make things right with the Lord won his salvation. I pray more will be willing to make that same sacrifice. What good is our material wealth if our soul is doomed to that fiery hell forever?

Thank You, dear Lord, for the power to forgive our sins when we repent. If we strive to make things right with You, our home is established forever. I have known for some time that if someone strives to takes care of You, You will also take care of them.

*Jesus, six days before the Passover, came to Bethany. Mary
took a pound of very costly perfume of pure nard,
and anointed the feet of Jesus and wiped His feet with her hair.*
John 12:1-11

Jesus Dines With Lazarus

I am so pleased to write this entry tonight of a wonderful experience. I am at the house of Lazarus and I feel it might explode with the joy contained inside. Today is another one of those days where my Father has blessed me abundantly. If anything else happens before this day ends, I fear my joy-filled body may burst at the seams. I am holding my newest granddaughter, Sheridan Grace, as I write. She fell asleep in my arms and I could not bear to lay her down.

Passover celebration is almost a week away. As we did for so many years, Jesus, James and I came to Bethany to Lazarus's house for a dinner prepared in honor of Jesus. I longed to have all my family together again. Of course, we have a big crowd with all of Jesus' followers. We have become a little family.

I remember when Lazarus' father, Simon, would prepare the grandest feast for anyone who came to the Passover. He always opened his house for weary travelers. We met him through a friend, but after that first time, he insisted the house would be ready for us the next year. Jesus and Lazarus became such good friends over the years, we could not think of staying anywhere else. Simon has passed away, but I can see his children have received his servant's heart. My family will always be grateful to the man who so generously took us into his house.

I have not been here for Passover since Joseph's death. I am glad James finally convinced me to return, so I could witness the memory created by Mary today. As usual, Lazarus' sisters were performing their own unique roles. Martha busily performed the duties of keeping the house in order with all the guests and making sure enough food had been prepared to serve everyone. Mary sat at Jesus' feet listening to him and his followers discuss some miraculous happenings.

At some point, Mary took a pound of very costly perfume of pure nard, and anointed Jesus' feet and wiped them with her hair. The fragrance of the costly perfume filled the entire house.

Judas' face immediately turned red as he asked Jesus about the waste of the expensive perfume. "Why was this perfume not sold for three hundred denarii and given to the poor people?" he asked Jesus.

Most of the followers thought Judas wanted to sell the perfume and put the money in the treasury. He may have, but only so he could dip from it, as I have again noticed him doing. I have tried to talk to Jesus and bring it to his attention for some time now, but the proper time has not presented itself. I almost wanted to shout for joy when Jesus sternly rebuked him.

"Let her alone, so she may keep it for the day of my burial," Jesus said. "You will always have poor with you, but you do not always have me."

My burial? What is he talking about? He is only thirty-three years old. Why would he be talking about his burial? He mentions his home in heaven in one breath, his body for ransom in the next, and his burial in the next. How are we supposed to know what he is talking about? His words make no sense. Even his twelve are confused by the words of his teachings. Give me wisdom, Lord. I need to know the meaning of Your son's words.

As we were dining, I got a wonderful surprise. Judas, Joseph, Simon, Leah, Sydney Katherine, Zachary Joseph, and their new baby, Sheridan Grace, arrived at the house. What a glorious reunion. I had never seen the new baby. I did not realize it had been that long since I have been home to see my other children. They said they knew we would be here so they decided to close the shop for a few days and come to visit. What a joy to see all my sons together laughing and having a good time.

They said the carpentry business had been doing well, and had more than enough work to keep all of them busy for some time. I think they were hinting for their two brothers to return home to help.

My heart skipped a beat when Jesus rushed to hug each of them. As I remember, the last time they saw him, they were ready to tie him up and take him home. Obviously, he has forgiven them, and did not hold any grudges. I think James must have told them he and I had been baptized. They asked questions and listened to Jesus talk, but I am not sure they were convinced of the need for this baptism. Jesus could not hide his pleasure in the fact that they were receptive to his new message.

Leah shared the good news that she may be expecting another child. She and Simon seem so happy. They adore each other and their little children. It took only a few seconds for Sydney Katherine and Zachary Joseph to steal everyone's heart. We have not laughed and rejoiced so much in some time. The reunion revived everyone's spirits.

Simon's house has always been open and full of people during the Passover feast, but tonight it appears to be bursting at the seams. No one seems to mind. I am writing as I look over my grandchildren and their mother who are sleeping soundly on a cot in the middle of the floor. All the men have gone to the roof or out in the garden to sleep under the stars. If a storm develops, we are in trouble. It will be wall-to-wall bodies in the house. I would not care. I am enjoying seeing everyone so much; I do not care how cramped we become.

Dear Lord, thank You for such a wonderful family. The boys still adore their big brother even if they are skeptical of his message. I again pray that You have opened their hearts to the message Jesus now preaches. Help us to understand that Jesus needed our disbelief to declare a message and, I have to say, it worked well. I pray You will allow us to have a good visit.

Sarah and Elizabeth come to Visit

Just when I thought God had blessed me beyond measure, I received even more blessings. My heart is overflowing with happiness, as I write this entry tonight. I cannot believe what happened today. We got up early this morning and Mary, Martha and all the other women busied ourselves preparing the morning meal for the house full of guests. Salome and I both worked as hard as we could to keep up with the other two sisters. While we worked, the room filled with laughter and kind words.

In the other room the men were participating in a tournament of senet. Words of advice and encouragement could often be heard along with the shouts of victory and the groans of defeat at the end of each game. Every year we have been here, Jesus and Lazarus would keep a record of their wins and losses. I am not sure who is ahead at this point. My heart fills with happiness to see them all taking a break from the turmoil of these last few days.

We were cleaning up everything when I spotted a movement in the doorway. To my amazement, who should walk in but Sarah and Elizabeth with their families? It seems Sarah had planned to visit Elizabeth and celebrate Passover at the synagogue in Nazareth. When she arrived at Elizabeth's, they went to visit their brothers, but everyone had gone. Then they decided to pack some things and come to Simon's house, because they knew everyone would be here. Oh, what a wonderful celebration! And what good news both of my daughters bear—they are both with child and should deliver within a short time of each other and a not long before Leah. What a wonderful gift—three grandchildren. My Lord is so wonderful!

"I am going to have a girl and name her Mary Elizabeth," Sarah boasted with the same determination as when she told me she had met the man she would marry. I will never forget that day she came home from the well those so many years ago after seeing Joel there.

Sarah said Doctor Luke comes by quite often to check on her and see if they have heard anything from us. I hope the kind doctor is doing well and will continue his writings.

Elizabeth said she does not care what she has as long as it comes quickly and is healthy. That is Elizabeth. She will take whatever God chooses to give her and will never complain. To her, every day is a gift from her precious Lord. I love her attitude and caring disposition. She is so considerate of everyone. She steals the heart of all who come in contact with her.

Mary, who gratefully chooses to do anything but housework, has taken all the children on a walk through the outskirts of town. She is like a mother hen with all her little chickens. I wonder why she has chosen not to marry and have children of her own. She would be such a good mother. Sometimes our Lord chooses to allow women to be mothers to other children instead of their own. Perhaps God knows how thankful mothers are for women like Mary. There were days when I wanted to scream at the demands of all my children. Sometimes a kind neighbor would come by and ask if they could borrow a child to help with a project. I thanked God for the timely diversion. He seemed to know when I had reached my wit's end.

Dear Lord, thank You for family and dear friends. This is such a good beginning of Passover week. I just pray it will end as wonderful as it has begun. Everyone seems so pleased to see each other. It is such a wonderful feeling to see everyone getting along so well.

Jesus, therefore, six days before the Passover, came to Bethany where Lazarus was...
so they made a supper there,
John 12:1-2

Mary Prepares to Celebrate the Passover

Why is my heart so heavy tonight? I should be rejoicing over the celebration of the gift of our precious Lord when he delivered our ancestors from the bondage of the Egyptians. Instead, I am experiencing that anxious feeling only a mother can describe.

I should be especially happy today. Last evening I watched all my children follow Jesus into the water to be baptized. After the bountiful meal, they listened intently to the words Jesus said. As he spoke, Sarah bravely spoke up and said, "I want to receive this salvation you are talking about, Jesus. How can you offer it to everyone else and forget your family? Why did you not tell us about this before?"

James and I stared at each other and smiled. If she could only remember how many times her brother has said the very same words in her presence. Only today did God open her heart for receiving the promise of the salvation Jesus has been proclaiming. I am beaming at the thought that we shall all again join each other in that heavenly kingdom of which Jesus boasts.

We have enjoyed a great feast in preparation for the Passover celebration. All my family and dear friends are present, but now it is time to send my children back home where they belong. God is telling me they do not need to be present to watch as their brother is delivered to his Father. Although it may be a glorious reunion, they could not bear the thought that they will never see their dear brother again. They have no idea anything is happening. They see the crowds gathering and the signs Jesus is performing. He is just their brother doing the good things he has been doing for some time.

Thankfully, James agreed to return home to help Elizabeth and Sarah travel with their children. I see God's plan taking shape with everything that has happened in the last few days since we have arrived at the home of Lazarus. God knew that would be the only way James would ever leave Jesus at this time.

Jesus' followers, Salome, the other women, and I will be the only ones left to view the glorious reunion when my heavenly Father descends from the heavens to lift up His son to join Him in that glorious kingdom. I am sad, but I know heaven is such a wonderful place and Jesus has said he is looking forward to being with his Father again. When he used the word again, I wondered if had been there before? I wanted to ask, but he disappeared before I had a chance.

There is something brewing I have no control over. I feel the tenseness in the air. All my children are here and we have enjoyed the laughter and fond memories of family and friends for a few days now. Last night, when Jesus mentioned Joseph and how he loved to hear him read the stories to all the children, there was not a dry eye in the room. Little Jesus sat in big Jesus' lap as his uncle told the same story Joseph told the last time he held Sarah in his lap.

Jesus is preparing to share the Passover supper with his friends some place near Jerusalem. I heard him send two of his followers off today in search of a young colt. I wonder what he is going to do with a colt. I remember Droopy, the lowly donkey on which Jesus almost entered this world. That trip to Bethlehem over thirty-three years ago is one I will never forget. Or the happenings in the lowly cave lit by the brightness of the star that led the shepherds and the kings to our humble abode. Jesus appeared to the lowliest and the highest during those few weeks we were there.

As I look outside today I am amazed at what has happened since then. The town and the roads are full of people wanting to see Jesus and catch a glimpse of Lazarus whom Jesus raised from the dead only a few days ago.

I wonder where all those masses of people waiting to see Jesus come from. I am not sure where he is now. I know he had been in hiding before he came to Lazarus's house earlier this week. He knew he would be safe from the scribes and Pharisees in the home of his friend. No one could have gotten close to Lazarus' house. They would not have tried this close to Passover. They know how important this celebration is to our people, but really, they do not care. If they want to make a spectacle of Jesus, now is the time to do it, because everyone is here to celebrate this glorious holiday.

I wish I had the peace I used to have when Joseph and I would come to Jerusalem to celebrate this great event. All my peace has turned to anxiety over what looms over me.

Last night before everyone reclined, Jesus hugged each of his siblings and planted a tender kiss on each forehead. Emotions were high when he finally made the rounds and moved outside. Elizabeth and Sarah were at my side for some time asking me why he appeared so preoccupied.

"Mother, Jesus should be happy like he usually is at this celebration. What is happening to him?" they asked.

"I think your brother is preparing us for another period in his life," I told them through a smile that held back a surge of walled-up tears. I could not cry and let them know the fears I have of what may happen.

I think God has enlightened me somewhat about this promised kingdom. I wonder if I would have willingly accepted this challenge had I known the consequences. This heavenly kingdom Jesus talks about does not resemble the throne of David as I had anticipated.

In our earthly home, Jesus learned the life experiences he needed to teach all those parables these last three and one half years. His visits with his cousins, where he learned to sow the seeds of the farmer and cast the nets of the fishermen, prepared him for his teachings. His well-rounded childhood provided everything God intended for him to learn. I pray my God is pleased with the life we provided His son—the only life we could. One filled with love and compassion for all fellowmen.

I only wonder how one will attain this heavenly kingdom and what type of sacrifice one must offer to enter. I am afraid of the answers I might uncover. My beautiful little baby who captured the hearts of the lowliest and the highest; my young toddler with his outstretched arms and little feet running to meet his grandparents; my young boy standing tall in the synagogue as he recited the words of the scripture as clearly and accurately as the most noted scholars; my teenager as he sat with the leaders in the temple; my student as he wrote and recited the beautiful prayer for his graduation ceremony from the synagogue; the loving brother who so carefully cared for the needs of his siblings, has now captured the heart of the world.

I recall pleasant memories of the obedient son who repeated the death prayers for his earthly father the twelve months after Joseph's death; the loving son who breathed life into my miracle child when her entire body had already turned blue due to lack of breath; the grown man who is wise beyond any earthly measure and whose knowledge exceeds that of the most learned scholar. He was *my* son. He is now the son of his heavenly Father.

My dear Father, I thank You for these few days of celebration with all my family and friends and the laughter and the love You gave us to get through this time. What does the future hold for our son? I know he is Your son, but You must not forget he is my son also. If You must call him back to You, please make it quick and painless. I do not see how You can let it be otherwise. As a loving Father, I know You cannot bear to watch him suffer any more than I, a loving mother, can. You know I will accept whatever You have planned. As always, I remain Your bondservant to do Your will.

We all know the rest of this story. But do we know it through Mary's eyes. I ask for your prayers that God will give me the words to write *Mary's Journal of Jesus' Death and Ascension* to be worthy of His blessing and your time.

I pray you received a blessing from this second journal of Mary.

I appreciate any and all comments of my work.
Please follow my progress and address any comments to:
jesusmyson@live.com
www.jesusmyson.com
Facebook @ JesusMySon
Twitter @ AuthorMBailey
Blog @ jesusmyson.blogspot.com